THE
VIRGIN'S
GUIDE
TO MEXICO

a novel by

Eric B. Martin

To Sr:
A true champion
hope you enjoy it

THE VIRGIN'S GUIDE TO MEXICO

a novel by

Eric B. Martin

MACADAM CAGE

MacAdam Cage
155 Sansome Street, Suite 550
San Francisco, CA 94104
www.MacAdamCage.com
Library of Congress Cataloging-in-Publication Data

Martin, Eric
The virgin's guide to Mexico / Eric B. Martin.
p. cm.
ISBN 978-1-59692-210-5 (alk. paper)
1. Teenage girls—Fiction. 2. Americans—Mexico—Fiction.
3. Mexico—Fiction. I. Title.
PS3563.A72376V57 2007
813'.6—dc22
2006103272

Manufactured in the United States of America
10 9 8 7 6 5 4 3 2 1

Book design by Dorothy Carico Smith. Cover art by Tim Brennan.

Thank you Juvenal Acosta, Ariel Dorfman, Guillermo Fadanelli, David Lida, Jay Mandel, Meredith McMonigle, Kate Nitze, Ethan Nosowsky, David Poindexter, the Fulbright Program, the Grotto, and the Xel-Ha.

This book is dedicated to Joaquín.

PART **ONE**

One

She has never been inside a bus station before. Until a month ago, she didn't know Austin had a bus station, or where to find it, or who or what the hell went on there. Her mom would be disgusted—although what does she really know about her cold and mute deceitful mom—to see her common little girl lined up behind two crusty senior citizens, a family chopping it up in Spanish, and the pale woman with an ass the size of Arkansas. So that's who. Ugly runaways and old folks and Mexicans and asses sized for Arkansas.

At the counter she pays cash money for the ticket, keeping her eyes dead and mouth straight so as to be forgettable. It's one of her inadvertent talents. She is famously forgotten far and wide, all over town, even in her own home. True, that home is stupid big, with more rooms than the three of them know what to do with: dad's leather office; mom's white pink woody study; a disgusting mirrored master bedroom with dueling walk in closets and bathrooms plural, his and hers; the guest room where no guests ever room; vast zones for living and cooking and wash; the basement cave of daddy's billiards where satellite TV projects large size, two four seven, three six five.

Her room is on the ground floor, in a lone finger of the house that hooks off toward the garden. This suits everyone just fine. The walls are painted peach, no joke, but the walls are barely visible because the place is lousy with books—childhood treasures, Euro classics, Beats, Plath,

3

Huxley, Exley, bubble covered jet trash. Her room is never really neat, but this time she has left it more than slobby, condemned The Maid Also Known As Esperanza to hours to make things right. The plan started out clean and clandestine but then every piece of clothes she owned came to audition for the ark. T shirts, cargos, sweatshirts, jeans. Shoes: needs an elephant boy and sherpas for her shoes. Photo albums. Last year's high school yearbook. A box of old letters from middle school, round handed notes folded into triangles, *Hey Alma, do you still like Charlie V?!?* until she sat bedazzled on the wall to wall, choking on the stale past crumbling through her hands. Enough. Enough with books in pretty lettered spines that stare like doe eyed toddlers *please don't leave me here behind*. Don't listen. Don't be an ass.

It took hours. Hour after hour in that totally messed up room, shopping her personal mall for what's right to bring along. This is where the killer imagination comes in. Close both eyes. Simulate a future. A girl in flight. A girl alone, hunting Earth's most gigantic city for the only man who can tell her what she needs to know. Is there running? Clubbing? Formal dining? Her mother might be shocked at the list of leftbehinds, but Alma thinks she did okay. Time, that little bully, will tell.

The bus is not full. There's a seat number on her ticket, but mysteriously the senior citizens have decided to annex her rightful place. She mentions this to them, quietlike, standing in the aisle with impatients bunched in tow, but the old couple shake their heads and wag their index fingers back and forth like synched uptempo metronomes. Impatients sigh and shift and stamp behind her. She must tell the old finger wags again, in Spanish now, and silently scratches words on the chalkboard in her head:

> *creo   que   usted   está   en   mi   asiento*

Crap it's slow up there, every word sold separately, although there's this feeling—like a deep low bass thump getting louder, hard to tell, she thinks it's getting louder—ever since she started to study her mom's native tongue, in secret, just one year ago. There is Spanish in her somewhere and it's trying to get out, but before it can the old wags strike her mute, shaking their ancient heads with vigor as their fingers hit *allegro*. Silenced, she presses her lips together and drops sullen to an empty seat, where she leans her forehead against the tinted window and mumbles to herself. *Creo que* old people suck.

They stop in San Antonio, at another backdoor bus station in a rude hole part of town. More Mexicans get on. This might still be America but not on this bus. Autobuses del Norte. Gotta be tough to find someone who drops south off the map on an Autobús del Norte. American buses must be more organized: surveillance, records, questions about who and where and what on earth she's doing. The Mexican bus, on the other hand, could give a fuck. No one asks her nothing.

Fresh bodies press onboard. Outside she can see enormous packages tied up in twine, dead bodies and crates of dynamite loaded into the cargo bays while the empty seats fill up. See now it's stressed out now with all these people coming on. Old people suck, they suck, they really really suck because there's going to be a problem—they're in her seat, she's in someone's seat, not even ninety miles from home. But there's no problem. The vacant spots are filled without debate. Unlike her freakish mom, real Mexicans don't fret or fuss or panic, not in their natural habitat, see how the free range untamed Mexican rolls with punches, makes do, adapts? Outside, back in Texas, all cargo is dispatched and the driver bumps hands and fists with his main man at the counter, leaping theatrically aboard, hissing the doors closed and the AC up high. They slip out through San Antonio's quiet Friday morning streets, find the highway, and get gone.

In Laredo, the bus veers away from the US border booths to drop her at a makeshift station near the high fenced bank of the Rio Grande. Only a few of them get off here; this line is bound for Nuevo Laredo and then the city of Monterrey, four hours deep in Mexico. She's never been to Monterrey, or Nuevo Laredo, or even Laredo for that matter. She's never been to squat, and that's part of the point.

The station is even more disappointing than it first appears. First the serial killers' bathroom and second no locker for her bag. The vintage AC system doesn't stand a chance against the midday August heat. Hotter than a June bride in a feather bed, her daddy would say, probably *is* saying right now as he steps between the glass steel building of the office park to the big red SUV waiting in God's only square of shade. Whatchu won eat? he's drawling super Texan jovial to a chummy sales rep or VP Branding or vertical partner opportunity. They got Friday ribs at TJs and lasagna at the Giovanni's. Salads, yeah, caesar taco chicken green, they got it all, salad probably wouldn't kill me neither, sure I'm watching my weight too, you know, just from comfortably afar. Blah blah blah. The big mouth bully. Everyone's best buddy in the world until their world ain't what he wants.

She drags her bag over to the counter, leans there heavily on her elbows to look friendly and short. At 5'9" she would tower over the dwarf in demi uniform who ignores her while he decodes a computer print out like it's a declaration of war. When he finally looks up he glances at her tits but finding little there hunts around until he spots her hair. Her hair is not so bad.

Do you have lockers?

Lokoust?

Lock ers. She points to her bag, turns an imaginary key in the air.

He watches her and sniffs and smiles as if she's just unlatched a chastity belt. Low curs. He shakes his head. No, we don't have it.

¿Sabes dónde? There's the beat.

No sé decirte.

Every Wednesday night for one year, down at the community college, Alma has been cramming this language into her brain, where she built a sturdy grammar cabinet and filled the right drawers up with words: verbs here, nouns there, feminine, masculine, pluperfect, subjunctive, *por* and *para, ser* and *estar.* She's always been an extraordinary student, of everything, as long as it takes place in a classroom, but the trick with language, she read somewhere, was to get the basics and the structure and then go fall in love. Madrid. Buenos Aires. The *gap year*, the Brits called it. Don't go straight to college. Explore your holy cow. What a great plan except here she is packing stolen credit cards and chatting up some perv who works for Autobuses del Norte. Not quite strolling down Las Ramblas, is it?

¿Lo dejo con tigo? she tells the guy, pointing at the bag.

Sí, cómo no. His voice rises in mild interest.

Sólo una hora. She glances at the schedule on the wall. *Voy. En el bus. A las cuatro.*

Está bien. He puts his lips together tight and pouts with certainty.

She keeps her small black backpack of essentials—the goodie bag—and leaves the rest with him, hoisting the duffel to the countertop while he watches without a hint of help. She's brought too much stuff, this she knows already, maybe he knows it too. He pats the duffel twice with both hands and swings it out of view.

A las cuatro, she says again. *Gracias.*

De que.

She sits down on one of the benches to examine her map. Nixon High School looks far. North Jarvis Street starts somewhere nearby, although she doesn't know where the five hundred block might be.

That's probably not a good idea, someone says to her.

Above her looms the frontside of pale Arkansas, packed into dark blue jeans and a whore red T shirt, shiny, tucked. Cheap black boots, well shined, unscuffed. The woman's voice is country, she could really be from Arkansas from how she looks and sounds. Or Missouri.

What's not.

Your bag.

It's not safe?

Is it ever? says Arkansas, snorting like a wild horse and turning her attention to the parking lot outside where someone useful has arrived. She nods. Just a word of the wise. Her boots click martial along the floor as she departs. Climbs into a jacked up Tundra and disappears.

Alma sneaks a look at the counter where the guy is watching her. Is he a bad man? She heads back to look for signs of scumbag, unfurling her spine like a fist and expanding to her full height. More Godzilla than girl like that but that's the way things are. He waits for this strange tall teenager to come, curious what such teens might say.

The street Jarvis? she says in Spanish.

He squints into the glare of question. That way, he says, tossing a pigeon into the air. Right here, close.

Is it safe? She watches his face.

On this side? he says. Of course, Laredo's very safe. The other side, well, be careful, no? Lots of *rateros*. She doesn't know the word, but from the look on his face she can see what he means.

Rateros are like goddamn bastards? She is showing off, now, her best gutter Spanish.

He laughs. More or less. Where did you learn that?

But she shakes her head. That conversation doesn't interest her. The point is, bucko, are you a bad man? Do you empathize with others? She's looking for the truth but all she sees is that wide nose with mixed blood firing through his capillaries. One of his ancestors was raped by some dumbfuck savage from Extremadura who clubbed an Indian girl from Cuaultla. She feels for him, with roots like that, but he better not do her wrong. We all got roots. Screw Arkansas. She says thanks and see ya later and leaves the duffel there with him.

Outside the heat is funny. He he ha ha ho. She sweats promptly as she walks, the thin straps of her bag cutting damp canals into her shoulders and back. She's wearing tan shorts and a light blue tank top, new sneakers and white peds, her long hair tied back in a high ponytail. She's in disguise, in other words, dressed like her mom might dream her up, some normal J. Gap Lands Crew girl—but ugly—out for a little stroll. The streets are dead, at first, like something killed them. There was once a lively little downtown here but something beat it senseless. This ground beneath her feet's flipflopped from Mexico to Texas to plain ol' USA, as feisty locals gave gringo's dream the finger and started their own damn city, planted a thriving Mex Jeckel United Hyde spleening smuggled cattle, weapons, booze, drugs, cars, casinos, migrants, *maquiladoras*. She knows all about it. She reads. The border has a long proud legacy of all fucked up.

If she were her mother, this is one excuse she'd use. To grow up here, on both sides of the dotted line? Transplanted, fatherless, orphaned, alone? No wonder she's some frozen bitch. But Mom won't even tell this story. She'll talk about the cute paperboy on the Tex Mex bridge she crossed each day for school who called out made up head-lines BEAUTY CAUSES TEN CAR CRASH! She'll mention the hole they lived in if Alma won't tidy up her room. But just try to connect the dots and she'll be very clear: Mexico has nothing to do with it. Look at the woman. The Arabian calves, the tiger thighs, arms of cabled steel. Our lady of the triathlon. No one's ever seen anything like it. Her teeth light the darkness and disintegrate men's stitches. Skin like Swedish chocolate, black eyes and hair as the pit of the soul. There's no accent, no stories, no Spanish. It's like nothing but Texas ever happened.

Alma knows better.

The address on North Jarvis Street is farther than she would like it to be, but she strides on through the blaring heat, flapping her arms lightly to cool her smooth shaved pits in the breeze. North Jarvis isn't shy for traffic. There are tinted chromy pick ups, yupped out Lexi, pimp convertibles, bland sedans, meticulously rusted pieces of crap. There's even a public city bus that lumbers by, headed for the airport, or so the placard says. Holy shit, she thinks, watching the big beast gun a yellow light. Her mom rode that bus or its older cousin, twenty something years ago. Back when she was a Mexican hoofing it cross the border and then out to Nixon High School, full speed ahead.

A real live Mexican. Now that must have been something.

Recognizing the house is out of the question. Her mom has never described it and no pictures of the place seem to have survived. She's looked. She's turned all her parents' sanctums inside out and found horrible things: thin leather ties, self improvement books, stacks of Playboy magazines, hemorrhoid cream, huge credit card receipts, pamphlets on vasectomy, a cheap manila twist top vibrator. She's found old address books and diplomas, expired library cards and a Bible in Spanish. She's found that her mother who doesn't speak Spanish speaks Spanish, that her mother who doesn't have family has family, that her mother with no legacy's got legacy. But in all these searches she's never seen a picture of the first American house her mother lived in. The house of Elma Watkins, where all these lies and transformations must have first begun.

From the outside, 532B North Jarvis doesn't look like it could transform much of anything. The front face needs a paint job, needs some straightening and uncrumbling, needs a little love. When there's a gap in the traffic, she takes two quick pictures with her daddy's digital, filling the frame to close perfection from the far side of the street. Then she crosses, mounts the front stairs, and knocks on the blue door twice.

Yeah?

Hi. Hello?

Yeah?

Yeah. Um. You don't know me, but my mom used to live here? I was kind of maybe hoping I could come in and see the place.

Huh?

My mom, she says, shouting over belly laughs from failed mufflers passing by. She used to live here. A long time ago.

Yeah?

Yeah. I'm putting together an album, you know, of her past? She's in a coma, they don't know, you know. I just thought if I could take a couple pictures.

The door opens. He looks about two or three years younger than her, fourteen maybe, short, with straight dark hair flopped out spiky over his eyes. Got his uni on: black DisdainD T shirt, baggie jeans, white high tops. She knows which lunch table this kid sits at. Behind him, three huge chords are rocking out at optimum distortion levels. The stereo is pissed and screaming.

Whut? He squints through her into the unwelcome light, trying to figure her out, but Alma has no lunch table. He doesn't know that though. He doesn't know the geeks don't want her because she's too rough and the Goths don't want her cause she's too soft. She's too good for the Mexicans and too shitty for everyone else except the few she's known since preschool. He doesn't know about the soft shale sediment that lies beneath her toughest talk, the layers of baby bawling at recitals and dances and on the softball field or the time when she got her first B, the time she time she time.

My mom's in a coma.

Oh.

She was shot. In the neck.

He blinks.

It was a robbery at a convenience store.

He frowns guiltily and skips his glance along the ground as if she's saying it's his fault. Shit, he says.

She grew up here, long time ago. Can I come in, take a couple pictures? For the album.

Yeh. Sure. He shrugs and lets her in.

It's a tiny house, a one story job that goes straight back. From the front hall she can see the small backyard through the combo dine/live/TV room and past the kitchen. The other two rooms—bed, bed—are off to the side. The place smells like old canned soup and marijuana. No one else is home.

She follows him down the hallway. The whole house is carpeted except for the kitchen. Dark blue carpet, dirty and old. Linoleum worth carbon dating with a big sweet stove cum center griddle they probably don't make anymore. The kid likes the kitchen best too, she can tell, plops himself down on a stool by the door. He watches her looking around.

Your basic shithole, huh. He fishes a lighter and green ceramic pipe out of his pocket, clamps them together as a package, and offers them her way.

No thanks.

He glances at the plastic clock on the wall, and she does too: three and change. This information seems to please him. He lights up and takes a huge ambitious hit, showing off his young suction before pushing an expert cloud into the room. He sneaks a look at her, expecting wild applause.

How long y'all lived here?

I been here all day. He has outdone himself this time, launched himself into a loose orbit around planet Zortna. I cut, he says.

Yeah?

Yeah, fuck it. The music stops suddenly. They can hear the car sounds outside.

You go to Nixon?

He nods.

My mom went there. She lived in this house, and she went to Nixon.

Which room?

I don't know. She takes the letter out in case this is his way of saying bullshit. He leans forward and together they read the beautiful handwriting on the yellowed envelope:

Hermelinda Montes Figueroa
Casa Elma Watkins
Jarvis 532 "B"
Laredo, Texas 78043
EE.UU.

Mom's a trip, huh. He takes the letter from her and flicks the blank space where the return address should be. Bet she stayed in the front room.

Think so.

Noisy as fuck. S'my room. Me and my mom. Old bag's back *there*.

She's taken the camera out now, and backs herself into a corner of the kitchen to take a picture best she can. She takes another one from the other direction. The kid figures prominently in both of them, leaning forward off the stool and tilting his head and splaying his ruddy fingers in surf's up position.

I'm gonna go take a few more, okay.

Yeah, he says, laughing. Yeah yeah yeah.

She gets the dining room, the hallway. She gets the front bedroom with its old school bunk beds, its humid sour boy mess. The thick shades of all four windows are fully drawn so that no natural light interferes. Her camera flashes once and then again. The curtains open and the bunk beds disappear. A couch slides in from nowhere with two old lady chairs and a little scratched up coffee table and a writing desk in the corner. Her mother is sixteen years old sitting skirted on the couch with her knees together while Alma's pseudo namesake Elma Watkins pours ice tea for two in the other room. Sugar, sweetie? she says to the orphan who curls up on the couch each night and stacks her carefully folded clothes there in the corner, kept invisible from guests with a concealing quilt. Not that there are many guests. Mostly there's just Elma and mother, one spinster history teacher and a fate gored straight A student who were not meant to live together for a day or a week or two whole years but what else was there to do.

I slept on a couch, her mother told her once, one rare occasion when Alma was ten.

On a couch?

Yes. All my clothes fit in two little piles.

After everyone died?

A red couch. They were in Alma's bedroom, her mother brushing Alma's hair as if she might find something.

You were lonely.

I was looking for you, her mother said, smiling with all her teeth. Face wiped clean of memory and grief.

Hey, like, which convenience store? The kid's standing in the doorway now, watching her be in his room.

It's a stoned riddle that takes her a second to puzzle out. Oh. No, you know what? I lied about that. My mom's not in a coma.

No?

Might as well be sometimes but not physically technically at least.

Yeah, huh.

She did live here though. Couch and chairs and skirted knees are fading into the crumpled monuments of dirty clothes. She needs to ask him but she's not sure how. I just wanted to see it, she says. Sometimes you wonder where they come from.

It's a shithole, huh.

She shrugs. I'm going to Mexico City.

Yeah, right on. That's where she's from, huh?

D'you just say? Somehow the kid's still holding the envelope in his hand, how could she forget, but now she reaches out to yank it hers. You read this?

He shakes his head. I just remember, the old bag used to talk about her Mexican. He's walking down the hall now and she follows him into the other bedroom. The kid flicks on the light and what she sees is not the quilted bed or wicker chair or antique dresser with forged iron hardware but a picture of her mother hanging on the wall.

The girl in the photo is so soft and sad and beautiful that Alma about falls down. Must have been around Alma's age except a different species. Simple white dress, long hair pushed back under a thin head-band. Alma stands with both hands propped against the plaster, staring at her young mother in this constellation of frames. Her mother stares back. Can I tell you something? her mother asks.

And that's mine, the kid says, stabbing at a ferret faced teenage mother holding a newborn in her arms. There's me. Man your mom was hot. What's your name?

Ashley. She starts laughing. She lifts the picture and pinches it between her fingers, hard.

You're lying right?

Yeah, I'm always lying. I'm a big fucking liar.

That's cool. I don't give a shit. She's not really your mom.

I know. Except she really is. They look at the picture together. Is there, like, anything else? Any other. Stuff.

The kid almost smiles. You can ask old Watt yourself. He glances at the clock radio by the bedstand and she shoves the picture in her bag. Should be here soon, he says, worry bunched up above his nose.

She. She must be old as dirt.

You think? He's in the hallway now, pulling out the bottom drawer of a massive file cabinet, old rollers rumbling like thunder coming in. Shit in here somewhere. He yanks an accordion file the color of dried blood. Check this crazy out.

The file bulges with old mail, and junior pulls it out until: same envelopes, same script. A few of them have little doodles on them, carefully drawn little birds and pigs. She reaches but he jerks the letters away from her, out of reach.

What's it worth to you.

A sob shoots up her esophagus but she gags it back. There's a penknife in her goodie bag. She could stab him in the throat. She starts to say something—what do you want?—but she can hear her voice squeak up already. This kid wrings her grandfather in his grubby little hands. *Abuelo.* For the first time it occurs to her that she might really find him.

Twenty bucks, she whispers, fumbling with her bag. You see, I gotta. My mother's only. She can't even talk right.

Your mother's only what? He smirks at her, waiting for her latest lie. He waves the letters like a Japanese fan.

Listen. You ever wonder. She twirls her hair with nerves but makes herself stop. Why life's so fucking angry? She's about to say *your father* but she thinks better of it. You've seen my mom, she says, so why am I like this? You know? She waits for something smartass but he doesn't say a thing. Do I look like, I dunno, some fucked up looking family? Do I hate all this bullshit here because I should be down there? You know what I'm saying? All the lies they tell us?

For a thin moment she spots his brain pit of compassion but then he dances back from her, waving the letters around. You're the liar, he says. Panties all on fire.

She sighs. Twenty bucks, okay?

Twenty? He shoves the missives halfway down the front of his pants and looks her up and down. You want these letters? He waggles his hips. The letters dance.

What, she says. She tries to work some spit into her mouth. What, what, what, you want to see my pussy, what? He reddens and her too but she grabs the letters and throws the twenty rolling through the air.

No hey listen, the kid says as he lets go, ashamed ashamed ashamed. No hey I won't tell anyone, okay? He keeps nodding, as if to that invisible beat. I was just playing. Mexico City. Maybe, like, I should come with you.

She says nothing and slips by him to the front door, pulling it open and drawing the hot air in behind. He doesn't move, statued in the dark pupil of the ruined room. She pulls the door closed.

Her long legs reach out into fairytale steps as she makes the house disappear behind her, shoving the letters and the picture in her bag. She's not scared, not that she knows of, but for the first time since she left home she feels her heart cough and chatter.

Two

One of the many things she loathes about herself is that she studied French. For four years she sat with the sassy Austin Spice Girl Blond Brigade learning the language of frogs so she could what? Stroll through Paris arm in arm with Bitch Spice and Slut Spice to wink at randy French guys and power shop? What a fool. Fool Spice trailing sullenly behind, loathing self while her companions merrily ponytail along, that Bitch Spice classic cheery high tie swinging side to side, Slut Spice's fall or flip or fade bobbing vertically up and down. Two bolts of gold flashing through the air, flagging down the nearest passing boy.

And Spanish? *S'il vous plaît. Donnez-moi une fracture.* Spanish was for morons, for the feeble minded, for shirkers who couldn't handle French or Latin or even German. The Stupids studied Spanish. Football players, slow white trash, stoners, skaters, high C students. Mexicans. Mexicans studying Spanish. *Vraiment incroyable.* What good is Spanish, her mother would say, when you're already Hispanic for your applications? French is so old and beautiful. You can always pick up Spanish later if that's really what you want.

French sure ain't doing her a whole lotta good here on the Mexico side of the Guerrero Street bridge, where night is falling faster than a whore's drawers (her dad, yakking steady on the celly, heading home from work) under thick cloud cover that means rain at best. The border is busy, maybe it's always busy, what does she know, but tonight there are cars and people lined up long with intentions north and south. Getting away from it all, out for the night, home for the weekend, just plain home.

Southwise, the border is so easy it makes her wish she were an FBI most wanted with plutonium and designer drugs and live babies in her bag. The US simply lets her go. See ya. Feel free to beat it any time. She walks across the bridge, across the pitiful piddle of Rio Grande and into Mexico, where the Mexicans are waiting for her. But despite the impressive build up, the smart fences and weaponry and too tight uniforms, the long and short is that she barely flashes her passport, fills out a form, hands over some cash to a morose bureaucrat in a small bank booth. His hair has recently been cut by someone angry. He gives her five triple stamped receipts which she trades in for the pink tourist card, good for ninety days. From there she bustles to the next event: a playhouse traffic light at waist level with a button on the side. If the light turns green Mr. Playhouse Guard waves folks free and clear into his waiting country with a disgusted flick of wrist. She watches as he admits convicts, pimps, bigamists, child molesters and abductors, arms dealers, dope fiends, terrorists. Green green green green. They're letting everybody in, with everything they got. She starts to fear the law of averages, she fears red and the great unknown, Officer Playhouse snapping on his favorite cavity search gloves as she steps up to bat. Pushes the button. Happy happy green. Tax evaders, evangelists, runaways.

Ladies and gentlemen: Mexico.

How long has she wanted it? Hard to say. Ever since what Mother never told her; ever since Kerouac crossed the border with stoned Sal and Denver what's his name; ever since her dad said no and Mom said nothing; ever since she stopped eating meat; ever since she decided she must be someone somewhere but not anywhere she'd been before. She'd wanted it a thousand times without knowing what it was. One day Kerouac was not enough. The *migas* at #3 Tamale House—not enough. Austin not enough. Austin has definitely failed. She has lived too long on the greedy isle of Westlake, where life is but a dream of pretty houses and the Blond Brigade and pools and big backyards and nut brown help from the other side of town. Nannies and lawn men and maids. She might be nominally half Mexican but she doesn't look it, she looks weird for real and besides they can smell the Westlake on her. She stinks. And they stink too, they're not the Mexicans she's looking for. She knows what the real Mexico can be, she reads, it's more than uneducated peasant painters and roofers and gloopers of cement. Cilantro choppers. Cleaners of things dirty. It's more than a few assimilating Mids and Ups straightening out their accents and buying Beamers and following the Blond Brigade from store to Saks to Gap. It's more than these new American dreamers abandoning their homes for cash. Mexico is the confluence of two mighty lyric cultures, mortar and pestle and pomegranate seeds, B. Juárez and Sor Juana, Tonantzin and Cardenas, the Virgin G. and Leona Vicario and Frida friggin' Kahlo, revolutionaries and poet nuns, goddesses and artists, Spanish speakers of the truth. It's true she would have settled for Argentina or España if things had gone that way but fuck it this is Mexico! This is where she's from! Her roots! *Tierra!* This filthy dusty shit strewn street right here!

Mexico's first wave of hawkers does not know what to make of this ugly big bagged tall girl staggering with disappointment. Doctor? Hotel? Tequila? What do such girls want? She wants things they don't have but they won't leave her alone. The jerky rats, these must be the *rateros* sung of by Señor Bus Counter, who turned out not so evil in the end. Cross the border *et voilá.*

She shakes off a few but two rat bastards, bored, still linger and follow her so close they're touching without the physics of the thing. Come on, she says. Please, no, thanks, go away.

Blankets, they say, hammocks. Folk arts. Doctor. Clean cheap hotel. Those are the words but it's the way they say 'em, there's something mucous there. Doctor, they try again, their best bet, the most obscene.

Leave me the fuck alone! she says, her voice sliding up too high. She can't breathe in this panic of men. They laugh, smile, and let her flee.

Where is she now? Her feet in flight have landed her impossibly already off the beaten track. No one on the street. Texas lurks behind steel and wire on the other bank. There should be shops and cabs and stuff instead of this neighborhood that seems deserted, poor and barely residential. The buildings here look sick, diseased with spinal fungus or bugs. Her bag's too heavy, Señor Bus has loaded it with blond embryos and guns, she's so alone, she can't live like this, something's got to give. But at the next intersection, life blossoms to her left and she almost runs for the commercial fold. *This* is where she belongs, for now: a small square with iron benches, *taquerías*, curios, trinkets, shoe stores, carry out bars, *farmacias* touting valium and tequila. A woman calls out to her in Spanish, come here and eat some tasty tacos, but she shakes her head at all that meat and crosses the street. Sits herself down on iron bench. Two men stroll by, staring at her fat knees with cuddy bovine lust. She covers the rest of the bench in duffel bag.

The sky has not been nice for the last hour but now looks ill, sagging lower and lower and turning green. It needs to rain. It needs to do something, and sure enough as she sits there the clouds join witchy hands and start ringing slowly round the rosy in that mad tormented way. Texas knows what that means, and looks like Mexico does too, because when she glances down again the streets are drained of people, the doors and windows shut. Somewhere close and soon, Dorothy's headed for Oz.

She leaps up to the curb. Across the street gapes the taqueria entrance packed with refugees, where the taco matron bosoms through and waves to her again: get over here quick, room for one more. But the intervening traffic won't stop. Cars race by bumper to bumper. She leans forward with intent but these Mexicans won't let her cross.

The first drop of rain hits her forehead like an avocado pit. Then the low rider heavens open fire. She ducks and covers as rain sharpens and sure enough, on the pavement, drops have started bouncing in real unliquid ways. Fucking hail! Wild hard pellets dent her from every direction, and she's about to throw herself in traffic when a car stops sharp. The passenger door gapes open.

¡Venga! An old man driver reaches out and flicks his frantic hand downward as if smacking an unseen child on the wrist. *¡Rápido, rápido!* She throws her duffel onto the seat and dives in after it and pulls the door behind.

There is nothing to say at first. The sky chucks rocks at them but the driver keeps his calm. The wipers wipe. She can't see one damn thing but somehow he's conjuring up a path through the percussion and the violence toward the slave and organ markets and the ditches made for dumping virgin dead. Men die, she knows this, women too, in accidents and crimes, she flinches with each tick and pock, they die but how can she if all the world's a book and she the reader and finally the hail has backed down into rain, strong but sane at least. The old man looks at her and that's when she realizes she's in a taxi.

¿Estás bien? the driver asks, peering into her face for answers. She nods but he doesn't seem to see it. *¿Hablas español?* She shakes her head and that's the truth, right now she can't. You are okay? he says in deep accented English.

Yes. Thank you. She props her nose against the glass. The rain looks like it's going to stop but the sky's still good and weird. If they've got trailer trash in Mexico it should be flying by any minute.

Where you going?

I don't know.

I take you there. No problem. He waves at his taxi meter hiding low down on the dash. Don't worry. It's okay. You go to Laredo? His lilt is hideous strong, but for some reason he's easy to understand. He speaks slowly, choosing only words he's met many times before.

No, I stay here. Now she's talking like that too. I have hotel.

I take you. Good hotel.

No, she says. She's found her little notebook where she wrote down the name, a place sanctioned by the guidebook. Hotel Ajova, she says.

He shakes his head, turns the car off the main street out of the line of traffic. Rain completely on the wane, now, although real thunder clears its throat somewhere behind.

No. No good.

I want to go there. He's about to say something else but she gets there first. Please.

Please. He tilts his head unhappily and drives her through the narrow gutter flooding streets to the Ajova.

As the guidebook has promised, the small pink building sits slightly off the layman's map in a no man's land between the border and the Monterrey highway. It's clean, cheap, and the crappiest hotel she's ever set foot in. Her mom would piss her pants. Dad punch out a wall. Alma flips over the U shaped security bar, turns down the air conditioning, and strips off her wet clothes. The naked girl in the mirror catches her eye and now she has to look. Hair brown, not auburn or brunette or sandy—brown, exactly like the word says. Receding. She's got the highest forehead in the West. Her head itself is kind of square, not Mama's round or Daddy's long but some weird Irish robot head. Small mouth, thin lips, big nose, black eyes. The skin reddish, sort of Porky the pig skin that sun does not exactly tan but irritates into a rash. Brown hair, square head, black eyes, red skin. Oh she confuses people. For the love of god, they cry. Sweet Jesus what is that thing.

It's hard to say exactly which feature is her worst. Quasimodisms rule her from boxy head to prehensile toe. Here in Mexico, in the yellow light of her cheap hotel room, what impresses her are not the 36A dents where breasts should be, or the sausage legs, or the fur that plagues. Tonight we have a new winner: ladies and gentlemen, the neck. It has been rising in the rankings and finally tops the charts as the big thick fattest and least feminine neck she has ever seen, the kind of neck that brings to mind not kissing but bile and peristaltic motion. Her whole body is a failure but right now it's this neck makes her most mad, oh my god she hates her fucking neck. No child wants to nuzzle here. No pretty stones or diamonds would look right. This neck is built for 1st and 10 and then her shoulders…she throws herself sideways out of the mirror's kill zone, hurries into the bathroom, sets the shower to scald and by the time she comes out her rain chilled skin is warm and she smells like pink jasmine and it doesn't matter so much that the puny little towel barely fits around her. Plenty of hot water here at the Ajova. The mirrors stay steamed shut until she's safely into her best tough girl disguise: Pvt. Sacco's fatigues, gray large tee, some old Vex boots with the leather chipping off.

Ah. Mmmn. Much better.

Her documents suggest her mother used to live here in Nuevo on a street named Dr. Mier. She doesn't need the doctor—not anymore, not with these latest letters pointing her to Mexico City's Zapata Street—but still. Nearby and she's got to see it. With all the lies her mom's served up, there might be twenty cousins living there. They throw open the door and wrap her in their cocoa *primo* arms and laugh at all her jokes and feed her fruit and show her pictures and try to paint her nails, pressing mom's teenage diaries in her hands. Maybe tomorrow. Right now she's happy sitting tight. Flips on the telly, finds the Spanish MTV, opens her book, and reads peacefully for fifteen minutes or so until the people next door fucking get too rowdy to ignore.

At first it sounds like they're building simple sturdy furniture. But soon they're erecting stone cathedrals and steel skyscrapers, slaughtering live donkeys, cats, and humpback whales. The hooves and claws and huge tail fins smack against the wall. She gapes at the plaster and cranks up the MTV where a Spanish replica of Meme Chose drones '80s style over synthetic poppy din. The androgynes are playing as loud as they can but their wimpy synthesizers are no match for these super fuckers. She almost smiles, embarrassed and amazed. It goes on and on and on. She wants them dead.

Shut up, she whispers. Shut up, she says in a normal voice. But that's as far as she can get. The biggest wimp in the Americas fishes out her iPod, dials up Screaming Panda, and cranks it to brain bleed as she starts her book.

The book says that Sor Juana Ines de la Cruz was an illegitimate child prodigy who became the most important Mexican poet of the seventeenth century. This took some doing. Mexico in the 16 somethings was no bastard feminist's delight. But Juana was smart as shit. A stubborn geeky little weirdo who didn't eat cheese because it makes people dumb; chopped off her hair as punishment for learning grammar slow; tried to dress in drag cause only boys attended school. She was reading at age three, semi collegiate at ten, court favorite by fifteen, accomplished poet by eighteen, nun at twenty one, Church foe at thirty, dead by pseudo suicide at forty three. The book blows, the famous author's got something large and wordy up his woo, but she still gets the idea. Juana rocked.

That's Mexico, she thinks, pumping her right fist. That's what's burned into my DNA. All I want.

The music ends and she removes the headphones. She listens, lowers the volume on the TV. All clear. She searches around for a movie, tries her book again, debates whether or not she's hungry, flips her mirror self the finger a few times, reads the guidebook, looks at the map, listens to the telephone's electric tenor dial tone, wonders what the hell she's doing, gets out her black writer's notebook, writes the date in neat block print at the top of the page, I am Sor Juana, she writes, and then just like that next door they're building furniture again.

This is what people do. She closes her eyes. Her father's voice is low and chuckly.

Hey little sister. Hot as a June bride in a feather bed.

You know I like to sweat.

Place on Manshack?

Yum. See you there.

Click. Click. This is what her father does, what people do, and this is how they do it, yeah do me do it do it to me, the awful things said in Austin on Manchaca Ave. or the blasphemy next door, *dios dios* and more *dios.* She packs, straps on her goodie bag, hoists the duffel to her shoulder. The door shuts quietly behind her as she fee fi fums to the front desk where she tries to bitch dude out but he won't get off the phone. So fuck it. She's gone.

Few cars pass on the wide and soundless street as she stomps off toward her best guess of the border. It's two blocks before the sounds are completely left behind. Maybe they never are.

The air is warm again, most traces of the storm sucked up into dust. The sky has cleared except for one last cloud that hurries to refuel. Tilting dangerously, she lugs her heavy bag under the filmy streetlights of Nuevo. In Juarez, up the river, she knows they rape gut females by the dozen and dump them in the drink. Downstream in Matamoros they ran out of Moors to kill but armed robbery is sport. She reads. Border = bad. It's middle of nowhere, Friday night, Tex Mexlandia far from home. Theoretically, she's in deep shit.

In practice, though, the streets seem fine. A devoutly residential neighborhood—no stores, no shops, no late night peds. House after house after house winks with lights, dogs bark in a chorus line. Three cars and SUVs drive by but none of them are taxis. The last, a huge white tinted Mastodon, pulls up beside her, looming like a dump truck mated forcibly with hearse. Dopemobile. She keeps her step steady as if she knows exactly where she's going. What else can she do? But the fat boy isn't interested in her, keeps all mirrors shut as it accelerates gently out of sight.

Then she steps off a curb and feels the fear slip off her like a clean silk skirt.

A month ago, one summer night in Austin, she'd found herself on the East Side lost alone, looking for a party, cause East Side parties must be better than the Westlake shit, dope for coke, actual dancing, not all oral sex and flavored vodka. The truth was she had never been to an East Side party. She had never even crossed this part of I35 without Nathan Katie Jay as backup, and even then, where did they really go? Now or never. Get used to it. Jay and Katie gone, Nate a sudden piece of shit. The thing was she should have been gone too. She should have been headed for Buenos Aires or Madrid, that was all she'd asked, one year, rent her an apartment, give her a little leash, a little break, a little faith, a little time, how fucking hard was that? Was it a crime to want to be a person for a little while? All those straight years of A perfection and surviving high school crap, waking up every day and thinking *I'd rather slit my wrists than go*. But she went. Earwig. Cousin Itt. Hey aren't you this month's centerfold in *Popular Mechanics*? Those extra brains there in your ass? Her parents might be liars but she thought she knew them better. She thought she knew they'd see a girl who wanted it so bad she went behind their back with Mr. Sterling and called up Harvard to defer. And Harvard congratulated her! They recommended it! They thought it was a grand idea to postpone her humiliation at a new school! And who knows, maybe she'd be happier in Spanish? Anything could happen, except it couldn't, when her parents said no way and by then it was too late. Her hallowed spot was gone. January was the best Harvard could do. Not only no Madrid but starting halfway through the year. And until then she was stuck here, screwed, stuck in Austin, stuck with the Blond Brigade, stuck with one semester at U of fucking T, stuck with her angry dad and Nazi sympathizer mom who had screamed like Alma'd knifed her in the thigh. Stuck. She was going to have to learn to strike out alone or die. So there she went: party, alone, East Side, Friday night. The streets twisted and bent on her, the buildings shed their paint, the gutters filled with glass. She hit the lock button twice, turned the radio high, someone's nostalgic grunging. Passed concrete porches of beery men who stared at her car like they might like to eat it. She could sell her fear, she could put it in a box and detonate and blow a city block to bits.

A red light had forced the car to stop right where three young refurbished *éses* stood on the corner, kicking air, gangsta steady, watching her. And she was so mad, scared and mad, she wanted to cry, no matter what she dreamed about herself here she was just another little Westlake puss in the deep dark part of town, scared out of her enormous wits. The light turned green but she didn't know which way to turn. Shit. Shit. The East Side Austin bad boys watching her, flashing fingers, chopping it up, laughing and bumping and strutting in place. Here they came, chests out against spotless wife beaters, hands half cupped against their crotches or stretched out wide in a universal embrace. Dark stains and letterings of tattoos came visible. Then the light turned yellow and her fear went on ahead of her. She rolled down her window. They knew the street. Take me with you, huh? three jockeying for position, I be your guide, don't let him in your car that boy stinks, toilet for a mouth, I'm the only one can dance, girl. By the time she hit the party she already felt high. And driving home that night she started thinking: Mexico?

Bugs buzz harmless around the lone streetlight in front of her, its flicker strobing against the only street sign she's seen yet: Dr. Mier. Hell lo. Ready or not. Her cousins wait at 68. She dares.

She walks where cars should be because all sidewalk ends. On both sides of slim Dr. Mier concrete rules, and many of the buildings look unfinished, with dark steel rebar sticking out of the roofs like swizzle sticks. Maybe one day someone will build a second story, but in the meantime these roofs have stocked up on dogs. Dogs rush to the rim to greet her, barking down the block like children singing an old fashioned *ronde*. She doesn't badly mind the barking, dog's right after all, but a few of the nastier beasts do this trick where they rock back from the ledge and then scramble up again, stutter stepping as they lean into empty air like divers. It's convincing, first few times, these dogs about to launch onto her meat somewhere. Shoulder, thigh. As a rule she's fine with dogs but that's a dirty trick. Fuck you doggie, she says to one of these raging Rottweilers in the sky. And fuck you doggie too. They take offense and bark a little faster, staying put, swearing back.

If the houses have numbers, she doesn't see them often. 213. 128. At least the direction seems correct, consistent. Her mother walks past her in the opposite direction swinging arms and hips, headed for the store or plaza. *Oye, nena ¿dónde andas?* Her mother shouting friendly back. Nuh, she can't see it, can't see it at all. Wearing what? Mama unhappy with the uneven pavement, embarrassed by the crumble, wrinkling up her pretty nose at the smell. No. Easier to picture the young woman all grown up in Laredo with a letter in her hands.

My daughter,

I understand why you won't write me but I am your father and
you will never have another.

(translated from the Spanish by Alma Katherine Price)

Maybe the first thing Alma will ask her grandfather is what he did to deserve erasure. Maybe her cousins will have something to say about that. She's getting close. 72. A vacant lot. 66. She checks the envelope again and then turns around to stare at where the house should be.

The lot is not as vacant as it first appeared, but 68 Dr. Mier is spent. Burned. What's left is a concrete shell of a once one story home, now blackened like an old kiln. She swings the duffel off her shoulder and gropes around inside until she finds Daddy's tiny titanium flashlight. The ruins light up in front of her and she steps inside.

The floor's crumbled into concrete apples, the walls thin shattered cinderblocks. She leaves her duffel there up front, tucked back half concealed in rubble, and faces the rest of the building unencumbered, nimble, animal and quick.

Mom grew up in a shithole. Even with the fire's blunt remodel job, anyone can see that. A Mexican shithole. A Mexican *border* shithole. Does that explain it? Does that explain today's woman of steel who runs and bikes and swims as if that's how to reach the promised land, who rules house beautiful in short skirts and tight tops like some beefcake might show up, who loathes things cheap, who sometimes drives a truck and sometimes a silver 6 Series convertible, who denies her accent and won't speak a word of Spanish, who doesn't drink, who doesn't read, who believes in dinner, believes in men, who who who who who who who. I had a pretty hard childhood, was all she'd ever say. I guess I don't like looking back. Yeah, Mom. I guess.

So much for cousins. Alma takes a picture anyway, and the camera flashes eerie on the charcoal walls. This isn't Mexican. This isn't anything. The border is the problem, with all its copulating and the hailstorms and the narcos in their Mastodons and Blades, the goddamn bastards, the little stoners, the phony Dr. Mier. Fuck Laredo, and fuck

Nuevo, fuck all residents from El Paso through to Brownsville, they are no use to her. She has her marching orders. She has Mexico City.

From somewhere near the street, she hears mammals coming into the house. They move gracefully through the rubble, not making much noise, probing through the dark. She cuts her light. She picks up a rock just smaller than a baseball. The mammals are talking to one another now in Spanish. She gropes her way back into the dark of darkest corners, squats down with her arm cocked.

A few rooms away, the voices whisper like her child mother talking low with siblings when someone was napping here in back. It's true: the voices are young. Kids snuck out to play at night, pawing through her mother's ruined house, braving the inexplicable light inside. How old? It's late. Don't they believe in ghosts? They must be twelve at least. Twelve if she's lucky.

They whisper. What's *español* for double dare ya? They're headed back here, no doubt about it, they're moving down the hall through the rubble. Think. One B+ her whole life might have cost her valedictorian—and thank god what would she have said to those people, I hate all your fucking guts and thanks for making me feel small?—but all these brains gotta count for something. Back door. But it's too late. She'd still have to brave the hallway. Plan B then. Plan B is let them gain the door and then light, roar, rock.

Not yet. Timing is patience is everything. Not yet. Not. Not.

Where are they? No twelve year old but her has ever been so quiet. She can wait them out. She can wait forever except forever's coming fast. Breathe through the mouth. Her back dents into the wall where Grandma used to hang their clothes. *Abuelita's* dresses bury her in cotton and rough wool. The old woman is not old as she pulls apart the hangers and leans down to kiss her *nieta* on the nose. The girl smells bleach. *Aquí estoy. Ahora sabes.* Now do you feel better?

No sé, Abuelita. Tengo miedo.

Afraid of what? Listen to your accent. My little *gringa*. The City would laugh us out the door.

How do they know it's really biggest in the world?

It's big enough. Too big for you.

But Grandpa.

Grandpa's dead.

No he isn't. He isn't after all.

Well. Go home, *mijita,* your mother must be worried sick.

You don't know my mother anymore.

I know this is no place for *gringas* or *chilangas.*

I don't care.

Ay, cariña, you'll see, things are harder when you're dead.

They come for her and she fires. The rock finds its way through the door's mouth and thuds against the wall. She turns on her light. Everything is empty. She gets another rock and works her way up front. Empty. The whisperers or ghosts or tricks of sound have left. There's no one on the street either. Really? Ghosts? No ghosts in Texas but Alma's not in Texas anymore. What were they saying, what were they murmuring to her then? I might never know, she thinks, as she prepares to leave.

Instead she knows immediately. Shitty little ghosts. Her duffel bag is gone.

What they've got is the pale blue Fungicide T shirt Katie gave her and one irreplaceable photo album, plus Kerouac, Nin, Allende, Dahl, her white Pumas and black Martens, Jay's old Lees that fit her perfect. What she's got is her goodie bag with money, credits, notebook, pens, wallet, guidebook, Plath. Sunglasses, camera, iPod, two Rolexes of Dad's. Notebook. It could be worse. It probably will be, if she doesn't hurry up. If she can survive her own stupidity she can always buy new things.

Third intersection she hits is the most promising she's seen yet. The street has four lanes and real live traffic and a bar there on the corner with a dirt parking lot beside. Music booms from the long low building, slipping out the propped front door and vibrating into the night. From this distance it sounds like clown soundtrack, fast with lots of zany horns, tuba bass, accordion bouncing away beneath. Smoky rooms of rubber noses and floppy feet, men polka in pajama sleeves, painted smiles melt in heat. As she moves closer, the music changes to something slower, romantic, waltzing clowns in love. As if sensing her approach, a single hand emerges from the doorway and pulls the door rough shut.

In that new muffled quiet she hears voices in the parking lot. Familiar voices. They're not whispering anymore. Her heart no longer bangs triple time the high school fight song *hit 'em hard see how they fall! hit 'em knock 'em get the ball!* She can hear them pretty good.

Surrounded by an old gray wooden fence, the parking lot wraps in an L around the bar and that's where she finds the kids, hanging out where Dumpsters and guys pissing on the wall should be. Three of them, small, boys, ten tops. *Niños.* Little rascals. In the middle of their triangle sits her duffel bag, its belly zipped ajar. One of the kids holds Jay's jeans up to the light, examining the frayed knees with disgust. The others continue to dig for treasures, fighting one another for position. Her mini dryer. Bathroom kit. They look happier with that.

No one's seen her yet. She's been creeping up the flank, crouching low between the pick ups. Get as close as possible, is what she's thinking, so that when she freaks them they'll just drop everything and run. Should she scream in Spanish or in English? *Vete o te mato.* No, wait, plural. She can't remember the plural.

Her goodie bag bumps the mirror of a multi ton truck, and synchronized boy heads snap toward the sound. Now. Plural. She leaps out and toward them, shouting English that's my fucking stuff you fucking fucks!

They freeze. All three of them, paralyzed with surprise, their young eyes huge in the dim light. They stare limp as prey resigned to grisly fate. What is their fate? She stops two long steps from impact and in that hesitation she sees them see her: not a creature double feature, not an angry ape, not the boogeyman, not in fact a man at all. Girl. The faces thin and sharpen. Little men. They retreat from her, but slowly, pulling the bag as they go.

No, she says. She points a finger into the void. Get. Now. *¡Ahora!*

The Spanish is a mistake. They check each other and giggle, girl's a giggle, top to bottom, look at her. And suddenly they have something like a plan. It's not worked out yet and in that now or never she closes the gap, grabs the duffel with one hand and swipes at them with the other.

The tug of war begins. Four bodies stumble in the space squared off by building walls, a wooden fence, and cars. The boys hang on for dear life as she cranks the bag around, hoping to shake one and then the other in this crack the whip, but they've obviously played this game before. She's still shouting at them. Doesn't matter. Too much fun. The contents of her bag continue to centrifuge away. Kids are talking to her now, swearing probably, and now she screams, really screams like ax murderers are coming. They don't pay any attention at first but then, suddenly, the boys all let go at once. She staggers back a step, almost falls but keeps her feet. Get out of here! she yells, get! and this time they nod in agreement, turn and run without a word. Hitting the wood fence one by one by one, they vault clumsily over the top, the smallest having problems but he makes it without help from his buddies, who offer none. Just like that, they're gone.

Then she turns around to exit and sees why.

Backlit, their faces dark, five men stand spaced apart like gunslingers, their long distorted shadows thrown by streetlight to her feet. There's a big man on the left and then the others are shorter than her but wide, with working arms that bulge out of their tight shirts. These arms do things. She glances at the spot in the fence where the kids went over but the big man breaks from the group and beats her to it.

She stands up straight and clasps both hands in front of her, hoping her voice holds.

Gracias. Rateros pequeños.

The men punch one another with delight. *Órale.* In unison they move closer, talking all at once. They may be good brothers and fathers and loyal husbands, but as pure geometry the situation's grim, angles of escape dissolving fast. *Mis cosas,* she says, waving one hand at the debris. This time no one hears her. No one cares.

They've reached the perimeter where her things begin, picking them like carrots, shaking them triumphant in the air. A man with clippered hair and dark blue jeans leans down to grab her sweatshirt and instead tips over, falling heavily on his side. He rolls onto his back snorting like a happy hog and stretches out his arms and lies there peacefully contemplating sky. His friends roar. On a scale of one to ten, she's about to shit her pants.

Are you okay.

The one that's spoken is the youngest of the bunch, and the closest too, two steps away. Early twenties, decent English, or those three words at least. In his hands he holds her mini photo album which he offers to her, extending his arms out long so he doesn't get too close. She takes it.

Thank you.

What are you doing here. He's clean shaved and almost handsome, longish hair slicked back into a helmet with vast quantities of gel.

I don't know. It's. It's a long story. She imagines Nathan there instead, Nathan you will not believe this, but Nathan is not there and the guy just shakes his head. The men behind him are calling and whistling. He bends down and stuffs Jay's jeans and some tampons quickly in her bag.

You're alone? She doesn't answer. You need to get out of here, he says.

I know.

I have a car.

Just get me to a taxi.

He leans toward her and she smells beer, cigarettes, gasoline, and cologne. You don't understand. He sighs and his breath is somehow eucalypty. Stay close to me, he mumbles. Don't say anything.

Two buddies stand grinning at them from a step away. The one with a yellow baseball cap puffs out his chest and pokes the young guy roughly in the shoulder.

Oye, güey, ¿quién es tu novia? He's got the revving engine lilt but the young guy doesn't find it funny, shaking his head with his eyes. Gheelfren, the yellow cap says to her, tipping his brim and winking slowly. *¿Qué bonita, no?*

Preciosa, says buddie number two. This one's wearing a Minnesota Vikings T shirt about eight sizes too small, so his big shoulders, chest, and arms puff out like a Macy's Day parade. He steps closer, bumping young'en back the other way. The kid is tongueless, xraying his own feet.

Pero descuidada, says Yellow Cap. You need to take care of your things, my love. He holds out one big fist and opens it. The thick fingers curl back, and a pair of Crayola red panties bloom in his palm like an exotic flower. He waits for her but she doesn't move.

You got the wrong girl, she whispers.

Your pretty things, Yellow says. Splays his fingers through the elastics, a childhood cat's cradle, keeping his eyes on her all the while. So little for a big girl like you.

Leave her alone, Boyo says softly.

What. Yellow glances at him, smiling murder. What did you say?

Here comes Boyo. She takes the smallest step conceivable to her left, to see if left is possible, but the others are watching her.

Nothing, Boyo says. She can't believe it. Nothing! It can't be nothing! His eyes meet hers for half an instant, angry, and then flick back to Yellow, submissive with old fear. I didn't say nothing.

All right then. Yellow turns his attention back to her, her panties skewered in his outstretched hand. I think these are yours, no? he says. Don't you want them?

No, she says. She can barely hear her own voice.

They're very pretty. They both stare at the red underwear as if it's a crystal ball. You don't want to lose them. Why don't we make a trade?

Please, she says. Please don't. Boyo won't look at her, if he'd just look at her maybe her future would return.

A fair trade. Give me. Yellow stares at her belt. He has clear ideas

34

where this is headed but then Minnesota comes to life, reaching out one doughboy arm and plucking the panties gently from his friend, grinning like electroshock. Minnesota, then. There must be one right thing to scream or say. Minnesota is a father, Minnesota has a sister, Minnesota has a mother, Minnesota's wept. The big man brings the red red panties to his nose and presses them against his face, inhaling deeply. He holds the panties out in front of him and lets out a big hum before he stretches out the waistband and snaps them on his head like a shower cap. No one makes a noise, no one, not a dog on the block or a star in the sky, not until he yanks them down over his face like a wrestling mask, his eyes bugging from the leg holes, and that's it, that's the last straw, all of them are laughing and staggering like the drunks they are.

She runs.

She runs.

She runs and someone grabs her. Hand wraps briefly around her waist. It's there and then it disappears and she knows only that she runs, runs serpentine through men and trucks, the photo album pressed Bible hard against her chest like it might save her from what's next. But when she looks back to see who's coming they haven't followed her at all but still stand laughing laughing in a sloppy semicircle, where Yellow has replaced his cap with an old black thong while the tall guy's trying to strap her white bra onto the fall down drunk. The only one who looks at all is Boyo and that's her last vision as she rounds the corner, Boyo's sad black morning eyes with her red panties bobbing up and down behind him. Her undergarments dance and sing as she hits the main street with its lanes of traffic, raises her hand to stop a cab or swear in faith and make all of them, all of Mexico, disappear.

Three

What wakes her, finally, is a road crew mutilating pavement out-side her hotel window. At least the racket is American. She reaches into her goodie bag and checks Daddy's Rolex. 11:34. Holy crap. She had to risk the credit card last night. Daddy's Little is on the map now.

An hour later she's out the door onto Laredo's streets, washed, rest-ed, fresh. The workmen are done for Saturday, and the square is quiet and abandoned. A bored taxi driver catches her eye. South of the bor-der they might still be dancing around with panties on their heads, but here in Texas civilization rules.

So where we headed, miss?

I need to do some shopping. You got a Tony Patra's?

Hasn't made it down here yet. There's a Diggstown up off 35?

Diggstown. How about Picky's?

Yeah, we got one a those.

Picky's, then.

You betcha.

The man boy section at Picky's, with its world of dark dulled col-ors and shapeless pants, proves even more lame than she imagined. Never paid much attention to boys' clothes. They don't so why should she. But now she has to study a little. Loose, drab, straight, boxy, logos, sports caps, vertical stripes. This is what it means to be a little man.

She's no mama's girl but she still finds it painful buying stuff so bulky, cheap, and crass.

I want to wear stuff out of here, she tells the salesgirl. I didn't want you to think I was, you know, stealing.

No. We wouldn't think that.

In the dressing room, she assembles herself. Baggy faded jeans, bunching up around her sneakers. Sports bra. Never needed one before—no tits, no sports—but now she needs a tight elastic band to strap the little flesh back. Untucked T shirt, oversized, crimsony with white ribbing on the sleeves and neck. Adjustable blue white logoed baseball cap, long hair tucked inside. The rat kid in the mirror swims in rotten clothes. Wimp. Dork. She looks perfect. She dumps her shorts and tank top in the trash, charges it, and hits the Diggstown for accessories. Big loathsome two strap backpack because she can't risk the sling. Black wraparound sunglasses, skinhead style. Shiny black red moonboot high tops boykind seems to like. Piece by piece she vanishes until she finds the sign of no return.

The sign says boys and men eight bucks. Odd looks await her there inside. There's the barber and a kid in the chair and the buddy flipping through *Sports Fever*, waiting his turn. He takes a break to stare at her a while, trying to figure her out. The barber and the chair kid too. But she sits down and grabs her own mag like she knows what she's doing.

Sports Fever is not the best place to browse for hair ideas. Most of the guys are wearing hats and helmets. And the rest of them are black. Finally she finds something, a white baseball player with his hair clippered on the side, left a little longer up top, a touch spiky. He looks like a meathead. It might work.

The kid steps out of the chair. His haircut shows short on the side but not clippered, gives his head a little volume, and then left a little long and mildly boxy in the back. Up top there's enough length that it lies down, and he's had it combed straight back and held in place by gel. He looks like a million million kids that age, he looks impeccably normal, looks like Skoal and pimples and PS2. That, she thinks, that's the cut for me. He gets his buddy and they vanish quickly, without a word, but tossing her one last suspicious look. Fag. Dyke.

She stands and approaches the chair. The barber's face knits in thought, and then—she sees it happen—gives her the benefit of the doubt. Before he can say a word she hops up, removes her cap, and places it on her lap. He almost gasps. In all other things her genes have screwed her but Alma's got her mother's hair. Long, dark, thick, a little wavy, shiny. Her hair is almost beautiful, down to the middle of her back. The scent of hotel shampoo fills the silent air. He's about to reach out and touch it but stops himself, redirects his hand to cover his mouth as if in haut stylist contemplation.

I want mine just like his.

Okay. The hand comes down. He seems relieved. He bibs her fast, gathers her long hair up in a one handed ponytail, clicks his shears twice above her head. She closes her eyes. The weight departs. She promises herself there'll be no bursting into tears. She opens. The breath comes deep and quickly through her nose. She tries to laugh but air stutters from her in a hypothermic shiver. The girl in the mirror has recently escaped from an insane asylum perched on a lonely hilltop where they perform experiments.

Stepping away from the chair, the barber holds the dead weasel of her hair and dumps it in the trash. Now he works briskly. Doesn't wet her down just snips and snips away. She almost cries out to stop him as he carves a curve above the ears—a new grim feature rising from obscurity—but he doesn't hesitate. Man's a professional. Man knows what boys like.

There.

He hands her the mirror and spins around to face the wall. Her new head is rectilinear. She nods. He spins her back and hands her a tub of orange gel. Boys do such things themselves. Her forehead looms huge as she pushes the hair back, trying not to freak. Her face is muttonous. Her tint and contrast lost. She looks like suicide. The barber pouts in satisfaction and nods slowly. It's a new day, he says and matadors her smock aside. She pulls herself together, snaps an imaginary piece of gum in her mouth, and jams her baseball cap on tight again.

Yeah, thanks.

Oh you're welcome.

She doesn't tip him whatsoever. The little punk in the mirror wouldn't, so why should she.

It's evening by the time she makes it to the bus station, where she rushes to the bathroom and takes her time to size up the what—what?—in the mirror. The Whatwhat looks a little like her dad, to tell the truth, if someone shoved a bike pump in dad's skin and then inflated. If Dad's white skin was rubbed raw. If someone really fucked him up. With her hair in a dumpster, she's pretty much free of her mom. Her tiny breasts are gone. The Whatwhat is ambiguous. Better with the cap on or off? The problem is she looks about twelve right now. The sunglasses are good though. And frowning's good. Make a muscle in the jaw. Slit the eyes. Ugly works. Context. Maybe some older clothes would help. At least the timing's right. She just finished her period.

The next bus does not leave for two hours, and the only seats left are in the back, but she buys a ticket anyway, mumbling in her lowest key. She retreats to a corner and pretends to read. Turns the book upside down, slumps low in her chair, picks her nose, spreads her legs a slut's length apart, rocks her knees back and forth. No one notices her. No one looks at her at all. Who knew she only had to be a boy to completely disappear?

In the seats across from her, four guys in their early twenties have sat down loudly and are filling up the place with conversation. Two white, two Chicano, but all four voices all American. The Chicanos are from Laredo, and one of them still lives here. The rest live up in Austin. They're headed off together and damn it's got them chatty. If they're on her bus these jerks will drive her nuts.

Dude and she was *hot*. Believe you got in there.

She pulled the rip but Sam's a stubborn bastard.

His *technique*.

Technique shit.

So where's the king? Ha ha ha ha ha.

Late.

Suprise, suprise.

If he got on the damn thing.

She studies them. For instance: the way they act oblivious to the world is different, not intentional, not blocking yet aware the way girls do, just clueless. Nothing out there concerns them. If it ain't blowing up or titty, they couldn't care less. Security. Invulnerability. What else? They don't quite look at one another.

Dude the king he's like an AK firing blind into the crowd. One lucky bullet flips some bitch on all fours and he's done.

And Sam's bazooka. One target, all night, everything you got.

Too much work for me.

You the land mine. Girl strays from the pack and boom! your dick is in her mouth.

All crack up again. They could do this forever. They could have the same conservation in twenty minutes and love it all over again. They're stupid, they're fucking idiots, but there's a rhythm there, a percussion, and she thinks she could get it. Like stepping into a double dutch.

How 'bout Dean?

They turn toward the blond guy, thin with great bones in his face. He hasn't said a thing. White smile. Deep laughter. Pretty cute is what he is.

D got *no* technique.

Last man standing.

Plus no standards whatsoever.

Sounds like technique to me. The one named Sam leans back and his eyes fall smack on hers. Bunch of dirty old men, huh, Sam says to her.

She clenches her jaw, keeps the mouth straight, shrugs. The jump ropes spin and spin. You probably got your angle too, Sam says. They're all looking at her now.

At that age? Shit, his buddy says, it's all confidence. Those little girls just dying for it, don't even know what *it* is.

That's the truth, Sam says. He points at her. Chase and ye shall receive.

These are the guys. Treated her like lichen. Called her Earwig or Cousin Itt. This is what Joey McKenney and Grant Pauls and Shawn Stettner are going to be in a few years. Not the all out jocks but Asshole Lite. Who's got time for Earwig? Life's too short for smart, weird, homely girls. But despite all that she wants to say something. She wants to hold her boy head high and not slink her way through Mexico. Mute. Deaf. Shame, assault, discovery. Rape. Rape. She fights the panic in her throat as she leans into their crossfire.

Well, she says as gruff as she can, I. She sniffs to get another breath and lets her head nod slightly. I go for the ugly ones.

Ugly how? She's failed. A freak even in disguise.

You know, she tries, the ones who think they're ugly? When they look in the mirror? You know they do. Her voice is a little shaky, she doesn't know where to put it. She leans down low in her chair, pulls her brim down over her eyes. In this glare of boys her smushed boobs feel like 44 double Ds. She thinks of her father murmuring bawdy with his buddies on hot Austin nights, in a bar on a boat on the long front porch at home.

'Cause the ugly ones' the *wild* ones, she mumbles. She grabs her knees so her hands don't tremble. Her daddy whispers and she repeats. You know what they say. Plain on top, fire in the hole.

They all stare at her for what seems like a long long moment and then laughter ripples through their fine teeth down the row.

Goofball.

Child prodigy.

Gotta start drinking on this shit. What time is it? Where the fuck is he?

The one named Sam leans toward her, holding out a fist. She rolls up her fingers tight. Her nails dig into palm as she puts it out there and they whack knuckles. Ouch. She hopes she did that right. She wishes Nathan could see this.

Where you headed? he says.

Monterrey.

Yeah? Us too.

The 9:30?

Bus? Nah, we got a big ol' truck, we picking up a buddy down from Austin. What you got going down there?

Nothing, she says. Family.

He nods. This sucker's getting married in Monterrey on Sunday. We're making it a weekend. His eyebrows jag with expectation. MEH he coh. He pronounces it right, in an exaggerated sort of way. Square jawed with an army cut and mischief in his eyes. I'm Sam, he says.

Al.

He nods approval. She's so fucking good at this. She didn't watch these jerkoffs all those years for nothing. The next right thing to say is foaming on her lips when outside a bus comes hissing to a halt. Their much anticipated buddy has arrived.

Tall enough, bald headed, blue eyed and long lashed, full lips pursed in a half smile, he pauses in the doorway with the day's last light behind him, ready to dare the whole room to a fight. Instead he grins and struts their way, practically limping, hips forward, shoulders back, arms bowed out slightly to the side. Their faces light up one by one by one, watching him come.

She knows him.

Hey there Billy. His voice is soft and almost breathless, full of her daddy's East Texas drawl. He wraps a thick arm around the nearest one, manhugs him quick and tight. Well aww right. Goddamn brother E, what's going on? Big D. He slaps hands all around. Look like you're going to summer camp or something. Where'd you get the kid?

Without knowing it, she's risen too and stands in the receiving row, watching him come. Stupid. Now they must all see what she is, some fucked up gender mishmash shaped like a potato. And this guy. She does not want this guy looking at her. He's from Beaumont, where her daddy's from. Lives in Austin. Paints houses. He painted theirs, that's for sure, she saw him every day for a week last summer. He sweat like crazy, worked without a shirt, fast. Lee. Lee something. He knows everyone in Austin.

She watches him, deer stuck in lights.

That's Al.

Well alright. He evaluates as she looks him in the arms. The Kid, he says. He puts out his hand. She doesn't want to touch it but she has to, doesn't she, and so they shake, except he tries to do something like a snap off the end of her fingers that she botches badly. He frowns. We got The Kid. Every time he says it draws the sound out longer: kieeeeeed.

Catch a ride with us, you want, Sam says to her, grinning at Lee. I'm not sure I'd recommend it.

The Kid don't want no bus. Buncha onion smelling homos in there, man.

We can't bring him. How old is he?

It's good luck to have The Kid.

He's a minor.

Ain't no minors in Mexico. Shit.

Don't mind them, says cute blond Dean.

Al likes ugly ones, Sam says.

Not anymore. You with the king now. It's top shelf pussy filet mignon from here on out. Lee stretches out his arms, cracks his neck loud and quick to both sides. Mex e COE. Let's go, man, I'm hungry.

Five minutes later she's in the back of a huge pickup with extend-ed cab, four men inside, three out. She can't remember if she said a word but somehow here she is. They're turning onto the empty side streets of Laredo and heading toward the border. Jump out. Jump. Yellow Cap and Minnesota are waiting with her panties.

Where we gonna get bud, Lee asks Dean, winking at her.

Don't worry about it. Dean smiles. He looks like he hasn't worried about anything for a long time.

Alright. Lee produces a well loved lumpy cigarette. Let's smoke this real quick. He lights and takes a monster drag, burning a third of the thing away. Then Dean and they pass it. She tries to make it look good before she hands it back. They finish and flick the cherry sadly into oblivion as the US border booths come into sight. The air feels right whisking through her short hair.

They ain't got the kind bud over in Mexico.

We'll be fine.

Goddamn, that's it right there, huh. Mex e COE. Lee lifts himself up to the rails of the truck. Ahead of them, brightly uplit, a flag sized half a football field wags its wide bands of dark green and white and red. The screaming eagle splays in the middle, flapping his wings, rattling the snake in his claw. The bright white lights of the border put a halo around the cars ahead of them, the guards, Lee's bald head and Dean's golden hair. She can see his split ends, each tiny fiber that's come unwound and frayed. Class registration would have been in three weeks. It's winter in Buenos Aires and Nathan's in Atlanta. Sor Juana read Shakespeare, didn't she? Five brilliant thoughts go streaking naked through her mind so fast she can't get a good look at any one of them. Stoned.

Look at all that. Like Vietnam or something. Lee pokes at Dean's shoulder. That normal? Dean doesn't answer.

Yeah, she says. Her voice sounds low and nice. If she can keep her chin down.

That's normal?

Totally.

Damn war zone. They gonna mess with us, huh? Man they gonna mess with us.

It's cool, Dean says.

They gonna mess with us. Shit, you got a mint or something?

You got to push a button, Alma says. They both look at her. She should be scared of Lee who's stoned who stares who knows her but she's not. Yeah, you got to push this button. Just don't get red. She shrugs.

What?

They mess with you.

I ain't pushing no button. He smoothes back the tight skin of his head with one hand. You know they going after the bald head motherfucker.

Well, hopefully they won't give you the glove, she says. He's still staring so she mimes it, snapping latex on her hands.

Lee's eyes get huge and wild, a horse set to toss his rider. Fuuuhck that! I ain't going through there! They're in the middle of the bridge now, froze in traffic. Lee lifts his head up and peers down over the side into the trickle of the Rio Grande.

Dean's head bangs against the truck as he laughs hard at the stars pricking one by one through the darkening sky. He's just messing with you, man. He smacks Alma softly on the head. The glove.

It happens, she says. She can still feel Dean's smack and it feels good. No one knows it but she's powerful. Would not surprise her if her hands and feet are growing.

Try to peek through my backdoor. Lee still looks panicked as he checks the guards and dogs and fences waiting on the other side. My god. He's half laughing now. Shit look at all of those motherfuckers.

It's cool, Dean says again.

The guards wave them to a spot and they kill the engine, pile out. It's not funny but if she looks at anyone she'll lose it. The inspectors ooze suspicion as they circle truck and reach into the bed, feeling up the bags.

The guard says in Spanish: one of you come with me.

The guys exchange looks. Customs, one says finally. Lee points right at her.

The Kid take care of it.

She opens her mouth but the guard is already leading her over to the little room with the traffic light. Powerful. She follows.

For some reason, this time, there's no one else waiting. Feels like a set: the miniature stoplight, the xray machine, the guards with guns, small cameras rolling from the ceiling and off to the side. She walks up to the light and pushes the button before anyone can think about it. Green. She knew it. She turns around smiling, ready to go, but the guard shakes his head and points to the button again, stabbing a finger long range through the stale air.

That's not right, she's pretty sure. This time she presses her pinky against it for good juju. Green. Ha.

He shakes his head, points. She can't believe it.

¿Por qué? she says.

He's surprised to hear his language, even the little bit, or maybe it's her decent accent. Now he stares at her. *¿Papeles?* He scrutinizes her tourist card and hands it back.

Tiene que hacerlo una vez para cada pasajero. His Spanish is fast but she understands him perfectly. Once for every passenger means four more times.

¿De verdad?

Sí.

She pushes the button again. Green. *¿Está bien?* she says.

Three more times.

Three? Please, she says. My brothers are not as *pendejos* as they seem. The words surface without effort. Words crawl from their caves and bunkers and blink into the light.

He smiles. Your brothers?

Different fathers.

The guard grins. Bastardry and whoresons are funny. *Así es,* he says.

Así es.

Again, the guard says, still smiling, cajoling, pointing at the button.

She puts her ringless ring finger on it. She's got a bad feeling. She's running out of fingers. The red is out there somewhere, waiting to cast a sickly light and xrays into every cranny of their vehicle and insides. She drops her hand.

Sir? she says, the streetlight doesn't want us. *Semáforo*—how does she know that? Three times, she says, is enough, no? Three times, like a fairy tale. *Cuento de hadas.* Her mother must have crossed this bridge a thousand times and been bullied in this room. Her mother used her beauty but Alma has her wits. Her mother told her fairy tales but never the true Mexico. Three times is enough, she says and looks the guard in his left eye. Right brain. That's where empathy lives.

Está bien, he says. He shrugs and takes her back and shakes his head so slightly at the other guard and the two of them drift away to attend a beat up station wagon. From the look on their faces, they're going to take that shitty little car apart.

Let's go.

Two mammoth speed bumps later she's back in Mexico. And soon she's drunk. She's full of beer and guacamole in the parking lot of Los Jarritos and the guy named Eddie's pulling a Ziploc full of dope from his crotch. The two Chicanos from Laredo—short light skinned Cristobal, plump Willy groom—can't believe their friend's stupidity but Lee is very proud of him and happy. By the time they hit the Señor Frog's they're all stoned comprehensively. Boom boom boom boom techno trash.

There ain't no women here, says Lee.

Then they're back in the truck, driving into the desert, headed for Boys' Town.

Four

The road gets worse after the liquor store. Huge pavement holes snap open and take bites out of the truck. Out there in the blackness sits what looks like two eyes in the desert staring at the sky, and as they get closer she can see a kind of glowing race track twisted in a figure eight. A small walled city of shacks and building, bustling busy in the night.

Boys' Town, Lee says. The way he says it sounds even more sinister than it already is.

At the great gate, a giant dog stands guard alongside two cops with submachine guns. Everyone waves them through. A police substation squats there in the lot with cops propped against the walls, while inside an officer smokes cigarettes and types under fluorescent lights. Beyond, one building seems to lord over the rest and they park behind it. Texas plates and pickups everywhere. An insect march of men streams from lot to building, men in boots and hats and buckles, beef fed ranchers and fair haired frat boys, some straight eyed, some staggering. Lee catches her in full gawk.

You just stay close to the king, he says.

Inside the place looks like a dancehall except no one is dancing. Fifty sixty sexed out women circumambulate the room, locked in hand to hand commerce with keen male shoppers. The stares in this room could suffocate babies in their cribs. Some of the women are taller, some shorter, some have light skin and some almost black, there are blonds and a redhead or two, but somehow they're all Mexican. Maybe it's their mouths, the slight pouting frown of a Spanish speaking mouth at rest. She doesn't know what it is but it's Mexican. They wear short dresses and minis, halter tops and high heels and modified bikinis, they sway like sea creatures in the music and the heat. And Alma's drowning, choking on the human parts. She's never seen a whore before, although the word's a favorite with her so called peers for any girl who steals a boyfriend, or goes down, or doesn't, or wears tall heels, or doesn't, or anyone at all. But they have no idea what they're talking about, do they? At the far end of the room, she spots the gates of hell propped open to a dark staircase beyond, where instant couples reel past each other through the portal's gaping mouth, ignoring everything but business. Upstairs somewhere, things are taking place. She feels her ribs and hips contracting, like her own parts are turning themselves inside out to hide.

Her posse takes in the scenery. Not one of them looks repentant. Not one of them looks like an awkward Holden Caulfield who just really wants to talk. They sit down at a table, order beers, and gaze.

Alma's first sip demolishes half the bottle right off the bat. Imagine paying some girl to. Imagine thinking that was pretty cool. She closes her eyes as she sips again and sees her teenage mom, the girl in the photo who hardened into her mother. Oh God does this explain it? What happens to a young Mexican girl that makes her lose all hope? She opens her eyes and all she sees is penises. Penises in hats, penises in khakis, penises laughing hysterically at something another penis said. How poor can these girls be? How do they do it? How can they do it? That dark skinned girl in the pink top right there, how, please?

The girl in pink swings around and nails Alma in her sights.

Skin gelato smooth and perfect, big breasts and hips and butt, the pink whore struts her bare legs, tossing around her long black hair. She's wearing this trashy halter polyester thing that ties in front, two sizes too small. Silver four inch sandal heels, white micro sidetie that barely covers cheek. Halloween costume of a whore. Her nose is a little crooked but it actually makes her real and beautiful. She's not twenty yet, or maybe barely. Dollar lipstick, sand pink shadow, lots of charcoal eyeliner. Is she a runaway?

The unfed lions Alma's with start growling and Lee's up on his feet.

Hey little sister.

Qué tal papi. Her thigh is in his pale hand.

Tell the truth.

She smiles, reaches out, and cups the back of his neck. He leans in to whisper but licks her ear instead. She leads him away.

Goddamn.

You guys come here growing up?

Hell yeah, fair Cristobal says, looking over at plump Willy who nods but barely. Half the guys we know got laid upstairs the first time.

In unison they all look at Alma. Too late, she says. Her only hope's that her disgusted face resembles malicious lust.

Eddie tilts his head at her, flopping his hair to one side. Yeah right, he says. We're getting you some tonight.

Fuck, Sam says, we're getting *me* some tonight. I never been to a whorehouse. I mean this is a real live whorehouse. Guess I'll try just about anything once.

They drink to that but then Lee returns alone.

A hundred bucks! Goddamn. Never paid for it in my life. She should pay me!

Not cheap.

Get a white girl for that. Lee points at Cristobal. I can't speak no Spanish, come on now, get that down to fifty. I ain't paying no hundred dollars for some Mexican. I don't care how fine she is.

There other places. This the most expensive.

And the best, Willy pitches in.

Come on, Lee says, and Cristobal goes with him.

Now that she thinks about it, maybe she has seen a prostitute before. Not just in Kerouac and Fante, Nin and *Cops* and *Pretty Woman.* What about those women hanging on South Congress, faces missing, waiting for cars to stop? What about Lisa Reggio, who supposedly sucked off any guy who would gas up her old Bronco? These faces here are killing her. They smile and frown and wrinkle and purse. She is a person who hates people but the hate behind these faces must be advanced. The fat ugly man grunting on top of them, his mother for giving birth, *their* mothers for letting this happen, God, the government, CEOs. Mexico. The whole world for punching holes in them again and again and again. Is that all Nathan wanted?

She makes herself keep drinking. She wants to get as drunk as twelve year olds who raid the liquor cabinet for schnapps and Triple Sec and vomit up a lung, and maybe she's on her way when their table is beset by whores. A dyed buxom blond paratroops into Dean's lap, one hand disappearing between his legs like a ferret run to ground, and Alma jumps and races for the bathroom before that is her fate too. She finds an empty stall with a door that doesn't lock and no toilet seat which must be why someone's been shitting on the wall. To the sound of piss pounding an aluminum trough outside, she holds the door closed with one hand, lowers her pants and levitates and proceeds with quiet caution. She breathes through her mouth, trying not to breathe at all.

She'll sneak away. She'll find a taxi. Join the Society Against Whoredom. Anything God wants.

When she emerges from the bathroom, though, the guys are waiting there for her, ready to move on. The track outside is packed with matrons hollering in the doorways of unpainted concrete barracks, pulling girls out for show like dead rabbits from hats. Men wander in packs of three and five and twenty, drinking out of plastic cups, dipping in and out of places with the air of bookstore browsers. Lee stops to haggle a few times but he's just having fun. They pass the signs: dog show, monkey show, donkey show. There's no show she wouldn't believe.

I left my wallet in the truck, she tries, in her best indifferent dude voice.

Bullshit. Lee stares her up and down.

I don't care about shows, says Sam. Let's find some women. I'll cover The Kid.

Alright. Lee puts his face in hers. But you ain't going nowhere. I seen you before, he says.

Murk stirs there in her stomach. I think I might throw up.

You ain't throwing up. Don't lie.

Hey, it's cool, says Dean, stepping in close.

No. I seen this little dude before.

I never seen you, she says. Her accent's more East Texas than it's ever been before. She can feel the sweat bunching up there at the edges of her sports bra, about to blot her shirt like gunshots, but her voice is low and steady. When you gonna pick a *señorita,* anyway? We're all waiting on you. She juts her chin at him. She must be drunker than she thought.

His pupils get small and hard and then exhale. I got my eye on you. You ain't going nowhere. His hand comes at her quick and she blinks before he hits her, except he doesn't, just settles five thick fingers on her shoulder like a familiar sent to guide and to protect. We got The Kid! Not gonna let his boys down like that! The guy's a pig, right, he's a slimy pig dog and would sell her just for sport but under the warmth of that hand she gets an instant of how it'd be to be his friend. A calm sure loyalty there, unquestionable and strong.

All right, she says.

Alllll right, he echoes back. His big hand stays on her shoulder and Dean puts one on the other as they weave and sailor along onto an uncrowded stretch of track.

Standing alone, towering above the concrete shacks, a two plus story building throws festive yellow light and music as they pass. First Sam then Lee and then the others stop, contemplate the structure for a while. It's something out of a movie set, wood done up in the style of Old West saloon with a long front porch, swinging doors, small curtained gabled windows up above. A sign above the door explains *Cow*

Bar. They mount the front stairs, push open the swinging doors, and head in like badass strangers pulling into town.

Inside the place is empty except for four guys sitting glum and quiet who come to semi life as boys arrive. One of them sticks his fingers in his mouth as if looking for a bug and whistles shocking while the others wait to see what happens. Lee and Sam and company are already turning around, but the whistle stops them. From the second story, descending slut majestic down curved, showcase stairs, women begin to materialize. They're decked out like fake cowboys, with flimsy hats and belts and plastic pistols strapped to hips. An extra tall dyed blond in cut off Wranglers comes first, boasting an American flag halter top with patriotic nipples; a sheriff type in rawhide leather complete with fake mustache and silver star; the outlaw with her ammo belt crossed between double Ds; a redhead Dallas Cowgirl. Six in all. They strut over to their guests and lead them to tables over on one side. In the dim light, it's hard to tell what they look like although Alma gets a better look as they remove their hats and put them on guys' heads. The cow whores have long hair, heavy makeup with sparkles. Alma gets a hat on her head too from Sheriff who also removes the mustache and tucks it in her cleavage, reaching out toward Alma's neck. Alma jerks away and Sheriff gives her a nasty look before smiling. Her tongue looks fake.

Hello little man, she says, reaching down and pressing one long fingernail into Alma's thigh.

Alma glances over at the others as she smacks the hand away. They're deep in negotiation and paying no attention. *No quiero nada,* she says. *Lo siento.*

The Sheriff bites her lip, showing salt white teeth, and pokes her tongue out again to run it along the bottom of her upper lip. *¿Nada? ¿Cómo que nada?*

No dinero, she tries, fending off the Sheriff's hands with soft super kung fu moves. She points at her friends. They got all the money, and they're not spending it on me. *Cabrones.*

That seems to work fine. The Sheriff immediately leaves her to join a double team on Lee, who is squeezing butts for ripeness, trying to make up his mind.

Eddie is the first to rise and let himself be led away, and Lee is next, choosing the Sheriff after all. Cute Dean has managed to fall asleep alone in the corner, and no one can revive him. Maybe she can do that too, there's nowhere she'd rather be than fake snoozing over there but lots of whores are in her way. They crowd around Sam, last man standing. He leans against the wall, flirting heavily with extra tall in cutoffs. Her legs are muscular. High strong cheekbones. She reaches down between his legs and rubs like he looks cold, and they continue to chat amiably like that until Sam nods and smiles, concedes her point, and follows her to the base of the staircase. Alma sees him hesitate a moment, she hears the voice yelp in his head *what am I doing* but the echo must die away fast because he glances at her, shrugs comic ironic and marches on. As they start to ascend, Alma catches Cutoff's profile, watches the way she curves a bony hand around Sam's waist as if to lift him bodily upstairs. The bones around the eyes. The jaw.

Alma jumps up from her chair. Sam! Look out, she's a man!

Sam hears something. His name, perhaps. The music is loud. He turns back to her and waves with cheerful solidarity. He shrugs as if to say, isn't this wacky, ain't Homo sapiens something?

No! she calls out. Man! she shouts again. The pimp tenders at the bar start looking mildly alarmed, edging themselves off stools. She Man! she yells, ignoring them. She Man!

But Sam has already turned back to business, continuing up the stairs, and when Alma starts to run after him she finds one very angry Dallas Cowgirl in her path. Shit, she's a man too. They're all men, and this one is pissed.

You liar. The She Man's English is heavily accented. I call the police. You know Mexican police?

Right, sorry, okay. Every step Alma takes is mirrored by the She Man, they are dancing uneasily back into a corner, running out of room. I made a mistake, Alma says.

Dallas stares at her, and then grabs her jaw, holding her head firmly in her grip. Releases her. *Uta, ya veo,* Dallas says. Very slowly, inch by inch, she examines Alma from head to toe like a used car lemon she almost bought. *Chinga.* You a girl.

Blood pounds in Alma's head. Shame strangles her neck. No, she says. She waves Dallas off with both hands. I'm tired, I'm sorry, I'm drunk, sorry about everything.

I don't think so. Dallas slants her eyes down to Alma's crotch, pouts a wicked smile. No. Show me.

I just look young, says Alma. I don't even want to be here. They dragged me.

Who?

My friends.

Tus amigos, Dallas says, switching to Spanish, your friends have no idea. She winks at Alma, showing matching blue and silver eye shadow lacquered thick. Alma tries to step away but Dallas grabs her by the elbow. Show me, Dallas says. She reaches out with one hand toward Alma's crotch.

Not here. She can't think of what else to do. Dallas shouts something at the pimps and grabs Alma's wrist with a forehand grip and leads her upstairs.

The room is big enough for a bed but not much more. Dallas closes the door behind them. Let's see it, she says in English, leaning against the exit. You show me cock I fuck you free.

I'm not showing you shit. She holds out one hand like a crossing guard. I'll pay you. I'll pay you if you just be quiet and leave me alone.

Oye, Dallas says, talk nice, okay? Just show me, please? She's back in Spanish again, almost whining, stepping toward her, pushing her hand aside. Please? I'm so curious now.

How much. I have sixty dollars.

Dallas sits back on the edge of the bed and pouts. Girls pay extra, she says. Eighty. Dallas turns her head and examines herself in the mirror.

You think I look like a man.

No. I was just confused. I'm drunk.

You're jealous. I suppose you must be an ugly girl. She watches Alma closely, waiting for her to flinch. Your friends are not your friends. They don't know.

Alma passes her four twenty dollar bills, making sure their hands don't touch. Can I go now?

So soon? The money vanishes. You want everyone to think you're such a quick little bunny?

I don't care what they think.

Of course you care. We all care. She tilts her head back like she's about to laugh and instead lets out an enormous groan. She winks. I'm going to make you a man, she whispers. Dallas moans again and grabs Alma by the shoulders, spinning her toward the mirror like a postcard rack. You need to keep your shoulders up, she says.

I don't need your help.

You drop your shoulders too much. When you're a girl you're too tall, yes, but a boy? Stand up straight. *¡Ay sí, papi, más, más!* Dallas stands and demonstrates, hunching her shoulders up and bowing her arms out slightly to the side. You try.

He She reaches out and lifts Alma's shoulders, forcibly spreads her arms out slightly to either side. Now Dallas points to one eye, motions look, and then touches both sides of her face with her hands as she straightens her mouth, clenches her jaw, sucks her cheeks in a little, furrows her brow to get a wrinkle or two. A man with red dyed hair and boobs in D. Cowgirl getup. Why not. Alma tries the face, and sure enough this helps, squares her off a bit and gives her two more years right there. She looks at Dallas with surprise and Dallas winks, lets go a series of blood curdling cries, sits on the bed and starts bouncing gently up and down. She crooks a finger. Alma stands nearby, watching her creak and thump the bed to a steady beat.

When you look at me, Dallas says, you look too much at my shoes and thighs and clothes. Look at me. She points. Tits. Lips. Ass. *A menos tetas,* she sighs, especially if they're in your face like this? You stare, okay?

I know, says Alma, annoyed with herself. I know that I just. What if I'm shy?

Dallas snorts. You try not to look, but then stare anyway. You're a hungry fat girl. These are ice cream. *¡Sí, dámelo, dámelo!* Let's see you do it.

I am.

No, look at me. She stops bouncing and pulls Alma up to stand beside her on the bed, which sags significantly under their weight. They both readjust their balance. Like this. Dallas flicks her glance back and forth between Alma's eyes and chest, lingering below and then swinging back up reluctantly but does not linger long before dipping back to chest.

Like this? says Alma.

Don't look in my eyes like that.

Like what?

Like you're looking for the truth. You're a man, Dallas says. You look in my eyes to show you're stronger or to figure out what to do next.

Is that right.

Yes. It is.

They stare at one another, and then Dallas starts bouncing up and down on the bed again, hard this time, and Alma has to trampoline along as the metal frame bangs against the floor, bang bang bang until He She is one great breath of sound, the sound Alma might imagine making when she's in her room alone and everything must be quiet as a mouse, that's the sound and there's something real in it before the whole thing crescendos out of proportion and then stops cold.

I can go now?

Are you running away?

From you? She doesn't mean to answer but there's something in this room that reminds her of having friends.

From home.

Alma nods. That too.

I ran away, Dallas says, stepping off the bed and no joke lighting up a cigarette, leaning against the wall. When I was sixteen. Was it your father?

Yes. In a way she's telling the truth.

Dallas nods in agreement. Fucking fathers. They should have their dicks chopped off.

I agree, Alma says. They smile at one another.

I could touch you anyway.

Alma feels something rush in her, like her skull fell asleep and someone's shaking it back to life. She leans toward the door and Dallas grabs her thigh suddenly with one huge hand, one hand that controls everything about her until it relaxes to let the bruise begin already.

You be careful, Dallas says, the voice quiet and angry. Okay? It's a dangerous thing. If you're not more careful. The big head shakes, pulls a deep breath in through the wide nostrils.

I'll be careful. You be careful too.

Dallas lets the wrinkles come around her eyes. Thank you. She gives Alma's thigh a pat now and withdraws the painful giant hand, tucking it out of sight.

I'm probably lucky I met you, Alma says.

I won't tell anyone.

No. Do you think.

What, *mi amor.*

Could I get some of my money back.

Dallas snorts. You poor thing.

Yeah. Okay. She steps toward the door but Dallas gets there first and wraps her up in arms, squeezing her long and tight.

Good luck, *mijita.* You'll need it.

Behind her, as she leaves, there's the sound of Dallas flipping on the postgame shower, true charading to the end.

Downstairs she finds Sam and Dean sitting on the front porch, sipping bottled beer as they contemplate the perverted desert plain. She plops down beside them. No wonder Mom hates Mexico.

Where you been? Dean asks.

I tried to warn you, she says to Sam.

What.

It was a man, right? Your. She points upstairs.

Hmm, says Sam. Could be.

You couldn't tell? says Dean.

Blowjob.

And?

Pretty decent. He looks at Alma. A guy, huh?

I know it.

Like, had an operation or actually still a guy?

I don't know. Maybe still a guy?

Yeah, he says. Well. Something to write home about, I guess. He laughs. Oh well. You got to try to be open minded, right? He laughs again, enormously good natured. Alma almost feels something like affection for him.

Where were you, though? Dean again.

She gets ready to lie when the sonic boom comes from inside.

By the time they get in there, three impassive cold pimp faces look on as Lee roars red faced bile invective, shitgaahdamnmotherfuckerfaggotasssonsabitches I'll keeeeel you! His eyes threaten to pop from his bald head and roll like big blue marbles across the floor. With mild interest the pimps watch this mortally wounded beast in final flail before the end.

Lee! Sam shouts.

Lee whips his head around as the sound of his own name hits him like a rock against his cheek. Fuuuuuuck! he explains. It's a shim!

Sam steps in close, watching the pimps carefully. They look so relaxed they must be armed.

It's cool, says Dean, it's cool.

It ain't cool! Lee yells.

We'll get your money back, Sam says.

Already got my money back!

Now the pimps start to look alarmed. One peels off upstairs while the others half surround the mad East Texas man.

What is the problem.

Problem is! You got a bunch a shims up there!

One of the pimps has his hand resting ready behind his back. Something dangerous.

Look, I'll get you a better woman, beautiful woman, another pimp says.

Lee shrugs Sam's hand off and puffs up to face his audience. Fuck. You. Mother. Fucker. Alma thinks he's about to strike but instead he turns slowly, keeping his eye on them, and pirouettes so he can keep staring as he goes strutting out the door. Sam and Dean and Alma catch up to him outside.

Goddamn homo crazy fucking Mexicans. Jesus.

Man. I thought we were gonna have a blood bath there.

They don't want mess with The I. Lee kicks at the porch. You get one too?

What.

You know. He rubs his bald head with deep rue.

Yeah, probably. Sam shrugs again. Where you going?

I got to find a woman, Lee says as he lopes down the track. Meet you back.

They wait for the others. Discuss a recipe for brining pork. Turkey soup. Dallas sits alone somewhere inside. Dallas a little boy in Mexico, once upon a time. Dallas and Alma's mother's brother playing cowboy Indians in a summer patch of shade. And there's her mother watching, beautiful and swift. Mom watches and she's beautiful, that's all Mom ever does until she starts running, freed from herself and her beauty and her body, running faster than her brother and then neck and neck with boy Dallas until she pulls away and streaks into the desert, all alone. Then Sam's shaking Alma's shoulder as the sun peeks over the flat horizon and they stumble ghoulish to the parking lot where finally, miraculously, it's time to go.

Five

She's making out with Nathan in the grass. Lips dry and chapped. The sun has baked her skin car hood hot, and his hands feel cool there on her bare flank between hips and chest. His hands feel good and he knows it, but then he whispers something in her ear that makes her angry, something dumb she can't recall exactly but it pisses her off. She pops up away from him and hands on hip regards the familiar terrain of Barton Springs: kids pissing in the shallow end, teens stonin' and half bonin' on the slope, concession stand of sweet salt tasty crap, the dog people fawning over their swimming pets on the other side of fence. It takes a natural spring fed acre pool to render summer almost sane. Discreetly she unwedges suit from crack and steps down the grassy slope. Clear green water bobs below. At the base of the hill her bare foot slips and she stumbles into an inadvertent run, surrenders and launches. Somehow she manages a dive. Her body sluices into the cool water and she comes up with a gasping laugh. Barton Springs will cure you fast. Nathan is a prick but what can you do? He's ashamed of her, and she's ashamed of him for that. She treads water there, watching showtime boys fly off the diving board like sleek unstable molecules. Then Dean stands and drips and waits his turn, his blond hair matted winningly against his head. He nods at her and grins and high hops high into the air, twists like a parade baton and splashes. She waits and scans the surface. Just as she starts to worry he pops up right in front of her, breathing easily, his face an arm's length away at most. Water beads along the fine bones of his face.

Hey, he says, cheerful with surprise. I know you.

The jolt slips her head and thumps it good against the bed of the bucking truck. The sky's a blinding bleached blue white. She closes her eyes again. Someone has sandblasted her mouth. Her organs hurt. She sits up. They're hurtling through the desert in the morning light, rolling out a thin black road behind. It's bone dry land of dead out there, empty except for small platoons of Joshua Tree scarecrows and low agave shrubs that squat at their feet like pets.

Mornin', says Dean, holding out a red silver Tecate can wet with cooler sweat. He's sitting against one side of the truck, arm outstretched and resting on the rails, his blond hair flickering in the eighty mile per hour wind, and Sam sits opposite, exactly as relaxed, and there beside her Lee lies still, curled with both arms over his head like the world's one big grenade.

She yawns, her best strategy against vomit. Is there any, like, water?

Dean shrugs, retracts the beer, and fishes a clear bottle from a plastic bag. Not cold, he says.

That's fine.

She tries to drink slowly, thirst on one side, bathroom on the other. Dean pops his beer from the foam thermal koozie and slides a new can to reload. The koozie says:

Pronto Food Mart

Austin, TX

GET SOME AND GO!

A panic jabs her between the eyes. Can take the girl out of Austin but. Where are we.

Should be getting close, Sam says.

Monterrey?

No. Some town called Bust A Move?

They're having a party. It's on the way.

Fiesta. Sam grabs his tits and shimmies.

Oh Jesus, she says, covering her face in her hands, struggling to keep her voice tenor low at least. She shuts up. These idiots are the worst thing ever happened to her.

In for a dime, Sam says. Dean offers her a beer again with two hands and tenderness. You'll feel better, he says. Don't let that blood alc dip too fast. She shakes her head.

Okay, he says. He leans forward and clicks can rims with Sam.

Should be getting close, Sam says again.

There's no evidence of that out on the sun burnt flats, where a long train's crawling north. Big purple mountains sit blurred in heat haze. She sips her water. Stupid fucking Nathan. Or whatever—*Nate*. Nathan seemed to like her fine, but this new and improved *Nate* is cut out for better things than ugly Alma except behind closed doors. Traitor shallow fickle dick. Trade three *Nates* right now for one ice cold lemonade from Tastee-Freez. She hopes those Emory girls mock his teeth.

The road is all but empty and they pass the few cars or trucks as if the others stand stock still. The wind hurricanes its fingers through her hair. Puffy stupid fro but hey okay big wuup. Who knew the pleasure of short hair? She takes off her shoes, socks, rolls up her cuffs, gets current moving past her ankles, across her calf, almost to thigh. Sam and Dean are quiet, eyes wide open and mouths closed tight as the enormous space whips by. Guys, she thinks, sometimes do have a talent for shutting up.

The mountains creep closer until she sees green crowded at the hilly feet, a patch of color grafted to the desert. What else could be their destination? She hopes so. She's got to pee.

It must be early because the town's doors and windows are closed and no one's on the cobbled street but a black dog. Concrete. Trees. They bounce over a set of road tumors, pull onto a sidewalk. Lee stirs in his makeshift crib. In eighty seconds her bladder will burst and she'll scream like a girl and his Beaumont eyes will kewpie wide and hey now I know this little bitch.

This'z it, Cristobal says, swinging out of the cab. A half crumbling looking wall frames a red door shut tight.

Willy raises a finger. No one mentions Boys' Town, he whispers.

That's right, Lee says. He rises yawning from the dead. You heard that.

Oh we'll see, says Dean.

Seriously. It's my fucking wedding.

Where are we.

Bustamante.

Sounds like a good place to smoke some bud, Lee says as Alma jumps out to follow Willy into the house.

He can barely open the door for all the bodies there inside. They rest inert on cots and mattresses and bedrolls thrown into every inch of space. Despite the humanity it's cool in there. Long bolts of hair tuft out of the body tops and she can smell it too: women, the whole room through. Willy tiptoes and she follows winding through the sleeping maybe beauties who sigh and shift and roll. A dark brown eye opens briefly at her feet.

There's a stream that runs right through the house, beneath the surface, she can see in the little breezeway where the floor's peeled back. They dodge the filthy kitchen and emerge into a backyard of dirt and trees coated with one million miniature empty bottles and cigarette butts to match. Sitting big and calm in the middle of it all is a shirtless sweaty buddha who struggles to his feet as they approach, his arms outstretched, a burning cigarette in one hand and tiny beer in the other, as if he's wreaked this havoc personally, all by his lonesome.

Willy! Buddha bellows, and then hushes himself, drawing no no smoky zigzags with his cigarette in the air. He points up a set of outdoor stairs to a screened in room above. There's a landing halfway up where another few bodies are sprawled on bare concrete, moving not a lick. Sinners sleeping everywhere.

S'up Lalo, Willy says.

Same old shit! Buddha flinches at his own noise again. *Chupando,* he stage whispers. *Pachanga.* You wanna beer?

Almost.

How 'bout you?

That's The Kid. Lalo, *mi primo*.

Hey.

Should be a cold beer in the bathtub over there. We got some little *esquincles* cross the street running beers for us. They should be up soon. He holds up the tiny eight ounce bottle. These things like three sips each. I've probably had two hundred of them.

How many came down?

Bet there forty of us?

Make that forty six, Willy says. He glances at Alma. Seven.

Bathroom? Alma says.

Piss out there. Lalo waves at the yard. She hesitates.

Off the kitchen, Willy adds. She hurries away to find it as the two men start naming names.

Slowly, the house comes to life. Downstairs stirs, the women showering one by one by one while those in waiting clean the kitchen and the yard outside. Sam and Dean and Lee and them stay out of the way, careful not to interfere or help. Soon men and boys are descending to try their hand at bathroom roulette, and in their wake she sneaks up to find some rest. A few sleepers are still breathing heavy on wall to wall mattresses and foam. The Y chromosome *essence* is overwhelming, but she finds a corner and collapses anyway. Maybe she'll wake up in Buenos Aires or Austin or Mexico City, she thinks. Maybe she'll wake up dead.

What wakes her up is music. An oompah bass polkas under the bright gobble of accordion. She wouldn't mind changing her shirt but instead she jams on her cap and heads downstairs.

The courtyard buzzes bilingually, men gulping little *Coronitas* as they gang grill meat on an enormous smoker with the top off. She slips into the smoke and cousins, cousins and husbands of cousins swapping views on ribs, tornados, Rafael Palmeiro, the outlets of San Marcos, hand dug drug tunnels in Nogales. This could be Mexico. Inside she finds a transformed kitchen ruled by women who pause their conversation to find out who and why she is. She holds her ground but barely. Women really look. They see all that newness in her clothing and her hair and sneakers, her unpierced ears and chewed up nails, they see the pale spot on her neck where her long locks used to be. She keeps her head down and mumbles a lot and they finally leave her alone, returning to their cutting boards and vegetables and knives. Guacamole, potato salad, peas and carrot rice, *pico de gallo,* gold flour tortilla *quesadillas*, bright sautéed peppers and onions. Give her a room without meat, without whores, without liquor and men. She lingers, watching, until someone's mother hands her a plate.

Eat.

Under their approving eyes, she loads up on everything, drapes two warm corn tortillas on top, and finds a place to sit outside alone but alone is not allowed.

So where you from? the woman asks. She's Latina, whatever that means, she's got the blended skin and hair and eyes. All the women do, except for one tall blondie bride.

More sausage and *fajitas* out there, says her hubby, sizing up Alma's vegetarian plate.

Austin. Don't eat a lot of meat.

Oh you must be a friend of Willy's then. She's not sure if that's because of the Austin or the meat, but the woman's smiling while her man frowns completely. There's chicken too, he says. She knows these kinds of guys who'd feel a lot more comfortable if she'd just kill something.

Thanks, I'm all right for now. You all come down here every year?

The man sticks a big rib pacifier in his mouth and points at the woman. We used to, she says while he sucks and chews. Willy's my cousin. Fiesta's great when you're a kid. Safe down here, they let us run wild. We had a blast. Now we just come down to you know relax.

Leave the kids at home, the man says, winking in no particular direction. He sticks out the thumb and pinky of one hand, puts it near his mouth like a bugle, tilts it back and forth.

For now. The cousin sighs. They're so little, you know, it'd be kind of hard. We'll wait until they're older, she whispers, till there some other kids. Don't want to be the first ones. But it is nicer when there's kids around, she confides.

Family stories flow. What would it be like to have a history of one thousand relatives from both sides of the border who all knew each other's names and faults and business? For all Alma knows they're out there. Not in the burnt out shell of Nuevo but in the elephantine heart of Mexico. This could be mine, she thinks.

Meeting the family, huh? Lalo and Cristobal materialize when her new friends disappear.

Everyone's really nice.

Cristobal snorts and snores. Dull ain't just a river in Egypt.

Man's jealous, Lalo confides. He leans in close and Alma breathes in at least fifty hours of consecutive beer. Always wanted to fuck our cousins.

They say first cousins fair game now, says Cristobal.

Mexico ever said otherwise? They who?

Scientists.

Yeah well. Too late. What is that, a Coke?

Yep, says Alma.

That's what I mean, Cristobal complains, he's over with the Coke and baby crowd.

With a flick of his wrist, Lalo produces a beer like a magician's dove. *Emborráchate,* kid. They clink bottles and he watches until she takes a shallow altar sip. That's better.

Let's get. Cristobal lights a cigarette, sucks on it aggressively.

Where.

Fiesta. Lee and them already there.

The town square has a church and park and a little town hall there behind. A crowd is gathered watching an amateurish dance perform-ance. A crowd is gathered at makeshift street bars and around an old man spinning cotton candy. A crowd is gathered everywhere. Men and women walking around in boots and jeans and hats and belts and tank tops, skirts, and dresses. They stroll the crowded streets, examining the impromptu pavement restaurants, the aging carnival rides, examining each other. It doesn't take long for them to find Lee and Dean and the gang. There's a space in the crowd like it's been pushed out by wrong magnets and then, presto, white boys. The men stare. The women stare. Might as well be wearing costumes. Capes and fangs.

The vendors love them, though. The vendors smell a sale. It's a bar barker who's wooing Eddie and Sam and Lee and D, waving an enormous blue glass bottle and singing out over the din.

Tequila! Ba bum da da da da dum da! Ba bum da da da da dah! *¡Vengan! ¿Qué les ofrezco, güeros?* They get tequilas in small cups while Alma tries to stay invisible, avoiding drink.

Güerito ¿qué quieres?

Nada, Alma says.

No, güerito. The bar man sounds sad. *Ven, te sirvo algo, te va a gustar.*

The guys laugh. Wear E Toe, Lee says, what's he calling you.

Blondie, Cristobal explains.

Ain't no blondie.

Whitey, I guess you'd translate. Little whitey.

They think that's a laugh riot. Wear E Toe, Lee repeats in a mangled Chinese accent. Dean's laughing too, fine teeth glinting in the light. The real gut splitter here is that they're all more *güero* than she is, these Irish Italian Jewish Germans, whatever the fuck they are.

They sit in one of the street restaurants around a plastic table. They order a couple of snacks. No way she'd ever eat here. The others are digging in, though, crunching through the foul fried pork skin. The waitress is terrible and friendly, her young face stretched in permanent smile as she confuses orders and nearly dumps food on laps. Somewhere close unseen a live band has started up, industrial grade speakers pumping music through her rib cage and the town and deep into the desert. As far as she can see in every direction, human beings are getting good and drunk.

She sits next to Dean who's silent happy drinking beer and looking fine.

Glad you took that ride, huh? he says.

I wasn't sure at first. But this is alright.

Yeah it is.

They talk for a while, the two of them: he's from Oregon, in grad school, in Austin, sits on fully funded porches drinking beer and grilling meats, hits Sixth Street on Thursday night for girls and pool, haunts the cafés reading big thick tomes midweek. He knows a lot about exSoviet republics but will only talk about them when pressed. She could have a crush on him, no problem.

I was supposed to go to UT this fall, she says.

Yeah?

I just couldn't do it.

Yeah. Just because?

So absolutely more of same, you know? She must be a little drunk again. She can't remember the last time she didn't have a beer in hand. Soon she'll be sumo fat.

You might be surprised. It's a big place. But I can see what you mean. I might have some reservations if I'd lived there my whole life.

You know? I can't even imagine being a freshman with all the über-bitches and jerkoffs who made my high school a miserable crapass stinking hell.

Whoa, he says, smiling. He had a great time in high school, she can tell, great times is all this D ever has. His own personal blond brigade and closets crammed with letter jackets. He keeps smiling, flashing those mosque white teeth. She should hate him but he's too mellow and cute.

For you, like Austin's something new and laid back and whatever, but that town's my fucking Kryptonite. Every mile I put behind me, I feel better, I mean it. She wants to say the word *Harvard* and see what his face does but then she thinks he won't believe her.

So what are you going to do?

Next? She should grab her crotch in punctuation. Mexico City.

Cool.

Yeah, or like they say, bust. Don't tell anyone, though.

No, he says, surprised at the request. Always wanted to check it out. Got a buddy there.

You should, man, you should. It's wild down there, and cheap. The women are smokin'. She'll say anything to keep this going. I'm gonna get me a place, take some time off, write. Most underrated city in the hemisphere, you know, but it's gonna be hot soon. She sounds cool. Is he impressed? She wants to tell him the whole truth. She sounds like a moron. Her brain floats small in salt beer pickle.

He nods slowly. We got this wedding, you know, but then I was thinking of doing a little trip. Before classes start. Gonna hit the beach but maybe I'll go through Mexico City if it's all that.

She feels her heart go flit a flut with gooey happiness. That'd be cool, she says.

Yeah, maybe I should do that. My buddy's a wild man too.

She feels so safe. She wants to touch his arm. He's looking at her with friendship and respect. She deserves it. She deserves him. They are going to Mexico City together. She wants to sing and dance.

They sit there talking about the huge city and Dean's friend there who's some kind of journalist and they might be able to crash with him and should they stop along the way? but then The Witches show up and all conversations turn their way in carnal concentration. She's not sure why they're called The Witches but there are three of them: a tall dark skinny, a medium round, a nice pert short. They've all brought their boobs. The tall and short are cute and they laugh a lot, like cute girls do, or maybe Cristobal's funnier in Spanish. He and Dean and of course Lee somehow get pole position. Dean's got the short one, listening pretty, on constant verge of smile. Alma watches the little witch appreciate him openly, speaking English clear and slowly to make sure she's understood. She's teasing him.

Where's your hat?

At home with my guns.

Don't you know? You can't be a man in Mexico without a hat.

No?

No. She winks at Alma, trying to be polite. You too, where's your hat?

I'm gonna take a walk around, Alma tells them. What a bunch of bozos. No way she's going to Mexico City with him.

She walks. Who knows what time it is, but someone has released the teenagers from cages. They prowl around in packs, the girls slutted out in tight surprising everything—mostly knockoff jeans and a cheap red skirt or two—no matter what their age or body type. Thirteen, seventeen. Weedy, fat. Good for them. She guesses. She bets every inch of them's dissected with savagery. The dirty old men like it, leering without shame, slack jawed at the pube breasts and butts and hips while dangling limp scummy arms around their wives. The girls ignore them absolutely, with panache, saving all attention for each other and a few complementary boys who trail close behind, sporting lifetime supplies of hair gel that strap back volcanic black or occasional peroxide hair. They flirt semi professionally. Alma feels old. She feels like an old woman in an old chair on an old porch alone.

She sits on a bench and takes out her little notebook. *El County Fair*, she writes *old rides and games*, she writes. *Equipment from the States declared unsafe and sold in Mexico. Prize stuffed bears refurbished. Stuffed with guns and cocaine. Teens are vapid everywhere and all the world's a letch.* A layer of her outer self has been sloughed off, leaving an uncommon sensitivity at once thrilling, uncomfortable, and totally out of her control. She fills two pages quickly and it both excites and soothes her. This is who she is no matter what or why or where.

She finds the gang again not at the tables but crowded around a gate that says 90 pesos—Dance. The band plays on. Witches, Dean, Lee, Cristobal, getting along just fine.

How much is ninety pesos?

Like ten bucks.

Dollars? Lee sounds like he's been shot. Goddamn. He grabs Cristobal by the shirt. They think they got Bob Marley in there or something? Together they buddy up to the ticket window, talk there for a minute or so, turn and call to her.

You coming in?

She nods. Why not.

They wave her over. This is my son, Lee says, grinning at the woman behind the glass. He's retarded. He should be free. He's only ten. It's his condition make him look big. I had children too young. Gave me cancer. He rubs his bald head. Chemotherapy.

For a moment it looks like the woman at the counter will have nothing to do with them, but suddenly they settle on forty-five for everyone. Alma pitches in a tenner, the other guys split it three ways, and they're in.

Couples of every age crowd the dance corral. It's not a line dance, not exactly, but they're doing something unison to the heavy synthie beat. The band reigns cheese royale in tight light blue cowboy outfits, turning synchronized on the raised stage, exhorting the crowd to clap and roll their fists through the air and *cumbia, cumbia.* She loathes this music sure, but live with silly dancers it makes more sense. What kind of parties don't have dancing? Her mother said that once.

Come on, Alma, dance with me.

No. Are you drunk?

It's my birthday party. Come dance with your old mom.

I don't dance.

I'll teach you.

Too late for that.

The Witches are singing and fist rolling and have dragged their semi willing partners on the floor. Alma stands to one side and watches them and laughs her goddamn head off. Cristobal is decent but Dean looks like he's cross country skiing and Lee is getting shot. People are watching them, amused, although no one's so slayed as Alma. To her surprise, the couples last a couple songs before retreating to the sidelines where The Witches head off to the bathroom in full twitter.

Let's get a drink, Dean says.

You know how to do that shit? Lee asks her. He turns to Cristobal. My girl's already getting bored.

The Witches are very forgiving.

I got a spin but need some other moves. Hold on.

There's a dividing wall there that shields them from view, and he leads them there behind it. She's sure this pit stop's drug related but instead Lee says hey Crystal Ball now show me.

What.

How to do this thing. I'm getting killed out there.

To Alma's amazement Cristobal grabs him and starts dancing with him, quick quick slow, quick quick slow. Lee stares at his feet, committing muscle twitch to memory.

Yeah, okay, I got that.

Now roll out like this. The semi Mexican pivots back on one foot like a door swinging open, then shut, quick quick the other way, open, shut.

Aw, yeah, yeah, Lee says, doing some Quasimodo imitation to his own personal beat. Come on, D, he calls out, you gonna learn here or what.

You look like a fool, Dean says, laughing.

Yeah, but this fool's gonna be *in there*. Come on, D, they got their own big ol' house you want a bed to sleep tonight or on the floor in homoville?

All right. Dean glances at Alma. Give it a shot?

She has to keep herself from giggling. I guess, she says, shrugging.

He puts his hands lightly on her hip and hand and they start dancing. He's a pretty terrible dancer, but he smells good and she can feel the heat of his fingertips seeping into her flesh. She corrects him, pushes and pulls his shoulder the way Cristobal moves his.

Like this?

That's it. She lifts his arm and spins under it one way, then spins back.

Hey, that's pretty good. How did I do that?

They practice there for a few minutes, half a song at least, stepping this way and that and murmuring instructions counsel, and it's only when they stop that they notice three little kids hanging on the outside fence, staring at them in slack jawed disbelief. Lee fake runs at them, stamping in their direction like a bull, and they take off running laughing screaming to tell someone of the strange things gringos do. In the small silence before the guys all start laughing, she feels the thin thrill of male secret.

Alright, Lee says, s'enough of that. I think I got it. His face turns suddenly seriocomic with concentration and then spreads in a smile as he practices once more solo. It's his own version, no doubt about that, the shoulders still do some pretty crazy things, but he's on to something, she has to admit. He sees her staring and he stops.

Enough to get the king *in there*, he says to everyone else but he's still looking at her. So where's your pussy at?

She doesn't answer.

Cristobal pats her on the shoulder. I told The Witches to find you a cousin or something.

And what would you do with it? Lee steps up to her and circles, surrounding her single handedly. Stick a Coke bottle in there?

Aw he's alright, says Dean. It's cool. He's The Kid.

Lee nods and the guys relax and turn, start heading back, but at the last minute Lee sticks out a hand to make her trail behind.

You like boys?

I don't like anyone.

Don't lie to me.

Maybe I'm just, you know, a virgin. It's the first thing she can think of.

He considers this defense. Why? he says.

Don't know. Didn't plan it. Just worked out that way. She's not afraid to look at him. She's telling the truth. She's not afraid but she might cry.

He looks right back. Well I won't tell no one but let's take care of that tonight. You're gonna fuck this cousin. If she don't show up *I'll* find you one.

Maybe I'll take yours, she says.

He gasps with laughter, smacking her on the head. Maybe you will, he says, still laughing, his blue eyes all ashine, until she points back toward the dance floor. The Witches have been too long neglected, their table surrounded, crushed by men. With surprising speed Lee swoops in there and grabs the tall one and leads her off to dance.

By the time the band stops playing for the night she's drunk again, the guys are dancing not half bad, The Witches are all over them, the table of guys next door is trying to invite her to she's pretty sure a cock-fight but she declines. They stumble back through the streets to The Witches' house and sit on the huge dark porch, talking about nothing in particular and staring at the glitter bag of stars above. The square wooden house sits at the end of a dirt track, in an overgrown lawn with scraggly plants and two waltzing ancient trees. Alma sips her drink of lime juice, beer, and ice, with salt rimmed margarita around the top.

Are you happy? the short witch asks her suddenly in well accented English.

Can you tell, says Alma. She sits up straight. This is a happy thing right here. What do you call it?

Michelada. You never had.

No.

But you like.

From now on, this is all I ever drink.

Ha ha ha ha ha. You like Bustamante?

Yeah. What I've seen. Love your house.

It's our grandmother's, she says, crossing herself. We live in Monterrey, but we come for the fiesta. Since we were little, we come to her house. It's very old. Pancho Villa spent the night here.

Really? Alma feels like she won a bet.

Pancho Villa spent the night everywhere, Cristobal says. But that's not why it's haunted. Tell her about the ghosts.

Ghosts, the short witch explains. One makes a lot of noise in the kitchen. Breaks dishes at night—crack crack crack!—but when you come downstairs? She shakes her head.

And the other ones are how do you say? says the tall skinny one.

Make love, says shorty.

Do the nasty, says medium round.

Our grandmother was a witch. The ghosts used to stay away.

Bustamante is famous.

Many *brujas* come here.

Isa's a witch too, says Cristobal.

No. Short Isa wags one finger in denial.

You've put a spell on me a hundred times.

Bueno, eso está fácil, the tall one says, hefting her breasts quickly with both hands, and they're back in Spanish, off and running.

Alma can't believe it. The tall one even looks a little like Sor Juana, and the plump one could pass for Leona Vicario, and Isa's a ringer for Rosario Robles except young and dark and hot. What are they doing here with these jokers when they should be writing poems and revolutionizing and being great? Why doesn't one of *them* want to come with her to La Ciudad de México? They know what grandparents mean!

But before long Lee and Cristobal and their corresponding witches have disappeared and it's just Dean and short Isa and Alma. In the silence they hear sounds that might be intimate coming from somewhere outside or upstairs. Alma feels a cool trickle in her spine.

That's not the ghosts? Alma asks.

No. Isa smiles.

What's it sound like?

Do you believe? Most Americans do not believe ghosts, right?

I dunno. Maybe. She glances at Dean, waiting for a comment, but he's just smiling and running a finger up and down one short witch arm.

But you are different, Isa says.

I have Mexican blood, she says. The words sound strange to her. She's never said it, just like that. My mom.

Ah. You know I think so. I know someone who looks like you from Chihuahua.

Really? She didn't think there was anyone in the world who looked like her. My mom's from Mexico City.

And her parents?

I don't know. I think my grandfather's still there.

You don't know?

I don't know.

Isa looks at her sadly and then finally blinks. The woman was from Chihuahua, says Isa in a shiny brand new voice, she lived here in this house and married a man from town.

What woman.

The woman who died. He hang her from that tree because she sleep with a man. Many times. She fell in love. But her husband find them and shot the lover and hang her from that tree.

Some men don't know what else to do, says Alma.

Yes, says Isa. She gives Alma another long look before glancing back at Dean. You all think angry is the same as sad, Isa tells him.

Oh, I think some other things, he says, smiling. His hand continues its round trip up and down her arm.

Isa smiles back. What the dead woman did was come here every night and make love outside his window. Until the husband go crazy and kill himself too. It's sad, no? That's what we hear sometimes. Now I think they come only for fun.

That's *the* nicest ghost story I have ever heard, Dean says. The small witch examines him with goo goo eyes.

It's not nice, Alma says. It's not nice to be lied to and betrayed.

No, the short witch says.

I gotta go. I'm tired, I'm going back.

Goodnight. The small witch kisses the air next to her cheek. They both glance at Dean.

Later, he tells Alma. We'll figure out that thing tomorrow. I'm in.

In what, says the witch.

Oh it's a big secret, Dean says. But I can whisper in your ear.

Alma walks off slowly through the dark yard. She doesn't care if she never sees him again.

There was a moon earlier but now it's gone, and there aren't any street lights near this famously haunted house. The darkness is impressive, it's something she's forgotten about or never known. She can just make out the opening in the wall and the street there beyond, but she can't see the way the driveway dips. She stumbles and only barely catches herself before she falls and as she steadies herself she hears a rush in the air behind her. There, walking toward her briskly, is a body holding its own ivory skull in hand.

Be careful, says the skull.

A car passes by on the street and in the headlight's penumbra she makes out the face of the small witch carrying a white cowboy hat. She holds it out to Alma. Are you okay? the small witch says.

Yes.

I want you to take this. You are going to Mexico with him, yes? The City.

Sí.

Pues, es para tí entonces.

Thank you. She takes the hat, tries to hold it steady in her shaking hands.

Be careful, the small witch says again. In thirty years you maybe will look back. The small witch shakes her head. Dangerous, she says.

Alma touches the thin band around the crown, the well worn palo of the brim. She can feel its witchcraft spells and charms and hexes.

You are going to find your grandfather, Isa says.

I always thought he was dead. But there's this letter. He lives at 216 Emiliano Zapata.

Then you will find him, the witch says. Do you remember him?

I used to think I was a princess, Alma says. The witch can't see her blushing in the dark. That someone left me at my parents' door but one day I'd find the king and queen. He's something I dunno a poet or a writer. Never met him. I think maybe we're alike.

Yes.

I want to know what happened.

You are a *mexicana.*

Alma clutches the hat to her chest. Thank you.

The small witch nods. An old hat but it was *my* grandfather's.

What was he like?

He was a man, you know? In that time. She closes her eyes and Alma's sure she's staring at the dead. She opens again and smiles. Still, to be a man in Mexico a hat sometimes can help.

Thank you, Alma says again.

The witch takes a deep breath and lets it out and then leans in and kisses Alma firm this time, real and cool and on the cheek. *Pues, cuídate mucho.* Then she reaches out and takes off Alma's baseball cap, runs her hand through Alma's hair, and places the cowboy hat carefully on Alma's head. *Lista,* she says happily, disappearing back into the dark. The word means ready or clever or smart and Alma hopes she's right.

PART TWO

Six

Years later, long after she'd found their daughter and left Truitt and moved far away from Texas, Hermelinda could close her eyes and conjure up the wild pigs of Mexico. They had been driving for about an hour out of Laredo, plunging south through the desert on a smooth toll road. Moving fast. Good times, bad times, the way Truitt drove a car always made her want to lean forward and put her lips against his neck. But not with Charlie there.

"Just a dead spot," Charlie said.

"Dead spot my ass. Sat link don't do dead spots." The toothpick in Truitt's mouth finally came apart, dissolving into splinters, and he picked them off his gum and lip and flicked them into a plastic cup. "Thought you took care of that." He plucked new wood from the red-blue box.

"Dead spots happen." Charlie curled his medium-long hair behind his ears and stroked the company laptop like a cat. "It won't last."

Truitt nodded grimly. "Yeah," he said. "We're hauling butt." He tapped the steering wheel and big guitars and cymbal smash filled the cool air inside. "That little stinker," he whispered. Hermelinda could not hear him but she read his lips.

Outside, Mexico streaked by. She pressed her fingers against the tinted windows of her cage, sending wrinkles rippling through her hands. It was hard to know which line to follow or if they were all one great line, doubled and redoubled like intestine winding across every surface of her body, a single thread that if someone pulled all parts of her would come undone. She did her best to stay stitched tight. There was the loosening of skin around her neck and a slow waddling of the flesh at the back of her arms. When she sniffed in deep, something was going sour, might be him or might be her or might be that their girl was gone. She pulled her fingers off the cool glass, leaving five warm smudges.

"Charlie," she said, leaning forward. "May I see it again please?"

Think about you and that long ride

I bite my nails I get weak inside

Truitt was singing and he did not know it or hear the words but Hermelinda did. She always heard the words. A real American could sing an album front to back and look at her like a cow if she asked what they were singing about.

My lightning's flashing across the sky.

Looking for my lost shaker of salt.

If I leave here tomorrow, would you still remember me?

Happy Birthday dear Lindy.

That crappy song.

For her 40th he had brought a band and invited everyone they knew plus some she did not. A throw-down was what Truitt called it. A few people danced. Alma was there and then she was not. The sun went down and out came whisky, dope, tequila. Now! But they would not sing. *Pero allá tal como aquí en tu boca llevarás.* Hermelinda was drunk and old and counting what she had given up. *Payaso, Relámpago.* It did not happen often. Five cups of wine and she would forget the life she might have lived: fat, weak, ignorant, poor, humiliated, debased. She leaned back in her chair and watched Truitt with his shirt off, soft and prosperous, the outside like puffy risen dough that should deflate the moment something poked it. Scars on the inside of his lip from dipping days, she used to feel them against her tongue.

Where was Alma?

Charlie passed the laptop back to her.

```
hey mom and dad 'sup 'sup... shows rocked...
down in scintillating S.A one more night... no
worries, k?
    late, alma :)
```

Their little girl, their baby tramp. How many lies could she type a minute?

"So this comes from Monterrey?"

"Pardon?" Charlie leaned back toward her, pouted his full red lips in concentration.

"Can you turn that down a bit, Truitt. Please?"

The way you move, it's right in time

The way you move, it's right in time

"Truitt!"

"What?"

"Turn it down please."

Truitt turned it down. But he sure could use a blowjob right about now.

"I was wondering," she said, "how do we know this came from Monterrey?"

Charlie glanced at his boss again but finding nothing there he squirmed around in his seat, and the safety belt twisted into his neck and started to choke him until he managed to pry it up onto his forehead where it stuck like a crooked sweatband and then finally popped up free behind him. He glanced at her quickly and blushed. He was not very good at looking at her.

"When you send an email?" he said. "There's all this information that comes with it? And they you know like every computer has its own unique ID, and that gets an IP, which is assigned by the ISP you—"

"My god, Charlie." Truitt chopped the world in two. "Don't even bother. Honey, I barely get it and I'm the dot-com gillionaire."

"You were doing fine, Charlie." She smiled. The boy gulped and began grappling his seat belt again.

"That's his area of expertise," Truitt said, "give him some Internet, he'll turn off the lights in Finland. Says she's in Monterrey, she's in Monterrey."

"Or was," Charlie said.

"She still there," Truitt said. "She ain't in no hurry. Think she got all the time in the world. The little monster."

Maybe a monster, Hermelinda thought. Maybe a runaway. Maybe getting something out of her system and coming home.

A chorus of beeps began to chime from everywhere at once.

"Coverage," Charlie said, wrinkling his nose and pumping a sudden fist. He reached back and yanked the computer from Hermelinda's knees. Truitt was dialing up the cell phone as Charlie typed furiously, a big chord bolero rising to a mighty close. She sat back, straightened out her skirt, draped the thin white cashmere sweater across her legs. She could barely hear Lucinda now, singing softly to the busy men up front.

Although it was mid-afternoon, the toll road was deserted, the empty lanes reminding her of a road in dreams at dawn. Maybe that was why when she saw the ground ahead moving—a dark composite movement, side to side—she said nothing. Truitt was barking at his phone and Charlie bent into the insect chatter of his keyboard as the shifting mass grew closer. It was a brown pond lapping and splashing and moving across the desert to their left, moving like a flat ground-tornado toward the road. Hermelinda saw it but she said nothing because she had wandered back fifty hours to the cheese counter. Central Market. Ann Fowler looking fresh as the organic blue lake beans. Well hello there, Lindy. Lindy?

Hi, Ann.

Those steaks look beautiful.

We eat like lions when our activist's away.

Oh my. She starts at UT in a couple?

You know she does you phony gossip-whore. That's right.

Can you believe, college? Ha ha ha. Y'all lucky to have her close for a while. She doing that last hurrah with the girls next weekend?

Next?

In San Antonio.

She's there right now. I thought they all were.

Oh no next weekend. Surely sure.

Yes. I must be confused. The sudden rotten stench of cheese that marked the end of sleep: Camembert, cheddar, Gouda, Brie. Alma was gone.

Hermelinda left the cart there in the aisle. Left the perfect marbled New York strips and new potatoes, asparagus, pinot, all of it. She drove home. Outside Alma's door she found herself mumbling something in Spanish. She pushed the door open with her head and there it was, the messed abandoned lair. On the scummy bed she cleared a spot and sat there, reading the remains. Boy. Sex. Drug. Alma might be across town lying naked with a pierced and tattooed youth resting under the budget whir of ceiling fan. A party cabin on the river out in Hill Country, drinking beer and smoking pot. But Hermelinda did not think so. That was not what Alma did. This did not feel like the kind of lie a mom could just ride out.

It had been a long time since she had searched her daughter's room. Timidly at first, she ran her hand beneath the mattress and slid the drawers out of the night stand, checking in the spaces there behind. After that she wandered around, looking for a line to cross, wondering if there was some way to stop herself. There did not seem to be. She reached out and pulled the books down one by one, books books books books books.

> *Heartbreak Soup*
> *The Best of Roald Dahl*
> *Breakfast of Champions*
> *The Big Red Book of Spanish Verbs*
> *La Perdida*
> *The Story of O*
> *On the Road*

She did not look too closely but she noticed. Sometimes a piece of paper fluttered loose, a photo, a letter, a note.

DID YOU SEE JP'S HICKEY?!?!?

don't feel close to you like before but i don't know why

Nope—Jordan cockblocked him

Cockblocked? How would she know she found it when she found it?

She decided to call Truitt. She decided to sob on the phone while he tried to calm her down, what what what hold on I'm on my way. He was on his way and she felt a little better. He walked in the door smelling of whisky and warm lake water which was okay on Saturdays. His problem-solving face on, flow charts etched into his brow, spreadsheets in his cheeks. S'gonna be alright. Where is she?

I don't know. Crystal meth, she thought, cockblocked.

Why don't you. He waved casual Houdini to make her disappear. Lemme make a couple calls.

What will I do.

You. You could have a swim.

Of course! She still loved him, she had to, look at that. She nodded and changed into her suit and started laps while inside he worked the phones, his blue eyes small and cold, squinting to bring this problem to its weak and knobby knees.

She swam. Their pool was longer than most, for a house pool, but not long enough to really lose herself. Six or seven strokes consecutive were required for that, ten was really best, with ten she was a water flesh machine and nothing more or less. Out at Deep Eddy she could get ten. Out there in the early mornings with the young and aging women all fighting the good fight to keep their bodies right, but here at home she cruised across in four or five, a silly way to swim. She chugged it out for almost an hour anyway. Then she slipped out of the pool and dripped her way across the clean orange tiles to their beautiful house, to the door that opened directly into the bathroom. Feng shui designer-flow between pool and shower and bed, with lots of space between bedrooms, Alma's and guest's and theirs. Everyone keep your secrets, please.

He was still on the phone, agreeing glumly with someone on the other end in spaced uh-huh uh-huh uh-huh. He needed to figure this out. This was his fault. Back in Alma's room she surveyed the damage with satisfaction. She ripped the sheets off the bed and pulled a poster off the wall, tearing the corners. She was close. Her heart was going like she had never stopped swimming her 125th lap and counting. She held her breath and listened. She could not hear anything. How would anyone know what went on in this room? No Mexican child, she began to think. No Mexican child would ever live in such a dangerous, lonely room.

Ahead of them on the Mexican road, wild pigs, tons of them, were coming into focus as Hermelinda sank down on her hands and knees on her only daughter's floor. She pressed her face against the carpet and inhaled deeply. Then she started to crawl. Tiny particles of sand and dirt leapt as her fingers popped the carpet. Wild pigs were crossing tar as Truitt found Hermelinda there in the corner, pulling at the shag, she had some scissors and was gouging away at the edges, yanking staples from their mounts, peeling the carpet brutally back.

"We'll find her," he had said. "She'll be alright."

"Truitt. Truitt!"

In the front seat, her husband's head popped up at the last minute, flipping off his sunglasses, too dark for driving really, designed for the open ocean glare of tropical fishing in the Caribbean, he'd never been down there but someday he would, get some of his buds and hit one of those St. Somethings to fish his brains out, with the sun screaming off the water and special glasses a must, but now he heard his name, he heard his wife calling out to him. He zoomed in on that straight and empty road and saw it was not empty anymore.

A great conga line of whiskered boars shuffled across the highway just ahead of them. They were the size of medium-large dogs, but slung low and stretched out and rounded wide. They looked small and then they looked big. The last thing Hermelinda remembered seeing before the car left the road was a pink snout raised toward them in question.

Truitt hit the brake hard and the car lurched forward, hunched like an animal realizing a cliff. There was zero chance of stopping. His foot released the brake at the last instant and he swerved sharply to the right. The SUV tilted dangerously but took its orders, pulling parallel to the now-scattering line of pigs and skipping like a flat rock into the desert. Truitt fought for control. Low bushes clutched and spit at them as they flew by. He straightened his line and then hit the brake again. They skidded out into a slow and final J, coming to rest in the dry dirt sand, enveloped in their own curtain of dust. The engine seemed to gag once and then die. There was a strong, cheesy smell. In the confusion a man had replaced Lucinda Williams.

> *Too many nights in a roadhouse*
> *Too much wine, women, and song*

"Christ," Truitt said. He quickly turned to find his wife. "You okay, baby? We're okay, aren't we?"

She didn't say anything but he nodded as if she had.

Outside the heat slapped him once across the face but he took it as he paced slowly around the car, squatting to assess the damage. One of the plastic panels had popped off, and there were scratches and dings and marks everywhere but he couldn't spot anything serious. He got the car-jack tire iron from the back to clear away some of the dirt and sand. Why had he turned? They could be a fireball right now, dumbass Texas toast. He'd made a mistake, done wrong, should have kept calm and straight and burst those pigs against the bumper, hoping for the best.

He heard an engine on the road and when he turned to find out what was coming he saw two wild pigs standing there at eye level, twenty feet away, staring at him.

The pigs were brown and gray all over, spiky with an extra collar of punk rock jags around their thick, short necks. One of them was about two feet tall, the other half Truitt's height and five feet long with a dark razor-ridge down his back. Javelinas didn't usually get that big, Truitt thought, but this one had. He was a big ol' boar. The smell of musk mixed with the bruised rubber and oil and dust. Truitt stood up, quickly, but the two pigs didn't move.

"Go on now," Truitt shouted. "Git."

The big boar's mouth dangled open, showing off his pointy three-inch tusks. The smaller boar followed suit. Her tusks looked thicker, whiter, healthier. Big guy had got himself a nice young piece of ass, worn his tusks down chomping on her suitors, had nothing to prove anymore, not to her at least, yet here he was by her side staring down the most dangerous mammal ever made and his big red death machine.

"Come on now, whachu want?" The pigs didn't answer but skated to their right in unison, turning their big flanks sideways. They looked bigger sideways and they knew it. He could smell them for sure now, they were doing something deliberate and stinky to make their point.

"I'm pissed off too," Truitt said. "But things turned out okay, didn't they." Then he saw the crushed baby javelina wedged into the SUV's grill.

The piglet's head was the only thing visible, as if the SUV had opened its big hood wide and swallowed the rest of it whole. The head was perfectly intact. Its tiny eyes were closed heavily as if it were merely sleeping in the front of Truitt's car.

Truitt raised the tire iron and shook it at the pigs and they finally started to back away, moving toward the road. Sorry for the couple, but chances were they had three or fifteen more. Didn't get all those titties for nothing. He bent down and stuck the tire iron behind the piggy's head to pry it out. Then the little head opened its eyes and screamed and Truitt jumped about twenty feet in the air and that big boar came galloping out of nowhere to attack.

Later a dream would come back to him. He was standing on the roof of the SUV in the great desert, surrounded by hundreds, thousands of javelinas throwing themselves at the vehicle, driving their tusks deep into the tires, truffling into the dirt so that slowly, slowly, they sank this car into the desert and roiled over him like a horde of quilled sandpaper creatures, rubbing him to death in a great revenge of the pigs. But that was later. In the moment he did not hesitate. He set his feet and cranked back the iron and swung as hard as he could.

From inside, Hermelinda watched the long black iron rise and fall, rise and fall like an oil well, watched her husband hop and dance around the creature, some old movie Cherokee dance. Charlie was shouting in the front seat but she put her head back and closed her eyes. Alma was a little baby girl, with soft skin that smelled like sweet peas on the vine, Hermelinda could feel the weight and warmth of the body in her arms. She could feel the shiver and spasm of that little body in trial and error, trying to figure out how things worked, the mouth groping for her nipple, the tiny hand that tapped against her arm as Alma fed. The eyes popped open and Hermelinda stared down into the stormy sea green well. Listen to me. I will not love anything as much as I love you. But maybe I will never love you as much as here and now.

She heard the car door open and then Truitt was leaping in, slamming the door behind him, still breathing hard, hands shaking, blood on his pants. The engine roared to life and he gunned it back toward the road, dirt flying everywhere behind them like a dog burying shame. He glanced at Charlie's lips moving in horror or admiration, and then met her eyes in the rearview mirror.

"We're okay," he said, sounding sure of himself this time, angry and sure and urgent as she could remember. "Now let's go find that little bitch."

Seven

The strip malls. Hermelinda did not know that she would see them here. Big box, fast food, supermarkets. American stores waving their signs at her. The only difference was that sometimes she could see a piece of rebar poking up off the roof like a stray bikini hair. Her whole world in Nuevo looked like this, all this hopeful rebar pointing at God to say we are not yet finished here.

She will hate this, thought Hermelinda. She will not stay long.

"I don't want us getting lost," Truitt was telling Charlie. "You on it? I need your A-game here alright." They were slipping through light traffic like the other cars were driving backward. If there were police in Monterrey, Truitt did not seem concerned.

"I'm on it, Mr. Price." Charlie's little Adam's apple trembled.

She knew Alma would hate Monterrey from years of being expert in what her girl did and did not like. What made her cry. What made her squint and wrinkle and made her breath escape unordered. What made her Alma. Now all Hermelinda knew was what her daughter did not like, and this was almost everything. One day the tall and curious girl started to walk in mourning, stooping her head and shoulders. There were no skirts or colors anymore. There were no more stories at the kitchen table. There were no conversations. There were shrouds and single syllables. Hermelinda had spent her days and months and every-thing training to predict the future or reconstruct the past from Alma's

95

angle on the stairs or the treble of a cough or choke, to read face and hands when she dropped Alma at the movies or picked her up outside the library, to know what Alma meant by *nothing, nobody, some guy, not really, okay, sure, goodnight.* On Guadalupe Street one day Alma winced when Hermelinda touched her hair and soon there was no touching her, no looking in the eye, no kiss, no brush. Once a month the bills arrived from BookPeople and Waterloo Records and Hermelinda sat out by the pool to read the list of titles. She wondered if she did not love Alma anymore, because to love her was to know her, to know her was the only way to make sure her girl survived. And if there was something more important to Hermelinda than that, she knew she better keep it to herself.

Outside the window, beige and orange cul-de-sac developments flashed along the highway. This could be part of Texas but for the hand that squeezed her neck and the huge mountain in front of them towering over the sprawl. Texas knew nothing about such mountains. Alma might like that.

"Wonder how much these places go for," Truitt said. She checked the mirror for his eyes but he was not talking to her. Or Charlie either. He was just driving, cutting through traffic like he had been on this stretch since high school. She was ten years old when she had last seen this highway and the mountain and it had looked smaller then. There had been no cul-de-sacs. She had never seen a road in Mexico that led nowhere, nowhere but to someone's door. She was sure that things had changed but in her Mexico the American dream of suburbs was a fantasy as wild as waking up in bed with a Hollywood star. Now the desert slope was full of these thin lines that branched and curled off each other to dead-end treeless loops like ovaries. Every morning hundreds of garage doors opened and released cars that came wriggling home again at night. In twenty years the trees would grow but right now the developments looked impossible. Something unnatural was making them take root and stand.

"Ring a bell, Lindy?" Truitt reached one long arm back. His fingers groped for her like something small and blind.

"I don't remember anything." She fluffed her hair out on the side she had slept on.

"No, I guess not."

A red SUV not unlike theirs was winding through the curlicues in the hot desert sun. It did not make sense to Hermelinda that women were born with all the eggs they would ever have and it did not make sense to her that of the thousands that had left her body only one had gotten out alive. Only one had learned to read and swim the elementary backstroke, only one cried at her recital, only one wrote fantastic stories about a plague that wiped out white people, only one aced every AP class invented. Only one got into Harvard. Only one ran away.

"New new new," Truitt said. "Someone thinks they're making money out here. And if they're right, they're rich, and they're just getting started." He took a deep breath and she thought he might be finished but at times like this he was never finished. His voice could be midnight cicadas or a rainy afternoon nap but it could also be a TV commercial for something no one needed. "Think what fifty grand could buy down here back when you came through."

She leaned forward through the seats, sending Charlie to his corner and even Super Truitt startled, sticking one arm out to keep her from the windshield. "Will you just tell me where we're going? If anybody knows." She pushed his rodent hand away and slumped back, tilting her knees to one side, out of reach. The hand flopped once and gasped and disappeared. She could feel him trying to squeeze through the rearview mirror but she kept him out and kept her eyes outside. The red SUV had disappeared or transformed into a white bird flying up to burn to cinders in the sun.

"We know where we're going," Truitt said. "We're going straight to hell, sounds like, we're going to goddamn pieces."

"We know, absolutely," Charlie said. She had almost forgotten he was there. Floppy hair bobbed between the seats. "More or less we really know, Mrs. Price." His eyes settled on the corner of her mouth, crept down her neck, lost their center, and flew off into shards. It seemed like if she reached out and touched him he might blow like a tomato in the microwave. One day he would have children of his own. He would tuck them into bed at night and bathe their little bodies and this drive would be just a faded nightmare then. Charlie's head floated there between the seats and maybe he was seeing his tomorrows too, maybe he was licking his lover's thighs or jogging with a yellow Lab named Grady. She watched him open his mouth to try to fill the silence. His teeth were white and beautiful.

"We know exactly," Truitt said. He heard the rind in his own voice but there was nothing he could do about any of it. I never should have let you come, he thought. If he could have stopped her. Slapped her right across the face. Got that shit out of the way in the comfort of their own home and left her in the driveway, one hand against her swollen cheek. Who knows, maybe she wished someone would hit her. He sure did. It'd be relief to have some normal pain shoot up his leg and rage vomit through his heart. He felt the thick body of the pig again, the way the iron had sunk into its wild meat. He'd hit it with everything he had but would never tell a soul the thing was still alive when he finally hopped away. There were flies and vultures perched and it was going to be an awful end.

"I'm just trying to make conversation," Truitt appealed to Charlie, who refused to uncork his ass, chill out, relax a little.

The traffic was getting heavier and they floated through by inches. No one honked. A huge sign with arrows signaled *Centro* and Charlie pointed left and left then right at the last minute. They swerved across two lanes of traffic like a busted record needle, Truitt tilting his head as if to listen for the car crash coming but it did not come. Hermelinda closed her eyes. They eased down the ramp into the city.

"Professional driver, closed course." Truitt said. "Do not attempt." He looked over at Charlie and grinned and winked. He could still feel the bumper of the car he'd barely missed, an inside fastball brushing the hair on his arm. "Saddle up. Crazyass Texans riding into town. We on track here, Sulu?"

"Left at the light. Really sorry about that, Mr. Price."

"Yeah well let's try to save a crumple zone or two, for later."

They crossed a river and she could see the downtown although she did not understand it. Then an older neighborhood began. One story houses from before there was a Texas, many of them restored, narrow streets with trees for shade. Some of them had the little huts on top for servants. For a little girl and her two brothers and her mother plus the father when he came home. Truitt drove slowly now as Charlie's head rocked between the signs, the two men mischanting streets of heroes and the states. Zaca Texas. High Dalgo. Cam Petch. She read the green time off the dashboard. 3:06 should mean *comida*, rooms full of chubby men and women and vast amounts of food. The greasy little goat. The plate of rice. Orange jello.

"That's it," Charlie said, tapping hard against the glass. The car hunched to a halt. Outside sat a renovated colonial place with leafy iron work across the tall, deep windows. *Café. Internet. Cerrado.*

"Now how the fanny-fuck can it be closed?" Truitt slapped the gearshift into park and popped his door and threw himself from the car. The heat was out there, waiting for her, careening into the AC, whirling invisible tornados. She could hear Charlie tapping nervously at his computer, she could hear Charlie biting his lip, she could hear Truitt's boots on the concrete outside. She opened the door and stepped out.

She had forgotten about the color. About the light. The tinted windows slipped behind her and when she reached for sunglasses they were not nesting in her hair. The café was oxygen and blood, and next door a deep storm blue, and down the street trailed apocalyptic oranges and yellows kicking open doors inside her. A low-pressure system moved slowly through her chest. Her mother used to laugh at *gringos* for their missing colors. *No saben. Ciegos. No sé qué.*

Her mother.

Truitt was banging on the door, rattling the iron grillwork like a gorilla in its first cage.

"It's lunchtime, Truitt. They probably went out." His shoulders were one of the nicest things about him, but this one jerked like bad machinery beneath her palm. She had not touched him for a day. She took her hand back. In the reflection of the glass door, sliced up by metal grate, Hermelinda caught a glimpse of their faces behind bars. His face cinched tight. Her own features strangled beneath a sheet of plastic.

"Three o'clock ain't lunchtime. Three o'clock's just fucking stupid."

From the next building, a woman's head poked from the doorway, and soon the body followed. Her hair was cheaply dyed and shellacked straight, hanging stiff and bronze to the bottom of her shoulder blades. The woman wore a cheap artificial fabric blouse and skirt with a Tepito fire-retardant sheen. She was plump. She was in her forties and she'd done a lot of frowning.

"Hey there," Truitt said. "How you doing?" His twang deepened in a simple shorthand of nice relaxed good mood. "We're looking for the big *jefes* of this café. You know where they all went?"

The woman's head tilted in diagonal. She was listening to Truitt but looking at Hermelinda, and Hermelinda could feel those eyes touch each part of her distinctly, pricing her watch and shoes and necklace, pricing her chin and calves, holding up her dark skin to a color chart. She wished she had her sunglasses. No one had looked at her like that for a long time.

Muy buenas tardes, Hermelinda said.

The woman nodded. This was one possibility. *Buenas.*

¿Hace calor, no?

Sí ¿no? Algo.

¿Le pido un gran favor?

¿En qué le puedo servir?

Buscamos los dueños del Internet.

No sé.

¿Pero sí están hoy?

Pues, sí, creo que sí.

Truitt didn't move. He stared at Hermelinda and squinted at her lips. He looked mean like that and ignorant. He looked like he had forgotten she could speak it except for games in bed. Maybe he had forgotten she could speak at all.

"She doesn't know," said Hermelinda, "when the owners will be back." Or she might know, Hermelinda thought, but she was not telling.

"That's all y'all said?"

"That's all." He was chewing on something, some black thought about her, and he was going to spit it out but not here and now. *Oye.* He had forgotten who she was. She was not sure she knew either. "Just chitchat," she told him. "I studied with the best."

He almost smiled. "Ask her where they like to eat." He licked his lips. "Tell her time is of the essence. Tell her we're not fucking around."

Es urgente.

Pues, no, verdad que no, no sé decirles.

"Oh I got that," Truitt said, "I'm picking that up just fine. She don't know *mucho*, do she. Or she's not telling."

"They're back soon."

"We ain't waiting." If he had a gun he might have shot someone. "Thank you very little," he called out to the woman, moving back toward the car. "Thanks for a dirtload of nothing."

The woman was not supposed to stare at them like that. She was not supposed to understand Truitt's words but her face darkened.

Disculpe, Hermelinda said. She took a few steps closer and now finally the woman looked down at her shoes. The thing is, Hermelinda continued in Spanish, it's an emergency. My daughter has disappeared.

The woman's face softened. Ah, I'm so sorry. I don't know what to say.

"Lindy." He might as well have whistled for her. "Come here a sec."

The woman looked at her with worried eyes: you better go. I will go if I want to, Hermelinda thought, but she was going, stepping to the driver's side where Truitt leaned out the window. He passed her a business card together with a twenty-dollar bill.

"Give her this and tell her the minute they come back? She calls us collect."

"That's insulting."

"Money helps a soul remember. Money never hurts."

"You don't know."

"Just got to do it right. Excuse me, ma'am?" he called out slowly, as if talking to a halfwit. "When they come back?" He pointed at the café. "Back? You. Call. Me!" He pointed at her and push dialed a number in the air and then splayed out his thumb and pinky and answered the phantom call. "Hello?" He winked at her. The woman was inching closer as he ran one finger underneath the number on his business card. "What's the word for call collect?"

"*Por cobrar.*"

"What she said. I'm paying." He placed the card in the woman's hand, and then almost as a casual afterthought folded on the money. "For your bother," he said, "any eventualities, hey I mean I sure do appreciate it. You been an angel." He winked again. "Thank you. *Gracias.*" Grah-see-ass.

Hermelinda could not watch but then she did and the woman smiled and traded a look of profound understanding with her husband.

"Don't worry be happy," the woman said in English almost as bad as his Spanish.

"I won't, not one bit. Thank you darling." He pointed at her, put the imaginary phone to his ear again, gestured to himself as if they were two old friends across a noisy room, pantomiming a date.

Inside the car felt like America again. One seat one vote, the AC roaring and the smell of things refusing to give up their newness. Truitt turned down the air and Hermelinda could hear Charlie's fingers picking at the keyboard. The afternoon had dabbed a touch of sweat at the base of her neck and low between her breasts.

"Okay," Truitt said. "Here's the plan." He could win a country auction or a trial with that voice, he could conquer a meek nation. "Charlie's been reading up and says this town's safe as church on Sunday. Time's the thing here. She was in that edifice at 8:14 AM, which means it's still our hottest lead but we gotta—we have *got* to, people—cover some serious ground." He jabbed a politician's thumb at her. It was almost a relief to be talked to like that. "We drop Lindy off at the hotels," he said. "Bunch in walking distance of each other. Charlie and I do the bus station."

"Okay." Alone, she thought. He was smarter than he knew sometimes.

"We'll stay in touch by hand radio." Three science fiction walkie-talkies appeared on the dash. "Military grade." Two of them were silver but one was sleek and pink. She picked it up and he grinned at her with the left side of his mouth and she remembered why the Charlies at his companies half worshipped him and why she used to love him too.

"How are you going to talk to people?"

"Honey, I always find a way to run my mouth." He waved a picture of Alma through the air like he was drying it. "They'll get the drift. 'Sides, you're right here on the line." He hit the button on a walkie-talkie and the other two squawked.

"Truitt," she said. Charlie flinched at the intimate in her voice and got interested in architecture. There was a sensitive boy beneath the silly haircut who knew how to leave people alone.

"You got this, baby," Truitt said, and he reached out and squeezed her wrist three times like he believed in her again and was pumping power into her, the way he did at marathons, or when she met his parents, or when she pushed and pushed his little girl too many years ago. Then he let go and stopped the car. "Find her."

From the curb she watched their red SUV dart through traffic. Then she crossed the street and sat down on a park bench facing the main church, a pale yellow building with six bells and a loudspeaker wedged between two cherubs, blaring choral music filled with faith.

The churches from her childhood had more rococo and gold and plaster saints scaling walls because what was a church if it could not make a child or peasant gape? This church looked almost Protestant. These people were too tall. But then the gassy Volkswagon *vochos* swarmed past like windborne motes of dust, twirling around the huge flat monolith of orange sitting in the *alameda* center, and with the huge mountain in the background, the big orange rectangle, the church, the ultramodern buildings flanking left and right—this was Mexico even if she had never seen it before. She closed her eyes and the sound of the VW bugs was the childhood roar outside *Bisquets Obregón,* uneven pavement playing beneath her feet.

The North will be different.

Different how?

Stingy. Hermelinda's mother gestured, hand cupped around the elbow.

Papa says that's better.

Your papa says a lot of things and some of them are true.

Across the plaza, across the street, Hermelinda paused outside the first hotel, flipping through the photos. They had argued about which to bring because he chose the most horrible—Alma ugly angry tired sad—but he was not here now and she shuffled three to the top: smiling tight-lipped at a holiday party, laughing crooked on the lake, reading by the pool. She still looked like a baby when she read, the way the eyes loosened and the brow let go and the mouth slacked. Hell, Lindy, they ain't gonna recognize her, she don't smile but twice a year. Maybe not but Alma read, wherever she was now, she was curled up with a book and her eyes looked just like that. No, the pictures were fine but the first hotel lobby told her there would be no Alma here. The handsome bellhop wanted Hermelinda to inquire but she did not because her daughter was not so clever to stay in a place this nice.

The streets of downtown Monterrey were thick with people. Light skinned, tall *norteños.* She had forgotten about them. Any one of them would have been *güero* in The City. The races did not mix as much up north because here the Indians could be killed but not conquered. She must have been only ten years old when her father told her that. He did not care if his little girl understood him or not but she did. The dark pocked face and hands that moved like caged birds when he talked. You see, little one, that's why up north is not Mexico.

But it was Mexico. The mustached men walking in their immaculate cheap suits, hair gelled back against their heads, staring at women with casual lust. The long-haired business women in heels and short skirts. How they looked at one another! At her. Her shoes. Her fading pink nails peeking from two-inch cream Prada sandals. She slipped into the next hotel.

The lobby was dark, more shabby than it first appeared. No doorman here. Instead a high counter with a man parked there behind. He was reading something except when she approached he was not, only staring at his hands. He lifted his face and did something to make the lines there disappear.

Señora. His voice was deep and heavy with repect. How can we be of service. He slipped out from behind the desk and squinted kindness at her. His eyes did not waver from her own but she could still feel his gaze take in her toes, her hair, her breasts.

Yes. Perhaps you can help me.

With great pleasure. He bent his head and put his hands behind his back, waiting for her to show him how. You visit us from the DF?

No.

You must forgive me.

My accent?

Your pardon, please. I'm always speaking when I shouldn't.

I. She fumbled with her purse, handing him the pictures one by one. She tried to summon up the voice she used with their accountant. My daughter.

His brow folded up in valleys like a special Chinese dog. He ran his fingers over the photo. What a nice girl, he said. I'm sorry I do not know her, *señora.* She is with us in Monterrey?

Yes.

Many young people stay at The Norway. He sucked in his bottom lip until it disappeared. You are alone?

No.

Yes, because it is better that you don't go there alone. He smiled again but not for her, a business couple headed for the door. He glanced at the clock there on the wall. My colleague will be here soon and I can accompany you, if it conveniences you.

Hermelinda stared at him. He was horrible, this stupid little man with his pig eyes and crinkly face who watched the secretaries come and go in cheap shoes they had just propped up on their bosses' shoulders after lunch, this horrible little man with his syrup patter living off cheap tips, how would he make money off her missing little girl? She turned away from him and stared out the lobby windows at the line of stores and all the faces walking by, talking and laughing, and she did not hear what he said next because there at the farthest edge was Alma. She saw her daughter's eyes and nose and mouth magnified by some trick of glass and light and then Alma was out of view and gone.

¡Señora!

The liar! She must have screamed but now she ran. She was woodpecker gunfire clicking across the lobby floor, she was yelling at the little man in English as she kicked off her shoes and raced to the street in naked feet.

"Alma!" she cried out. "Alma! Alma! Alma!"

She ran through the thick afternoon crowd that gaped at this middle-aged lightning-quick madwoman screaming English barefoot in the street. *Pinche loca. Qué puta.* She shouldered through and took the corner and saw not one thing she recognized. They must be right. She must be goddamn crazy. She staggered sideways, feeling the sudden sore in her soft roughed feet. She leaned against the wall and cried until a very old woman touched her wrist and shined concern into her eyes.

Are you okay, my child?

No. Thank you. Yes. It's that I've lost my daughter. I thought I saw her in the street.

Ay, my love. This is what it is to be a mother in these times. She held Hermelinda's wrist firmly. Push the hair out of your eyes. Give me your arm, that's it. Together they strolled back into the promenade of people.

My shoes, Hermelinda said.

The old woman shook her head. We'll sit down, have a coffee, you'll feel better then. I know people. We'll take care of you.

The café was a real café. Leather seats and creased white table-clothes crowded with sugar towers. She felt the tile cool and somehow clean beneath her feet. The waitress made an effort not to see Hermelinda's shoelessness, licking her lips to grease the way for words that did not come.

Two coffees, the old woman said. She was strange and elegant and wearing a fine Italian wrap. Hair was white but excellently done. I'm Maria Victoria Cuevas Castro. Please call me Mariví.

Hermelinda.

Mariví waited for more, folding her hands in her lap. Hermelinda placed the pictures on the table. And your daughter?

Alma.

She does not look very much like you. Mariví handled the pictures carefully, her vein-ridged hands steady and calm.

I was a strange bug too, as a child.

Sometimes it happens that way. The old lady sounded like she knew this was a lie.

You know the song about the ugly duck who turns into a. Hermelinda closed her eyes and found the word there in the floating gardens of her mother. Lilies and a painted barge. *Cisne.*

I don't know it. The coffees were arriving now, puffing steam. Mariví busied herself with quantities of milk and sugar while Hermelinda watched glossy Alma curling in the heat.

She is beautiful to me.

That's how we mothers are. The old woman gently reached across the table and touched Hermelinda's hand. The coffee here is excellent.

Drink. You will feel better.

Hermelinda brought the cup to her mouth but it was still too hot. I don't know what to do.

Three times it happened to me, said Mariví.

How terrible.

Yes. Where do you live now?

Now? She wanted to ask another question but she could not think right. I live in Texas.

Mariví nodded. I thought so. I am often in Dallas. Monterrey is not so bad but. She shakes her head. There's a class of people you cannot find here. She winked. And shopping of course.

I thought I saw her in the street. Did that ever happen to you?

Mariví shook her head firmly. No, I don't believe in that. Village fairy tales. She pressed her lips together tightly. I'm sorry. It is too soon. My poor thing. When did she pass away.

Hermelinda jerked her hand back from the crazy ancient crone. She could feel a jolt of fear as the world ran out of air and blood ground between bare toes. My Alma ran away, she said.

The old woman leaned back and opened her mouth and then giggled, swatting at an unseen mite in front of her. Ay, she'll be back, my love. Mine won't. And here you are sniffing the ground like a bloodhound. Where is the father? Your people?

What do you want. That I stay at home? She was on her feet now, and everyone was looking at her, the whole café.

Mariví shook her head and clucked. The old lady would be dead with her own missing children soon. There was no reason to yell at her except the way that Mariví kept looking at her.

Where I live, said Hermelinda, mothers don't just stay at home and wait. Where I'm from? Women do things besides suffer. You know that, don't you?

Mariví said nothing, collecting looks of sympathy from the rest of the café.

Hermelinda leaned in anyway. This, she said clearly, for everyone to hear, this is no country for a woman.

Maríví hissed at her. The sound traveled around the room, hissing and clucking, snakes and hens. Hermelinda flicked a red bill to the table and walked out into the street, heading back to the hotel. My mother was a mop and my father left us to die and look at me! They were looking, these people on the street, but they did not know what they saw.

"Lindy."

The familiar voice slipped sing-song from her handbag over static.

"Lindy, Lindy, where are you honey over."

She fished the apparatus like a pistol from her purse. The feel of it in her hand, this expensive shining metal, calmed her instantly.

"I'm right here, Truitt."

"Where."

"Downtown."

"No dice here but we're gonna head back to the café soon, see if they back. How you."

"I'm hanging in there. I'm okay."

"Alright girl, you the best, don't forget. We gonna find her *to-day*, we gonna do it. You knock out those hotels, now, holler for any reason at all. I love you, baby."

"I love you too." She lifted her thumb off the button and stared back at the world around her staring at her. I am not one of you, she thought. *Fíjate bien.*

High above the street a green balloon drifted, floating through the air. Alma was somewhere, here, close, looking up into the sky and seeing that balloon escaped from a birthday party or a car sale or marking the scene of a crime, sailing up out of the hand of a small child pulled into the back of a van. From the earliest age it was hard not to imagine that something would happen to them. As far back as she could remember, Hermelinda had seen her little girl triple-pierced and studded, her thin body wrapped in skintight clothes. She was hanging from the middle of the room, swinging back and forth in uneven arcs. She was sitting on a toilet with a needle in her arm. Alma was a fetus that bled to death and a toddler tumbling stairs, she was a child pedaling into traffic, she was a pre-teen floating facedown in the river. She was flying through the windshield, she was a depressive twenty-something, a worker drone, an addicted barren housewife, a middle-aged regret, an old fat bitter crone. The green balloon was floating over Monterrey and over her daughter's head, it was there for everyone but only Alma and Hermelinda could see it. She is not one of you and I am not one of you and yet out there, thought Hermelinda, out there somewhere, my only daughter is looking for something she thinks you people have. But I know. I know you do not.

Street sand embedded grain by grain in the soft hinges beneath her toes as Hermelinda stepped through Mexico to collect her shoes. She would find them, put them on, and walk until they fell apart or until she found her Alma.

Eight

The turn came suddenly, a dirt road jetting off to the ripped dry mountains they had been eyeing for half an hour through the dawn's green light. It was not a bad road, not so far, although Truitt leaned into the dash with gusto and flipped to four-wheel drive, muscling them forward with no hint of slow. A huge bank of dust rose in their wake and rocks leapt behind the tires as they tore on and up toward the town hidden somewhere in the brute sierra. 31 km. Real de Catorce.

"This ain't on the way to nothing," said Truitt.

"Maybe they didn't know." Charlie tapped the map. "Looks closer than it is."

"This guy she's with?"

"Blake. Dean Blake."

"How do you think I should kill him?"

The speedometer said 49 but it felt like hundreds of miles per hour. A first-time driver on these roads was not meant to drive so fast. Hermelinda yawned for air. They were climbing and climbing and the world grew more blue the higher they climbed.

Outside, a shrine blurred by. Homemade dollhouse with the Virgin standing in the doorway. They were back in the land of virgins now, where families of dark *indios* knelt at roadside altars, praying for the dead. The air was different here. The air was thin and crumbled in her hands like crackers. Truitt leaned them hard around another corner and Hermelinda imagined reaching up with both hands and pulling back the parking brake. She caught a glimpse of Charlie's laptop and saw the pictures were still there.

She had not recognized them right away, when Charlie first fished them out of the computer guts back at the Monterrey café. It was the number that shoved the past in through her ears: five thirty-two. The effort of the sounds all those years ago, the determination to say it right and strip her voice of the accent that branded her worse than skin or eyes or hair. Terty. Dirty. Thurty. Thurty. Tongue poking out between the teeth. Five thirty-two. She was stepping down those stairs in her only skirt—dark blue—and white-white blouse she had cleaned by hand the night before, waiting for fat Mrs. Watkins limping there behind and flagging down the city bus to drop them near the school. Green vinyl seats sticking to smooth thighs in the heat. Five thirty-two North Jarvis Street. My god, Alma, what are you doing.

There in the café, Hermelinda had dropped heavily into a plastic chair as Charlie recovered evidence and pictures to the screen. Laredo. Nuevo. Truitt caught her weight and she would have told him then except Charlie was still finding things, tracking Alma's searches. fungicide band luis barragan peyote real de catorce mexico d.f. diarrhea vegetarians latin american travel. She would have told him but they were back in the car speeding toward the bus station, where they found the counter, found the ticket trail, Truitt bribing everyone in his path. The guy at the counter said the gringo boy had paid in cash but the man named Dean Blake, he used a credit card.

Gringo boy?

Boy.

Truitt had closed his eyes for a moment and when he opened them again he knew something that she did not. Pulled a picture from the stack and watched the guy nod before he flipped it at her like a flashcard. It was the ugliest photo of them all, Alma scowling dumpy in a baseball cap and loose jeans and too-big shirt, caught in some foul moment on some foul day.

Pero con sombrero, the man at the counter said, looking straight at Hermelinda.

She got a big set of balls on her, said Truitt, I'll give her that.

A *pueblo* flashed by now outside the window, a one-sneeze town of unpainted concrete and thatch. It must get cold here in the winter. The August dirt looked like it could freeze meat and fry bread, the land looked defenseless to the hot-cold sky and no help to human beings at all. Silver and gold sucked from hills like this, all up and down the high spine of Mexico. There was a mural she remembered from a school trip of her childhood, from The City, with almost faceless miners trooping from the darkness to the whip-gun drivers overhead. They were Indians, the miners, they were red brown arms stretched wide as the soldiers strip-searched the thieving lying animals for bits of shiny rock. The rock built cities and towns where no civilization belonged. The rock built Mexico City, block after block of The City's Centro, the rock kept building long after it was gone. The neighborhood of La Roma. Low rows of *vecindades* apartments squatting amidst turn-of-the-century splendor. There were children to play with in the long narrow courtyard and neighbors up to your armpits and laundry everywhere. Father there on the steps talking art and politics and mother slaving alone inside.

As they had walked back to their car from the revelation of the bus counter—arrived 3:45 in Real de Catorce!—Hermelinda said finally:

She is going to Mexico City.

Because some story you told her.

Not really.

Some old bullshit you yarned.

I didn't. You wouldn't let her go to Spain. Maybe that's it.

Bull-shit.

Bullshit fine but she is going to Mexico City.

Because?

Because she thinks she has family there.

Family who?

My father.

Who died.

But he didn't.

Didn't how?

If Charlie had not been there she did not know what might have happened next. Maybe, the young man interjected, she's planning to stop in Catorce on the way? He was like that cow they used to calm bulls bred for *corrida*, he looked at her, and she looked at Truitt, and Truitt looked out the window. Sometimes it worked and sometimes the cow was gored. Poor Charlie. Truitt still would not talk to her.

Roadside, a huge sign appeared with simultaneous speed bumps. They were flying and now they skidded and then the thump as they hit the asphalt mounds.

"Goddamn," Truitt said, "they let every mechanic in this country put their own bumps in?" He glanced at the sign again, the two black bumps on yellow, with the explanation *topes* written there beneath. "Topes." He rhymed it with ropes. "That's Spanish for 'fuck you' I guess."

Somewhere there was a woman who still loved the way he talked. Maybe this was the woman that he slept with south of Austin's river in the cheap motels. Maybe this woman was the one who lay naked in the cool canned air while he blabbed and babbled about swimming in East Texas irrigation ditches and funny one-armed oil men and Brother Jim's pussy-getting boots, and the sound of his voice was comfort and the promise that life was a wonderful story that this woman could be part of. The voice would take care of the details and sweep all cares away. One day the stories would start to repeat themselves and every night would seem like the same night, and that night would not be quite what at first glance it appeared to be, but for now the voice was full of money and full of carelessness and fun. That woman was not her and had not been her for a long time. They still knew how to talk to one another but what would they talk about now?

The end of the road came suddenly. There was no town there, no anything, only a dark hole in the mountain that looked like it had been drilled by an angry prehistoric worm. A man waving a white piece of cloth directed them into line behind a pair of pickups and an old '70s sedan that belonged on concrete blocks. They waited. The curious peered into the tinted glass of their vehicle, offering strange things for sale: a life-sized Jesus bleeding on the cross, mint green *chicles*, bright red candied *tuna* fruits, plain wool blankets, carved wooden birds with multicolored plumes. If she did not know better she could think the world looked so alive out there, alive with real people and real beauty, the folkloric warmth of commerce, men and women of the earth. But she did know better. She remembered. She watched the tunnel's mouth spit out cars and trucks and a midget bus that barely fit and then their waiting line was waved through.

Jagged hands of rock reached for them in the dark. She sank down low into her seat. We should not be here, Hermelinda thought, Alma should not be here, this town should not be here.

Truitt had never seen a fucked-up tunnel like this before but it reminded him of that scene in *Willy Wonka*, they're on a chocolate river boat and Willy's getting weird, chanting like a chocolate monk, the children shitting their little pants as they rocket through the dark tunnel past mysterious twisted glimpses and sights. There were doors in Willy's tunnel but there weren't no doors here, if something happened here you were going to die a horrible death, the death that you deserved for being inside a mountain. It was the kind of place that made some men give up.

He could see over the roof of the station wagon in front of them, but beyond that a truck blocked the way, and Truitt found himself locked in on that station wagon, watching the brake lights for signs of trouble. The core of the Earth might be a fireball but it was cold in there. He knew Alma's little heart beat a war drum against the world but she had no idea what Austin was or what real people were capable of. Whose fault was that? He might have lied about a thing or two but never about his family. Never the fundaments of who he was. Then again, we've all done things we don't understand, thought Truitt, and then the station wagon braked sharply in front of them and there they were.

The tunnel spit the cars out into a chaotic lot of dirt, people, and business. Here on the other side of the world, here in China, people were busy. Eating—everywhere and all the time these Mexicans were eating, cramming tacos into their mouths like that was the last one. Even from here—it looked like they wanted folks to stop their cars, that's what the arms waving outside were all about, they liked to flop their hands and whistle, they had a decent wordless language when it came to cars—even from here the town church was visible. Visible? The thing was massive, the town was mostly church. There was one reason a troubled teen came up here. Not gold or silver. Drugs. Truitt knew it.

"They want us to park," said Hermelinda. "Here." She hadn't rolled down her window but was in silent confab with the men and boys outside. Her body moved differently in Spanish. Just a half step quicker. If you saw her through a window you might think she was a Mexican. It had been a long time since she'd looked like that to him. Long before she was the brown girl smiling like music in his arms, tossling in that pool of theirs, late hot Austin nights. She'd been Mexican for a week or two, when they first started dating, but after that she was just smarter and more sure and better-looking than everybody else. You wanted to do anything for a girl like that, Mexican or whatever, to grab the tech cash rolling out from California and flash-flooding uphill through the streets of Westlake, to marry her, to keep her, to give her what she wanted even though it couldn't last. Look at this place! Look at this Catorce! They'd had it all once upon a time now didn't they! Sucked these mountains dry and now what remained was ruined splendor, drugs and dirt. He didn't want to park unless he had to, just as soon monster truck this motherfucker. Why hadn't she told him? What kind of person lied her daddy dead?

"The road must go on," said Truitt. "Find one for us, Charlie, will ya?"

He could hear her rolling the window down and *buenos días taque-rías*. There was a stillness to the resting Hermelinda in the real world but here in Willy Wonka's Mexico her hands were starting to move like a pack of coked-up butterflies. Her mouth opened wider. Her mouth opened too far for comfort. These were strangers. What was she saying? He might be an idiot when it came to Spanish but he held advanced degrees in Hermelinda. Shoulda left her at home, in that driveway. If she turned into a Mexican on him at least she'd understand it when he smacked her. If she stopped being the precious thing.

"We can get around," she said. The man on the other side of the window was grinning like she'd just flashed him tit.

He didn't look at her. "You got us a map of this here pueblo, Charlie, or shall I employ my imagination?"

The low road ran like a gutter at the lip of town. They came around the other side and parked on a tilted square. Boys came running as they stepped out into the thin mountain air. Truitt drank it in like hot weak coffee, feeling it burn its way through his body but expecting more. He chose the largest boy, handed him a blue twenty-peso note, pointed at the car, and then pressed two fingers under his eyes, flashing recon signs. "Watch that for me," Truitt said. The kid checked him sternly, a good recruit. "Charlie, go scout for Internet." He tossed his squire a walkie-talkie and the boys tracked it through the air like a fresh vein of color. Charlie nodded, and when Truitt turned around again he saw she'd already half disappeared, fine legs pumping into the crowd.

Hermelinda had never seen anything like it. She was wrong to think that Alma would never come here and wrong to think that she knew everything that Mexico could be. That Mexico could be your weightless wrists painted with sweeps of pale green lines from the cloud-streaked sky to the empty valley below. What a beautiful town this was. She could walk this street with Alma's arm linked through hers. The only thing Hermelinda recognized was the way people looked at her. The way Mexican eyes ate a stranger. Burned her from her pupils to her shoes. Breasts. Hips. Legs and neck. What she had forgotten about Mexico was the sex, the way it lingered everywhere. It was eight o'clock in the morning but every man she passed wanted to spread her legs. The women wanted her to stay away from their men and wanted her to know they saw deep down she was still just poor dark Indian trash no matter how much her sunglasses cost or what anyone said. They hoped she was alone and barren. Their husbands hoped she was a whore.

The church stood up suddenly in front of her, squaring its big shoulders and arching that gray neck to the sky. Church square thick with people buying candles and kaleidoscopes from the vendors there outside. Saintly panoramas, beads, incense, crystals, rocks, the saints, alarm clocks, key chains, earrings, *Virgen de Guadalupe* everything. It was cheap and tasteless and ridiculous but they were living inside it and they would never see until life flashed before their eyes or they just walked across the border and looked back at what they'd been. Hermelinda could not know what it was to stand behind a stall of *Jesús Te Ama* t-shirts and watch a strange Mex-Tex woman twisting her tennis bracelet in confusion, but she knew what it was like to cross a border and see herself at last. She glanced behind her to make sure that he was watching before she slipped inside.

The floors were built from wooden boxes used to haul out silver, but she was the only one who found this extraordinary. Everyone else was busy praying, praying hard as if they thought that worked. Too many things had happened to the little girl who loved Jesus and even loved herself. Loved herself because her mother did, and because her father loved her until he did not anymore. He was thirty years old then. He was ten years younger than she was now. She did not know what he was. In the end he was a man like Jesus was a man. Like every man was a man.

The church was organized into a series of altars that followed the life of Jesus, and at each station there were people chanting and mumbling and one small old woman moaning, but Alma was not there. Jesus as a baby boy. Jesus as a young man holding someone else's baby strangely, like a politician. Jesus as a martyr up there on the cross. She had seen all these before but what she had not seen was how Jesus looked between crucifix and resurrection. He lay there dead, encased in glass with black dried blood encrusted around the holes in his hands and feet and also a hole in his right breast. It looked like his heart had burst except she thought the heart was on the left side. She pressed her hand against her own chest but she could not feel anything, not on the left and not on the right, she could not feel her own heart beating. It would not surprise her to be dead. For everything she did with it, she had no idea how her body worked. And she was forty! Alma was seventeen. They never depicted Christ the adolescent but that was the one Hermelinda wondered about.

She sank down into a pew. She had never dressed Alma up in white and stood her in front of bleeding Jesus. She had never told her daughter that the body was a sin, that sex was shameful, that true love skipped over sex and went straight to God. No one had ever threatened her daughter with hell but Alma was still angry and ashamed.

She did not know how long she would have sat there if Truitt had not appeared in the aisle. He did not say a word. Silent. Unbreakable. Never crumbled beneath her grief. He could always look her in the eye like he could solve her problems, and that was why she had let him have her, all those years ago. Sometimes he could. He stretched out one hand and she took it and he pulled her gently from the church.

"There's a guy we need to talk to." It seemed to Truitt that this might be the first thing he'd said to her for almost a day. They stood against a pale yellow wall in the sunlight. The sun was crisp up here but did not give much heat. Her fingers felt numb. She looked like she'd been crying, Truitt thought, except she never cried.

"Who?"

"King of the trolls, sounds like." He kept her cold hands in his, hauling her up the hill. "The good-time man 'round town." He watched her face but her face was a stone idol, sheared straight off some savage temple. The goddess of big grief.

"For me he died a long time ago," she said. She didn't look at him. "I'm afraid," she said, and the simple word sent beetles through his bones.

"I know it, baby. If we don't find her here." It was steep going but he refused to slow. "You might have to call him. If that's where she's really going."

She looked at him asylum. "She can't find him, can she? Please, Truitt, she can't find him."

"She won't, babe, but just in case she does."

"No she can't! She can't, Truitt!" She was trying to jerk her hand loose like a bratty little kid. "He's," she gasped, feet flailing, "dangerous that's why I did it I'm sorry I'm so sorry."

She'd lost it. "I'm here, baby, I'm right here, nothing's gonna happen." Jesus H. befucking Christ. He held her for a while trying to think until he realized they were standing in front of the house where drug lord Paco supposedly lived.

The house sat there on the big nose of the ridge overlooking town and was about what he expected: a high sierra crack-house, mud and cactus and corrugated iron falling apart at the seams. Someone'd stuck a spiky sun made from wood and painted orange in the dirt out front like a pink goddamn flamingo. Truitt pulled her with him to the door. "She might be here," he said, "okay? Let's stay on track right now for a minute. Can you do this?" He waited for her to nod and then they both breathed together. In. Out. In. Out.

"Okay?"

"Okay."

Truitt knocked twice.

"¿*Quién?*"

"*Hermelinda Montes Figueroa,*" she sang out, before she even knew it, although she had not been that person for almost twenty years.

The door opened. He was wearing pale blue jeans and a bright red and yellow shirt in hippie streaks, unbuttoned halfway down his hairless chest as if this were the Yucatan. He was headed toward a beard if this was possible for him, and now he stood and considered his visitors, running fingers along his scruff. There was pleasure in this motion, a look in his eyes as if he had never touched his face like this before. The fingers pulled down through the black hairs and stroked the patch beneath full lips. One hand dropped to his hip. He looked almost feminine as he leaned like that against the door frame. His jeans were worn white with age, white with the habit of his body, white here and there and there in a shocking line that crept an amazing distance down his left thigh. She could not stop looking at him.

"*Qué onda*," he said, his eyes rolling slowly down her body from her halo to the tongue between her toes, "*señorita Montes*." His eyes moved strangely in cascading curlicues. Behind him, the room was dark. The man-boy made no move to invite them inside. He slipped a hand inside his shirt. He could not keep his hands off himself.

Truitt stuck out his hand and the boy took it limply.

"Truitt Price." Her husband's voice was low and filled with oil. "You must be Paco. You speak English, Paco?"

Paco shrugged.

"Oh I think you do, Paco," Truitt said. "I think you got your ways."

Lindy was staring at the little fuck like she might like to eat him and Truitt squeezed the kid's hand like water from a rock. Cocksucker's lids came open then, wide open, but the kid didn't squeal or anything, just the widened eyes that told Truitt he'd got his attention. "You know a little something about peyote, that's what I hear, Paco. When it comes to Lophophora you're the man."

"You know Lophophora?" Paco shook his hand free suddenly and stepped out of the doorway, pulling the door shut behind. "You know Lophophora Williams, mister?"

"Hey I grew up in the sixties. I read that book. I did my part. It was cool and all but it's a different world today."

"Castaneda was full of shit," said Paco. It sounded funny coming from his girly little Spanish mouth.

"Sure, a big dummy. *You're* the expert, right? That's why all the kiddies come to you."

"To me? To the desert."

"The desert." What did this kid think? That they'd come all this way to suck his supercalifragilistic technicolor dick? He wanted to get Paco's hand again and turn it into ashes but instead he started to stare him down. The kid's eyes wouldn't stay still. They were shaking in his head like flies. Drugs. "Come on now," said Truitt, nice and slow this time, to get through all that haze, "I think we understand each other, Paco. You know why I'm here. Why someone like me. Needs to talk. To someone like you."

The young man closed his eyes to think about this and then opened them and shook his head. "No. You are not ready for the desert."

"Got that right. I'm just a daddy, bucko. I'm just a pissed-off daddy looking for my little girl."

Her husband was showing him the picture now and Paco kept shaking his head. Hermelinda wanted to believe him and wanted to stop looking at him. It was only a little time before the white line worn into his jeans gave way altogether and what was there behind pressed through the fabric into daylight. It would fill her hands. It would fill her absolutely. She wanted it inside her. She swept her long hair off her neck and onto one shoulder while the two men stared at one another. She heard her daughter's name, the sound that should bring her back, and there was the picture of Alma, that ugly picture with the baseball cap. Her joints were softening, a liquid change in her neck and in the middle of her back, beneath her hips. The familiar that had not been familiar for a long time. She could feel the swell and the lips there pressing against each other and she reached down and adjusted herself. She did not care. Paco would slide his fingers and she would be something different. Not bloody. Not betrayed. Truitt had his other woman who did not see the blood there on his penis. Hermelinda could lie up here with Paco. The blood did not belong with the beginnings of a child inside her. Alma's little brother on the way. There was blood on Truitt and blood on the sheets and blood still coming as he banged on the bathroom door, Lindy, my god what's wrong, what's happening, the sobs wracking through her body. She would never come out of that bathroom. It was a hundred years ago and a hundred-hundred fucks ago and the other babies disappearing into the toilet's laughing mouth but she could not get out of that bathroom and she did not know how long it had been since she had tried.

"*Señorita Montes.*" The boy had somehow shut up her husband and was staring at her heart. "*Te digo algo de tu hija si se va este hombre.*"

"Truitt." She could not look at him, at either of them. "Would you give us a minute, please?" That was not the way to say it but she stepped forward and opened the front door whether Truitt agreed or not.

Inside it smelled like socks and sex and cactus. She stepped across dirt floor to where the wood began. When she turned around he was still leaning near the doorway, watching her.

You look like a dream of her, he said.

Don't say that.

I could see you in her. The figurine that waits inside the block of clay.

Please don't say that. There was no chair in Paco's hovel, only a wooden table and a wide low bed in the corner, and she felt so tired, she wanted to sit on the bed but was afraid of what would happen. There were green plant parts on the table like cells dividing stuck at four. Hermelinda pointed.

I need to see her. I need to see her now.

Paco shrugged.

Did you give her drugs?

She went to the desert. Found what they were looking for. He waited for her to ask again but she would not. They left for Mexico City, he said.

Is she okay?

More okay than you.

Hermelinda almost screamed but instead picked up one of the plants and held it in her hands. When?

Yesterday. He moved up beside her and took the plant away from her and put it back in place.

Is he a good man?

Neither good nor bad.

Did she tell you anything?

No. He reached out and touched her wrist and it filled her body with heat. But I can see inside. Inside all of you. Paco released her. There was something wrong with him, thought Hermelinda, something wrong beneath this beautiful wrapping. I can see your ancestors.

Not mine.

She saw them, he said. I can show you too. She moved away from him but he followed, pressing up against her somehow without touching. If you come with me you'll see her.

Where?

You'll see. All of them. All the living and dead. He reached out to touch her wrist again.

In the days to come—in Mexico City—Hermelinda would think back and puzzle what drugged-up Paco had really meant. But she had no doubt at the time. The beautiful boy grabbed for one arm and then here was Truitt yanking on the other and she watched them like two iron towers as she fell, as she sank to the ground, her cheek resting there in the dirt next to Truitt's boot. They were calling her name, Lindy, honey, *señorita Montes*, and she was calling out names too, calling for the missing again and again and again.

PART THREE

Nine

The subway station known as Insurgentes sits inside a centrifuge of cars like a sunken coliseum. Times Square neon signs loom overhead. Alma can get anywhere from here, theoretically, if she can pick her way through the pirate CD vendors and Mexico City skaterats and beggars so nasty they beg from other beggars. Down. Down to the wormhole through the city's guts, where if this were her first day in town maybe she'd be freaking out about all the polyester and the singing fat man selling electrical tape, or the blind orphan amputees, or the bureaucrats reading comic porn and cops in riot gear beating men back from the women only subway cars. Maybe she'd be more nervous if Dean wasn't with her, although he won't be, not for long. They pack onto the One Line, shoulder to ass to elbow. Either her bra is shrinking or she's getting really fat.

What a zoo, says Dean.

It's a city.

Hope this is worth it.

Big Red says.

Must be one hell of a cantina, Dean shouts, his breath stirring the hair of a small woman with her head shoved in his armpit.

Since they hit town two long days ago they have barely left La Condesa, a part of town that thinks it's cool. Thinks it's all history and peace. Trees fend off the chemical sun. Pretty people everywhere.

Sidewalk cafés. Art deco splendor. This is where Big Red lives, with the expats and the boho rich kids. This friend of Dean's from Jersey who knows everything but doesn't like Americans. What Big Red likes is the greasy goat *cantinas* feed you free when you order a few drinks, and his artsy friends and cheap cocaine, and gringophile *chicas* about ten years younger than him. He's going native. He's here to disappear. He's hairy and drives her totally crazy but at least the guy speaks Spanish and reads and knows the city and hangs out with real Mexicans who read and write and know Sor Juana from Dirty Sanchez. Dean has no interests except for girls and beer.

But he does look dazzling, even in harsh subway light. Blond hair twinkles. Smile shines. She maybe could forget he's all that she despises. Since Bustamante they've seldom been more than seven feet apart. He smells like rotting fresh cut grass. She would kiss him in a heartbeat, the loudest fastest heartbeat ever heard, she would rather be with him than all the Nathans in Atlanta, she would probably be his slave if he'd just ask her, but he won't, he never will, no one like him ever will, these good ol' golden boys the whole world greets with open arms and thighs. A few times he's caught her looking at him like she really shouldn't look at him. In Catorce. Last night at the Lobo. Drugs and lust and subterfuge don't mix. He's stupid but not that stupid. He's always drunk, which helps, she started wearing boxy glasses, which helps, but her boobs hurt when he looks at her, like they're trying to get out. All in all the thing to do is never see him again. He's bad company. He mistakes Bukowski for Burroughs, whose old house they passed this morning, where the famed writer started *Junky* and accidentally shot his wife. The place is a real landmark but all Dean noticed were the herds of pleated schoolgirls passing by.

Is this our stop?

We transfer.

The doors open and the crowd starts pushing out. Somewhere, here in the center, near the Zócalo, is the cantina where Big Red waits for them, probably with friends, and there's a part of Alma that wants desperately to join them and destroy themselves as planned. These friends know Burroughs from Bukowski. They read. They write. They talk for hours and never mention money and jobs and sales. For the past two nights she feels like she's stumbled into a dream of crisp dialogue and debauch, a Spanish cyclone of ideas she's never met before, and songs and secret histories and a key of laughter English speakers just don't have. They talk to her about the American invasion of 1847 as if it happened yesterday. She's afraid of their acumen and kindness. She's afraid she'll want to stay. She's afraid she might be wrong about what brought her here. She knows that the rest of the city is no Condesa, that she can't hide out forever with the hipsters and parks and markets bursting with the most beautiful fruit she's ever seen in her life. This isn't Mexico. This isn't where the Beats would come if the Beats were still around. Some Bohemian candyland with a little dirt and crumbling concrete and feces sprinkled in. La Condesa can go fuck itself. There are two hundred city streets named Emiliano Zapata, and her grandfather lives on one of them.

Dean puts his shoulder down and pushes through the crowd. Instead of following him, she ducks her head and lets a few people pass. And then leans back and rows backward, staying in the subway car, watching the people flow rapidly around her on each side. At the last minute she thinks *follow that ass!* but by then it is too late. The doors are closing. Dean is on the other side. Her things are stashed in a hotel room paid this morning for the week. Her map's marked up with yellow highlighter gilding the Zapatas. The doors close and she squats down out of sight. Her neck and shoulders feel enormous. A few stops later a seat appears and she takes it, ignoring the avalanche of stares. She tracks her progress beneath the city, astounded by such bravery, debating who will play her in the movie.

Next stop, Pantyland, terminal stop for line four with correspondence to—

She can't catch everything the loudspeaker says but the train is ending. She can see it on the map—the actual name is Pantitlan—on the eastern edge of the city. Except there is no edge. The pipes of people pump up the escalators and out into Thursday, 2:13 PM—where's everybody going? She has never seen so many people in her life, here, where the devil has built himself a nest of metal and concrete and extras made of sulfur. The city shows no sign of stopping. From here, the only form of transportation she trusts is light rail, but light rail doesn't go her way, which leaves her taxis known for kidnap or wild buses pawing asphalt. Buses made of robot corpses, with hand lettered signs that look like serial killers made them up. She's terrified of buses, no telling where they go. She should ask someone, but who? The people in a hurry or the ones who've been nibbling holes in their own clothes or the ones who stare at clueless gringo freak? And so she walks.

She walks for a long time. The buildings are gray. The streets are gray. The people are brown in a gray sort of way. La Condesa is La Condesa, but this part of the city was poured from the great cement mixer in the sky. No one's gotten around to painting for a while. The tops of walls are lined with broken bottles and pointy metal rods. The first few blocks someone with a knife is going to gut her like a fish and run her over and bite her fingers off and sic their dogs but she gets over it. She breathes and puts one foot in front of the other and after a while the city doesn't seem to notice her.

Zapata Street. Zapata Alley, Zapata Way, Zapata Avenue, Zapata End, Zapata Boulevard, Zapata Lane, Court, Cove, Circle, Drive, Park, Place, Route, Terrace, Gate, Circuit, Row, Arterial, Walk, Trail, Quay. Over the last three days she has marked every one of them on her thick book of a map. Some can be eliminated. Others can be slotted last. For the rest of them, she's starting on the right side of the city and working to her left.

Zapata Street of the far east looks like it winds into a dead end up against something known at *U. HABIT CERRO SAN JORGE.* What lies at the top of this Saint George Hill she doesn't know, but she's starting to get thirsty and hot and worried again. She's left the wide avenues and a residential neighborhood of cinderblock houses has engulfed her, with few markets or businesses or stores, so when she sees one—the tin sign says *Fanta*—she goes in.

At first the place seems empty. Cans on the shelves look old as art. No refrigerator. A dried ham hock thing rots atop a cheap aluminum scale. Someone has been calculating pi on a counter slab of butcher paper. She stoops to pluck a bottle of water from a plastic crate, and when she stands up there's a woman at the counter staring like Alma just shat on the floor.

¿Qué más?

Hola. Como, uh, agua. No, gracias. Sólo agua, gracias. She pops off the bottle cap and carbonation spews. She watches it foam along her knuckles and then shakes off her hand like she expected this to happen.

It's hot today, she says. Alot of hot, no? Alma's Spanish is slow but well pronounced, if people just give her a moment to think she's got the gift it's true.

Somewhat.

Yes. Alot of hot. *Alot* of hot. She tries to take a swig of water and ends up with supercarbonated spray all over her face. They maintain silence after that, waiting for her to dry. She's about to leave but instead she caps the bottle and says the kind of things she says these days, now that she's some prick who doesn't give a shit what people think.

Listen. Do you know why I'm here?

The old bag's eyes open wide. *¿Cómo?* She steps back into the shadows.

Too much, thinks Alma. Whatever you do you must stand up for yourself, her mother used to say, way back when Alma listened. Tell them who you are and what you want. Polite but don't back down. Next week I'll teach you how to live a lie. My name, says Alma, trying on a different voice, is Alberto Price, my mother is called Hermelinda Montes. Perhaps you know her. She lays down the water bottle and grips the counter with both hands for support. My grandfather, she says, my grandfather is Gustavo Montes. Gustavo Montes is my grandfather at 216 Zapata Street and I, I am searching, yes.

She speaks better than that, so much better, it's nerves, it's the city, it's something terrible's about to happen, but this declaration seems to impress the storekeep. Montes what?

Montes I don't know.

There's a lot of Montes. Something something something street Zapata.

Number 216?

Right there. The woman jerks her arm and here it is again, Mexicans tossing unseen pigeons in the air.

Yes, Alma says, feeling the hairs in her throat stand up on end. She swings her faithful goodie bag onto the counter and plucks the envelope from its protected spot. The woman takes it between fat fingers, flips it like a poker chip, and peeks inside, but Alma has removed its contents that begin

> My dearest Hermelinda,
> I may live forever because I refuse to die without seeing you again
> (translated from the Spanish by Alma Katherine Price)

Maybe her mother would have responded to this one if she'd gotten it. But she didn't, and it belongs to Alma now, and soon other things will too.

Look. Alma points to the corner where a return address belongs. A puffy fist presses down against the envelope, ironing out the wrinkles against the butcher paper. *Zapata,* the shopkeep slowly reads, *doscientos dieciseis. México.* The shopkeep scratches a tawny fingernail across the Z, trying to win a lotto prize. She shakes her head. I don't know.

Don't know what.

From the back of the store, a guy appears. Sixteen maybe. He looks like lard and Mountain Dew. The aquatic sound of his breathing fills the small space. The guy stares at her. It takes her a second to remember she's supposed to be his peer. She squares herself and frowns and nods like he showed up with gangsta rap. She feels phony and old.

This young man is from the United States! the shopkeep shouts, all but jumping up and down. Edvin, come and meet him! He is looking for his *raíces*!

Why? says Edvin.

My son will show you, the woman tells Alma. Something something there on Zapata.

Edvin thinks this idea is crap. He lets out his latest sniffle and retreats into the shadows again.

No thank you, *señora*, Alma says. But thank you.

Don't worry, the señora says. Edvin! Something something don't you something or I'll something! Alma's not sure what she's saying—so much harder when they're not talking just to her—but it sounds uncomfortable. The storekeep storms off after the apple of her eye and Alma runs out the door.

Up the hill she goes. She's out of shape. She's sweating. The thing she's learned about disguise is that layers work best. The air is mean and still. The neighborhood looks poor and she sees what look like projects up ahead. She's nervous again and she knows she should be more so but for some reason real Mexicans don't scare her the way East Side Austin Mexicans do, and plus there are no black people. Can't say it of course but black people are the ones that scare her shitless. Maybe that's how Memaw and Pawpaw felt when Daddy first brought Hermelinda home—well at least she isn't black!—although maybe they'd feel different if they knew about:

> *My dearest Hermelinda,*
>
> *It has been a long time since I last wrote but now there is no time. There are some things to say while I still can. The one that can be written is I celebrate your great escape and new life every single day. The others I want to write but live so deeply in my heart they won't let go unless they know you're listening out there.*

(translated from the Spanish by Alma K. Price)

Her mother got that one alright, when she was Alma's age. Did she write him back? Had she already started up this crap about what makes us all American, how everyone came from somewhere else once upon a time? And America was this idea, this feeling of security that made everyone sing the Hokey Pokey and put their differences aside. The thing was Alma loved that shit when she was little. She loved the Hokey Pokey. She loved to be the same. A little city Texan with her daddy's country twang. And in this scheme Mom was just another American dreamer who came from somewhere else. But Alma was a child then! She didn't know her mom was full of shit. They taught her to swim and bought her bikes and sent her on a trip to Paris but what about this? This view of the city as she stops to catch her breath, the waves of two three story buildings? She blurs her eyes and every building is a little rock in a great gravel parking lot that slants up toward the skies.

What are you looking for.

Edvin must know a shortcut because there's no way fat boy could catch up with her. He's not even panting, propped against the wall. He reaches down and shifts his package left then right then left.

I'm looking for Zapata. Her oversized cotton sweatshirt hides flabby arms and everything but is too hot for climbing. She should shift package in response but instead she scratches ass.

Zapata's dead, Edvin says. He points an imaginary gun at her and slowly squeezes the thumb trigger.

Carranza killed him. She points her own gun back.

They kill everyone, Edvin says. If her soaring grasp of history surprises him he doesn't show it. You're not from Mexico.

She shrugs. Edvin seems okay. Do you know a Montes?

Know a fuckload of Montes.

At 216 Zapata Street?

He frowns but points on up ahead. I'm going to show you something.

The street grades like a conch shell, curling up and up. Edvin is noisiness in motion. Swallowed scuba gear. His black sneakers grind the dust. He's talking to her or talking near her, fast and mumbly as she listens to inflection and waits for it to rise in question but of course it doesn't.

The route ends in a wall of dirt. The pavement stops, the bunkers stop, the dogs stop, everything stops. Except the projects. They are demi scrapers, three concrete towers planted up here like battle flags. Graffiti but no gangsta rap although tuba crackhead banda music almost does the trick. Now she's jittery. This is a place that photographs in black and white with cat's cradled police tape everywhere.

Where are we, Alma says.

Zapata. He points to the dirt beneath their feet and chops one hand through the air to indicate the projects. Zapata Zapata Zapata.

And 216? And Montes?

Who knows.

Can you see? she says.

Edvin squints at the multi stories without gusto and then walks into the projects.

Alma follows as closely as she dares, striding through the doorless way where a maze of halls and stairwells splits off in every direction. There are no people but a lot of stains. A woman appears and Edvin shouts at her Montes Montes Montes? Alma has decided she's not going any further but she follows Edvin anyway down a ground floor passage to a blank door.

Here?

No mames, güey. He looks older now, and angry. Do it.

She stops breathing and knocks twice.

The man who opens the door is not her grandpa. He's a midget, for one thing, and older than the Aztecs. His face looks like a dried shitake. Behind him she can see his one bed one bath coffin stinking in the dark.

Yes?

Señor Montes?

I am.

You? Alma thought this might be the building manager or something. You have a daughter? I, ah. I am. To search. My grandfather.

Please, come in, daughter. Son. His voice is nothing if not a croak but she can understand him perfectly. Daughter! But Edvin doesn't seem to notice, walking in there like he's come to case the joint. Montes blinks at her.

Welcome. You are in your house.

Um.

The chairs are vinyl things that have been covered in plastic, along with the cheap Formica table, the kitchen counters, and parts of the floor. Food clings to the old man's stubble like ticks. There's crust. And something's dead in the apartment. His hands shake as he pours apple soda into glasses no one's washed for sixteen years.

Drink.

Thank you.

Son.

Thank you. Edvin nods but does not drink either.

Mr. Montes, Alma says. Do you have a daughter that is named Hermelinda?

I have nothing, Mr. Montes says. Come see. He's flipping through a big stack of cardboard sheets leaning against the wall. From next door or maybe up above, the Rolling Stones come filtering through the walls. Here, says Mr. Montes. In his hands he holds a small unframed paint-ing of a young man standing scarecrow on a corner, his arms at straight right angles in a pantomime of street signs. Her art teacher—the clay colored Mrs. Andrews—would say the figure is photorealistic but everything around him is something else, oily and a little blurred. Alma's ready to contemplate a while but the old man covers this first painting with another and another. All the paintings show this same corner, sometimes empty, sometimes not.

I can't get no!

I can't get no!

When I'm driving down the street!

This is the house where I grew up, Mr. Montes says, half shouting over the music. The old man touches one finger to a recurring tawny building as dandruff rains around him. Drink. He pushes at her untouched apple soda. When he turns around she dumps it in the sink.

They are good, she says, ignoring Edvin's smirk. Here is 216

Zapata?

Guerrero and *Neptuno*. He taps the painting on top again. *Guerrero*, he points. *Neptuno*. It all changed. Everything changes.

No, here, this house. Apartment. She waves her arms around.

Here? He looks around the room like he's never seen it in his life. He shakes his head. I paint, he says. All of these.

Hey hey hey!

That's what I say!

Edvin taps his temple to indicate the old man's fucking crazy, although she thinks maybe she is too.

It skips a generation, Mr. Montes says. Grandfather paints and the father *rechaza* and then the grandson paints again. Your grandfather is an artist?

I don't know. Edvin's sliding toward the door. I don't know my grandfather. My mother's father. He lives at 216 Zapata. She's fishing out the envelope and Montes watches her like she might have a syringe to put him out of his misery. He examines the envelope carefully and shakes his head.

No. He wags his finger back and forth.

Thank you, she says. She puts down the glass and starts backing toward the door.

No, please, come, take. He's trying to hand her one of the paintings. Edvin slips a small radio into his jacket as he departs.

Oh, no, thank you, no. Edvin!

Please.

Very beautiful, she says. The fat boy's footsteps galumph into silence. But I can't.

I could teach you. You something something in your heart. He's smiling at her. Your grandfather was an artist and your mother?

My mother is nothing.

Sometimes it something something a generation. I could. Show, teach you. Learn.

I can't paint. I can't do this.

Yes, of course you can.

No, I want to write, she says, and her words are loud in the sudden quiet of the room. The music next door has stopped. I want to be a writer. She has never said the words before, not like she really meant it, not like that.

It's all the same. I will teach you. Stay with me. There is a sofa. See? His hands are shaking.

She should go find Edvin now except when has she felt like this before, this exact sensation of her body disappearing? High backed chair of the living room. Knees curled up into chest. She's holding Charlie's hand outside the Chocolate Factory and hiding Jacob Two Two under the bed. The back of the wardrobe's opening. The coin contains half magic. She's in the story now, and something incredible is about to happen.

But the sofa looks like it has a rash. The smell is awful. And what fucked up things has he done to the walls? It's all marked up with crayon or maybe paint, but now she can make out tiny little trees and tiny little girls, tiny little dogs and an antique car or two. There's a rifle, there's a moon, there's a carrot and a coin and a cloud that reminds her of *The Little Prince*. She's on her feet now but the music's starting up again and the walls are alive and Mr. Montes teeters on a ladder to put the red kite in the corner. She sinks back into the chair, watching its black and yellow tail. And there below.

That flag, she says. What's that flag.

That's for you.

Is that Texas? The state of Texas? In the United States? She could swear: the arrow and star and field of blue.

He chuckles to himself, lips pressed tight together, a tiny laugh that rolls there behind his nose and mouth. It's all for you, the stars and everything, you're in your house. Please.

She glances at the door. Big Red and Dean and a table full of smarty pants are out there getting drunk right now. Zapatas await. Nate's in Atlanta, Mom's in Austin, Katie's in College Station. I wish you were my grandfather, she says, and Mr. Montes nods, standing at the table gripping cardboard in his hands. Will you show me your paintings again?

I will show you, he says, I will show you everything, sitting down at last.

Ten

The hotel their daughter had chosen was not the worst fleabag Truitt had ever seen. It was pink, for one, and the windows had tiny little balconies, and there was covered parking. The neighborhood seemed decent. There were trees. No strip clubs or porn shops but a bunch of fake-leg stores. Pharmacies too. A medical part of town. He didn't really want to think about that.

The detective he'd hired was waiting for them outside. There was something not quite Mexican about him which Truitt appreciated. He was a big man but not by choice, with terrible hair and a clean new suit. The way he leaned against a wall made you wonder what he'd do without it.

"Mr. Price." The detective's handshake had some liquid steel to it. "Axel Eguren." Eguren bowed his head to Hermelinda and dumped his eyes off to one side. "Mrs. Price." English wasn't too bad, Truitt thought. Enough to do business in, at least.

"*¿Aquí está mi hija?*"

"*No, señora. Rentó un cuarto.*"

A room, thought Hermelinda. What business did Alma have with a room?

The detective was taller than she had imagined, taller and uglier, with eyes backed down into sockets trying to hide from the things they had seen. Wisps of drain-clog hair licked against his shiny head, and he seemed itchy from the cheap polyester suit or from all the European blood flowing through his veins. She had been afraid he would be a short dark man with fat Indian cheeks and a smile masking avarice and wrath, a man who might pull insects apart to pass the time. She missed Charlie, with his floppy hair and bright-eyed lack of gloom, Charlie who had never hurt a flea. She wished Truitt had let him come along.

Have you seen the room?

Eguren glanced at her husband before answering her Spanish with his own. No. I waited for you.

You go first. Make sure.

She watched him calculate whether she should be obeyed. Of course. With your permission. I'll return shortly.

Thank you.

He nodded and moved sideways past her and inside. She remembered that cologne, cedar and sage and dirty leather, how could it be she had never smelled it since?

"Where's he going?"

"Wait."

They waited for him on the sidewalk in front of the pink hotel. *Rosa Mexicano.* The color did not exist in Texas. The avenue was busy, four lanes buzzing around the wide median. Her hand began to sweat, her fingers sticking between her father's as he tugged her through the Sunday market there between the traffic, through the antiques and knickknacks and art laid out on the stones between flower stalls.

I think a cat vomited on that canvass.

Papa!

I think a dog just shat on it.

Papa! It hurt her chest to swallow all that forbidden laughter. She wanted to chant the word shit again and again and again.

Isn't there anything beautiful here, my Hermelinda? Anything except you?

Papa.

"You tell him to go up there?"

"Yes."

There was nothing beautiful and they would not buy anything. They would walk. Leave her mother and the boys at home and walk her father's city. His voice had an unfenced sound on Sunday, like it might leap up and nip her on the wrist. He was taller too. Sometimes he held her hand and sometimes he pretended, swinging there in sync with his fingers back to hers. He made sure to tell her never to go to the places they went. He looked dangerous and that was why they could brave the streets together. His skin was rough and pocked. His eyes were blood-shot. His hands and chest were thick. They said he looked like a gang-ster but he looked like her father. Women smiled as they passed. They dipped through the old Romita square and crossed the hundred lanes of Avenida Chapultepéc and wound through the mechanics' streets of closed shops and broken-down cars chained to lampposts. There was the strange Chinese sundial at the rotunda and they would both talk *ah-so-caca-ee-cho-chi-cha* as Hermelinda slowed, but a few blocks later they would arrive at the café.

Al Capone!

Hermelinda Linda!

Sit down, sit down!

Jovén, another table please!

She never saw them anywhere else, these friends of her father's, they existed only on those vinyl chairs with the crusty glass *lecheros* in front of them and huge fans spinning overhead, talking and talking and talking. Her father did not smoke but he smoked at the café. He was the only one without a mustache. Only one who brought a child. Only one in a suit. He was the oldest of his friends and the oldest father anyone she knew had. She sat at the far end of the table reading *Hermelinda Linda*, the comic book about the witch. Her father liked to pretend this warty hideous cartoon did not exist but one of the painters brought it for her. The witch taught aliens to cure their plague with sex and killed a bad cop on a motorcycle then brought him back to life. This witch was not for children but she was almost ten years old. Later on, one of the poets would lean over to relive the Friday show when TV's grumpiest Indian swore El Club del Hogar's toothpaste sponsor was turning his teeth brown! She thought she had forgotten but she had not forgotten. *Aniceto, Madaleno, gori gori gori, telin telin.* She looked down at her hands to find the wrinkles but what she saw was a simple copper crucifix.

Where did you get that?

Mama bought it for me.

False idols. The Church cannot be trusted. Anyone says you need me to get to God cannot be trusted. That's why we killed the priests.

Gustavo! You'll upset her!

She's not upset. She would have killed them too.

Gustavo!

You stupid Catholic bitch it's you they should have killed.

"*¡Aguas!*"

A stranger shouldered by her with something heavy on his shoulder wrapped in an orange tarp. She reached out for the pink wall. Truitt started after the guy.

"I'm fine," she said. She latched on to his arm which slowed him down but he dragged her to the corner anyway.

"Dick-lick."

The corner smelled the same. The air marched out of the Bisquets and whirled into tornados with the meat crackling in the carts and the cologne and gasoline and dust. *Tianguis.* Words and shards kept tumbling out of the grimy closet. At the other end of the closet was another door, and that door was banging open with its violent blinding light and Hermelinda turned back to the pink hotel because at least she could not remember ever seeing it before.

"I'm going in there, Lindy."

"Yes." She wanted him gone. "I'll come when it's okay."

Truitt wasn't sure what she meant by that but he went anyway.

Until he stepped inside he was thinking that so far Mexico City didn't seem very Mexico. The place looked more like Paris than Laredo, tell the truth, Paris with about a zillion acres of shithole slumland you had to drive through first. Inside the pink hotel, though, the lobby was no good. He used to fuck Faye Leblanc in a dump like this in Beaumont, the Star out on Route 6 halfway between his house and hers. From the outside things looked well kept up but inside same old same old, thinning carpet, bug-dimmed lights, mold and dead skin sweating from the walls. The sheets were clean at least if he remembered the Star right. The sheets were probably cleaner than Faye's pussy but neither of them gave a damn. The things women did in hotel rooms were different from the bedroom. He nodded at the desk jockey and pounded up the stairs.

"Eguren! Eguren, where you at?"

This was a funny game his girl was playing. Every time she used the bank card was like sending up a flare, she had all kinds of money but then went slumming anyway. Maybe that was a kind of conversation. I need you, Daddy, but I'll do it my way. Well fuck that. He could accept that Alma was unhappy and that he had something to do with it. Fine. But what did you do with a brilliant, strange-looking girl who'd built a safe room in her head? Look at Lindy, look at him, look at Alma and then what about the miscarriages—did that mean their codes were not compatible? Alma's brain was bigger than a Humvee but it was hard to get in there anymore. She used to love his stories about growing up in Beaumont as they'd lie there on the floor together, tossing stuffed cows in the air, or taking the truck out on the dirt roads near Reimer's Ranch. Then one day his stories sucked. The truck rides sucked. He tried. He built her twelve-foot shelves with one of those ladders that slide along the wall, and flew her out to L.A. to visit this rare-book store but she wouldn't pick out a thing. He thought they had a good time anyway. Made fun of the wannabes and double-D-list movie stars. They were good like that together, making fun of people. Naming them. The Blond Brigade. Dr. Rhino and his neighbor Minibar. Afterward he called the store and they sent over a first edition of *On the Road* that cost him eleven grand, and when Alma opened up the package he hadn't seen that smile on her since she was ten years old. Even he felt the rush. She froze there with that big black book in just her fingertips. He knew her then. That girl belonged in college, not Spain or South America. The world was a nasty place and he'd kept her from its nastiness. His job. But now. House-dog trained to bark the alphabet escaped into the wild. That's what he was afraid of, right now, very afraid and very angry.

"In here, Mr. Price."

"And?"

"Nothing." Eguren's horse head poked out of a doorway. Truitt leaned his way but didn't get too far as Hermelinda swept past him in a sirocco of Chanel and lunged into the room.

She did not expect to find her. She did not expect a room so small. A television hung from the corner of the ceiling because this was the only place it fit. A bed, a television, a phone, no closet, a shelf instead of drawers with a plastic bag on top of it filled with two water bottles and a sickly mango Gatorade. The smell of dirty Clorox. *Hotel de paso.* She had never been in one before, did not know where she learned the phrase. Not here. Did ten-year-old girls know about hotels that rented rooms by the hour, where you could walk from covered parking lots without stepping out in public? Did they know about the secretary or the neighbor's wife? If she reached up and turned on the television she was sure what would be showing.

"*¿Estaba sola?*"

"*Sí.*" Eguren answered from the hallway.

Alone, repeated Hermelinda, without a single thing? She poked at the plastic bag. Just this?

I don't know.

Hermelinda pulled the cover aside to check under the bed, but there was no under the bed. The frame was a solid plywood box. How did you find this place?

The bank card. Eguren edged into the room to face her. She used it across the street, at the Scotia Bank, for cash.

The Scotia Bank?

It's new perhaps since you were. He smiled like a poisoned rat. His teeth were orange. We have foreign banks now, they actually lend people money, what an idea, no? He was relaxing her, welcoming her back. And their machines are free.

What luck that you're a banking expert.

She was here on Thursday. Paid for the week.

That's yesterday, Hermelinda thought. Right here while she and Truitt trawled the hostels and cheap cafés near the Zócalo. How did Alma know about La Roma, where Hermelinda had been born?

And today? she said. How does your knowledge of the foreign banks help us with today?

He put his eyes away and stood there waiting patiently for whatever happened next.

It was going to be this man. This strange unpleasant man was going to be the one who told her something awful. These men were all the same. Their chests were full of stones. She stood up and took a step toward him and when he picked his head up she slipped into his eyes. She'd been in these eyes before. They were the eyes of the policeman when her mother died and the eyes of her husband when she told him not to fuck the other woman anymore.

"Is this," she told Truitt, who stood there in the corner like a thrift store lamp, "is this idiot the best you can do?" She almost poked Eguren but Truitt was not watching, Truitt was turning sideways and scooting past them into the room. Eguren did not flinch. "This is our big hero that will find her?" Her husband collapsed then, sinking down on his hands and knees at the foot of the bed.

He was on his knees with his head against the floor, not really moving.

"Truitt. Truitt! Get up, Truitt!"

Truitt did not get up. He reached out with both arms and jammed his fingers under the plywood bed frame, exhaled sharply through his mouth, and pried the whole thing off the ground. The bitch was heavy. His shoulders shaking. It sounded like a shell down there. There was a small pile of Alma's stuff in front of him, books in English, clothes, plus this old-looking cowboy hat, all shoved up toward where the headboard should be. He had no idea how the girl had managed it. "Got something," he called out. Books was good, he thought, books meant she was coming back.

Truitt was alive and inching beneath the bed, which looked like a great coffin swallowing him whole. His bad back arched to hold the bed aloft. Truitt inched and mumbled and the bed slipped back to his butt, tilted high up in the air, but Hermelinda would not help him and Eguren could not get past her if he tried. Truitt looked exactly like a dog digging for something filthy. She had never kicked a dog but she wanted to kick Truitt.

"You fucking liar. Your stupid dick."

And she did kick him. A place like this. *Cabrón.* She kicked and kicked. She kicked him and she left.

The wood frame flattened him as it slammed against his legs. He was on his belly in the dark, the pain digging cuffs into his thighs. He had to let go of the hat but then he didn't and his face fell down against the carpet that smelled like an old man's crotch. He couldn't turn and wriggling seemed painful. He wanted to tell her Alma was coming back and that he understood how this might happen, how even though they tried to work things out she might kick him under the bed from time to time.

Truitt wasn't making any noise as Eguren reached down with one hand but that was all Hermelinda saw as she backed out of the room and down the hall. Down the stairs. Truitt had taken the girl up stairs like these. He might have held her hand but she thought probably not. Hermelinda had forgiven him but it turned out what she had done was not forgiveness. What she had done was recognize: she lived in the world and these things happened, sad things, things that made a woman weep in her beautiful Spanish-tiled bathroom, several nights a week. Things in motels on Manchaca, which Texans pronounced Manshack. Twenty-six years old. He was not supposed to do that just like she was never supposed to see Mexico City again.

The city was waiting for her on her street. It did not care what she had done for the last thirty years. That she swam more than three hundred miles a year or stayed loyal to this man she barely loved or raised a girl who thought she could be anything and how many Mexican girls thought that? The two girls by the newsstand, what did those two think?

They were older than Alma, maybe, they were pretty and their skirts were very cheap and short. A truck or two slowed down to shout at them and these girls stood there like rock stars paying no one any mind. Hermelinda remembered that. They did not think that they would be anything. To create a girl who was truly free Hermelinda had cut her off from this. Those girls were not free. Alma was not pretty and was not Mexican and the world left her alone. To grow up slowly. To triumph with time and space and comfort and quiet to find herself. But not here.

The two girls saw her staring. What did they see? Her ratty faded flats, her dirty hair, the wrinkles splashed around her eyes, her pale naked lips, the small earrings that exaggerated the wattling under her chin, the cap-sleeved crew that made her arms look fat, the bare wrist, and the pants stuck somewhere just beyond capri. They saw her alright. She could not say how this had happened. She knew what not to wear. She wanted to tell them this is what your *mamá* would look like if you disappeared.

Forgive me, she called out before she even knew it.

They looked at one another as she came. The closer the younger. The whites of their eyes and teeth were blinding.

Forgive me, she said again, I want to ask you something. They did not nod and did not look away.

Where would you go, she said. Where would you go if you were seventeen years old? My daughter. It occurred to her that perhaps they would not tell her, perhaps they would take Alma's side. My daughter wants to know what she should see down here, we're from Texas, here on business, and she is bored. Seventeen years old.

The two girls looked at one another.

I used to live here, said Hermelinda finally. But everything I know is from another time.

What kind of music does she like?

Music. Hermelinda closed her eyes. The plastic case sat on the dashboard, a black and white stuffed animal plunging a knife through its own chest. Panda, she said, something Panda.

Banda? The two girls looked surprised.

No, no, it's rock 'n' roll, oh wait, there's another one called Fungus. Not Fungus. Fungicide.

Screaming Panda, one girl said.

Fungicide, said the other. Good stuff. She'd like the Chopo.

What's the Chopo.

In the Guerrero. They looked suspicious as they stepped away from her, throwing their arms in the air as if for help, but it was not suspicion just their *pesero* minibus bearing down.

She likes books too! Hermelinda called out after them.

Now they looked suspicious. Near the library? one said. And then they were gone, two pretty girls swept away by the city. Thank you, girls. Thank you. She raised her hand to wave goodbye.

From the second-story window of the pink love hotel in La Roma, Truitt found his wife standing on the corner, her hand raised in the air. In one hand he held the cowboy hat and the other propped him up against the glass. What was she doing? He spread his hand out inside the hat where his baby's head had been. Somewhere in that hand was hatred, somewhere in that hand was her mama brushing hair, somewhere in that hand were nursery dickie birds sitting on a wall, one named Peter and one named Paul.

"What do you need, Eguren." His wife was waving out there, her hand was in the air, his wife was angry, what was she doing anyway? "What do you need to find her. What resources do you require." The man was really taller than any Mexican he'd ever seen. "You need to hire a few men go hire them. You need to bribe a cop then bribe 'em. You need to hurt somebody hurt 'em. But if you don't find this girl. You understand me here?"

"I understand, Mr. Price," Eguren said.

"I know you do," Truitt said. "Now do it and do it now."

The man nodded, and Truitt turned back to the window. Her hand was down now, dangling by her side, but there in front of her was a taxi, one of those little VW jobs, its door mouth ajar like some hungry baby bird, and she wasn't doing what she's doing, was she, she wasn't getting in? She was getting in. She was stooping that familiar body of hers and folding it into that tiny green-white little car the guidebook said was pure kidnap express. He shook the window, trying to open. "Lindy! Lindy!" He heard Eguren leave his side, he heard the big man running like a herd of antelope. He saw the taxi close its door as if by magic, couldn't even see a driver, he could hear the big man yelling down the hallway, ¡no, señora, no! and then Truitt's engine started. Eguren burst down into the street below as the taxi pulled away and Truitt was off and running, hat tucked in like a football, running down the stairs to find his yelling hired man, Eguren yelling in her other language, yelling to this foreign woman, yelling words that meant to Truitt oh shit, Lindy, here we go.

Eleven

Saturday is just another day in the Montes household. There are no cartoons. There are no waffles. Instead there's a big water stain on the kitchen ceiling that looks exactly like America, complete with Maine and Florida and a couple of the Great Lakes, and there's nothing Alma can do about it. Since she moved in two days ago she's cleaned his dishes and taken on the hard crust of the seats and furniture. She's wiped down Styrofoam box liners the old man's taped together to form a kind of artificial wall. She's swept and scrubbed and done amazing things. If anyone visits Mr. Montes, they're going to be flabbergasted, but visits don't seem likely. That can't be her fault. She could leave right now this morning and she'd still be a hero.

Not that Montes seems to notice. The old man is out there. He doesn't eat. He doesn't sleep. He makes noises in between his nose and mouth. He doesn't leave the house and spit goes flying when he talks. The upside is he doesn't notice when she strips down to pants and T shirt and gives the bra a rest, which is a huge relief, except that she has to see her arms and breasts and belly again. The old man doesn't notice but he also doesn't appreciate she's saving his small life.

This morning he looks cheerful, though, sitting in a vinyl chair in clothes she hasn't seen before, watching her clean the kitchen. His hands dance in front of him like he's conducting orchestral accompaniment. He hums. That's all she needs for now. There must be something good in her to make an old man happy. She wipes down shelves. She cleans the fridge. It's harder than it looks. She's thinking about The Maid Also Known As Esperanza as she gets down on her hands and knees to start sponging down the floor, when suddenly he's there beside her with fresh bulbs in his eyes.

The smell is not so great but up close like this he looks about ten years younger, he looks flexible and spry and juiced with mischief. This little old man with nothing. In less than 48 hours she's brought him back to life.

It has been a long time, he says, since I was on the floor.

It's dirty.

It's beautiful. Everything is beautiful. He rolls to one side and sits with his back against the oven, legs spread apart, staring around at his kitchen. His belly bulges in a neat roll over his jacked up ratty pants. He looks a little like a baby. You have the eyes of an artist, he says.

They're brown.

What do they see from here?

From here? She sits opposite him, looking around at this dump she's been pissing away her youth on. From here, I see dust, she says.

He nods. Anything else?

She can't think of anything but then she checks the ceiling. I see the United States, she says.

Yes! he says, laughing like a child. ¡Cosa! You can see anything you want. He puts his hand on top of hers, the one that holds the sponge. Thank you. Thank you. And for a moment there, the kitchen floor of Mr. Montes's slum feels like a happy place. She can't remember the last time she did anything for anyone, not that they appreciated. This, she thinks, this floor right here is the best part of Mexico.

Did you always live alone, Mr. Montes?

I live with you.

Only since Thursday.

He laughs and spit shrapnel scatters everywhere.

You can help me, she says.

Yes. Anything you want.

She jumps up and pulls the map out of her goodie bag and he waits for her on the floor. They sit and pour over the pages together, their fingers tracing the yellow highlit Zapata streets.

I don't know much about him. Number 216.

So many.

I know. She feels stupid saying it but it's Montes so she says it anyway. I feel like he lives maybe somewhere very interesting?

Why?

I think maybe he's a writer?

Yes, a writer, yes, yes, that's something.

I saw some streets with writers' names over here. She flips and points to a grid of Dickens, Lope de Vega, Julio Verne, Homero and Ibsen and Hans Christian Andersen.

The old man shakes his head with vigor. Only strawberries live there, he says. Purely rich. His finger runs from the land of rich strawberries down the great avenue of Reforma. Have you been to the center?

I am only in La Roma and La Condesa and Chapultepec and here.

Look. He points to a constellation of Zapatas right in the heart of the city, then rocks back onto his knees and grabs the stovetop edge and pulls himself slowly to his feet. There's a dull hollow pop but she can't know if that's his knees or the thin metal sheet around the burners.

That's where the village lives. Let's go.

The light outside the building blinds them both. The projects seem less threatening than they seemed two days ago. And the view is incredible. It's clear, this morning, there's much more city to be seen. Fewer cars crawling the highways. The weekend, maybe. Montes leads her down the hill. A Saturday market has sprung up on what was an empty street, squat linebacker women with aprons everywhere. If she really had an artist's eyes, that's maybe what she'd paint, all those aprons or the stacks of ready sandwiches with tongues of sliced ham lolling out the ends or the men with wooden crates and soda bottles blocking off street parking spaces. She must remember this! She should be writing it down! Isn't that why she's not sucking Nate's dick and accessorizing and getting blasted with the UT Kappa Kappa Kappas come fall?

By the time they reach the city center she's given up trying to remember stuff. It's a little like being stoned, the way some image from the city storms her whole mind and then is gone completely. She's seen keening men roll plastic garrafons—*aguaaaaaaaaaaaaa!*—and huge silver canisters—*gaaaaaaaaas!*—down the middle of the street and gone. A horse and cart piled high with mattresses. A man ringing a hand bell runs in front of a trash truck like it might run him down, some guy pedals a stationary bike that spins a sharpening stone, hawkers sing their song about packs of colored pens, worth ten pesos, for sale ten pesos. And yet all that seems tame compared to the huge huge revolutionary square of the Zócalo, where most of the city's twenty million people skitter the colonial rink, plus more than a few tourists too, but Montes steers her past the National This and Metropolitan That and a street that roils with commerce behind and before she knows it the old man is pointing up at a street sign: Emiliano Zapata.

Here? she asks.

An artist could live here.

Could you? She tries to picture him in a cantina sitting with Big Red and Dean.

A younger one.

He is not young.

No, says Montes, coughing hard.

He looks like he's wandering off to die but instead his fingers find the few numbers on the city's walls, and before long it's clear that number 216 does not exist, that higher numbers don't always follow lower, and that what look like separate Zapatas on the map all conflate. In the end she sits down on church steps and crosses out not one not three but

Five! she tells Mr. Montes. Five is very good!

The old man looks pleased with himself.

By late afternoon she's knocked out eleven more, just by visiting three streets. One 216 reupholsters sofas and another is an office and the last one has been vacant for twenty-seven years. The good news is progress but the bad news is many of the others spiral out like splatter far from the city center.

Except. Except not too far from here, on the map at least, there's a neighborhood with more than four distinct Zapata Streets, including two very writerly looking dead end alleys, and that would mean finishing off twenty streets on her first day alone. Montes looks half dead again but she asks him anyway.

It's far. The truth is that it's a little *retirado*.

We can take a taxi.

A taxi? It's like she suggested hovercraft.

There must be a safe taxi stand here somewhere.

Very expensive.

I'm rich, she says. Didn't you know.

He tries his best to laugh and picks his cuticles ferociously. He takes a deep breath and then instead of okay says come I'll show you something.

She's not sure what he's showing her except a shitty neighborhood. Iffy. People on the street, more young than usual and wearing thuggy clothes. The vibe is homicide. This is the first time she feels like she would in black Austin, if she ever dared to go, which she didn't, and this is why. Bull Shit. She hears her daddy's voice, that macho Beaumont crap would translate fine down here. Daddy. A cloud of music hovers like a mushroom cloud, soundtrack for disaster. Three guys pop off a car hood and fall into step behind her and she tries to be cool but then fuck it fuck Montes fuck everything run run run Alma run!

She skids arounds the corner and hundreds of teenagers appear. They're wearing black T shirts. They're banging their heads. They're cranking Fungicide from six tweeters and a bench of wompy subwoofers. The street in front of her is full of metalheads and Goths and skatepunks, a river running left to right, piercings and plastic CD cases glinting like trout in the sun. There's Thwart and Wretch and is that an old school table hawking Iron Maiden tees? Gored By Bill, Rotten Stumps, Blood Donkeys, and then a bunch of stuff in Spanish. She can't believe it. It's a metal market.

Montes grins beside her, watching her drink in all that rock.

She makes herself stop staring. Somewhere in Nuevo Laredo some goddamn bastards have her Pvt. Sacco fatigues and old school Fungicide tee, which is what she could be wearing right now instead of these dorky jeans and sweatshirt. Her hair is at its dorkiest too, already growing out, but the demipunks and Mexigoths and grindcore *chicas* don't seem to notice. Just another loser asshole in a world full.

You like? says Montes. El Chopo is good, no?

She nods ever so slightly. She wishes he wasn't there.

From table to table she wanders, looking at the music, searching for a spread of mostly *español*. She'll get something for someone, she thinks, something really cool and Mexican. Nathan. A tight wrapped CD arriving in Atlanta with exotic stamps. What is he doing right now? What that compares with this, this right here, eat this, Nathan, eat it.

There's a break in the tables where the metal punk street crosses another, and there on the corner are two telephones siamesed back to back that cellies haven't killed off yet. She's been so careful, so far, to stay out of phones' way, and from computers, and from all the things that make here next to there. But now she laughs at them and then before she changes her mind grabs the receiver and her daddy's phone card and is breaking down how this thing works. The tone sounds deeper but surprisingly clear as it rings on the other end.

Yeah.

Is Nathan there?

The phone a couple thousand miles away clanks down hard. Yo Nate! Then there's nothing for a while. Montes stands against a wall, not quite watching her. The phone groans at her. Whut.

Nathan.

Yeah?

This is your conscience speaking, Nathan.

Oh. Hey. Whassup.

Whassup? I don't know whassup. Whassup with you, big Nate dawg.

Sorry, I was just. Allie. Hey. I was sleeping.

Course you were.

He yawns to prove it. We were at this thing last night.

Totally raging kegger.

Oh you know it.

Fine bitches everywhere.

Yeah, sure. Babes akimbo. He's pulling on his eyebrow, she knows it, the way he does when he's trying to figure what to say.

Is it everything you hoped and dreamed?

Well it's no Harvard, is it.

Fuck Harvard.

How's *that* working out for you?

Well, *Nate,* I'm sure it doesn't compare to life as studly Nate man, Texas Ranger.

Oh you know it, I'm all super Delta Phi Omega Ep. He's trying to hang but his heart isn't in it, and she didn't know it'd be like this, some bitter version of the way they used to play, the bile in every syllable, although they can swallow can't they?

Did you know they have stoner doom in Mexico? she says.

Oh I think about it all the time.

Thrash, grindcore.

Keeps me up at night.

The line's so clear, she wishes it would crackle, she wishes it would pop. He sounds down the block but feels six years away. Peers are passing in their studs and unis but the sky and strange old Montes remind her who and where she is. If you were embarrassed about me before, thinks Alma, you should see me now. Does he know her well enough to recognize her?

Nathan, really, time out, I need to talk a second.

What's up. His voice goes down deeper. He must be working on that.

Well. I'm not in Austin.

Fuck Austin.

Yeah. I. How can she say this? The thing about Mexican metalheads is that I'm right here at this like swap meet, right now, down in Mexico City, I took a bus and got a ride part of the way, it's a little crazy, okay it's a lot, but can you hear it? all around me? all this noise? and it's so cool, Nathan, you never seen anything like it. The words run out of her burning building. Nathan, god, I wish you were here, it's like, it's like every version of what we have but filtered through like a Mexicanizer, all the different scenes, like alternate versions of the people we know you know? Like a Mexican you and Kelly Roche and Katie and maybe even Fat Stu, completely through the looking glass. But then there's stuff you would never see anywhere else. Never. I had no idea, I mean sometimes I still have no idea, but I'm learning so much, sometimes I think, you know, I'm in over my head? but this is what I want, you know, I know that sounds stupid, but really, it's really cool, a little scary, but cool you know. You would be so, I don't know, I'm not making it sound right but you would be really into this, I think, it would be so cool if you were, you know, here, we were just like living here, taking a year off, just to live, just to get to know something else, and help me, you know, help me find out where I'm from.

Oh yeah super cool, those Mexicans really rock.

Nathan. Can't he hear it? With such a good connection can't he hear it in her voice?

Yeah. He does that thing where he exhales in little choo choo chunks. I been meaning to call, you know how it is, it's wacky, crazy, between arm wrestling the football team and fighting off hot Georgia peaches and eating okra, I got my hands full here. My comp lit professor's like this twenty-five year old who wears a three piece suit, no one has any idea what he's talking about. Apparently the end of history happened a while ago and no one told us. Did you know that?

No. Nathan sitting in a classroom, blue pen leaking in his mouth.

Yeah well you better ax somebody. Man. It's like a frat boy petting zoo in Rocks for Jocks, you would not believe these guys, I mean these dudes evolved from rocks, you know, we're like studying their ancestors. He snorts. You got the Rocks on one side and the Peaches on another, and the Art Butts and the White A Be Rappers, they're all here, it's like like when does it all stop? I bet hell's just a big high school too. There some cool people though. Trying to crack the lit mag code. I don't know. I guess who are we kidding to think you ever really start over, you know?

Sure, Nate.

He inhales again and she knows what he's about to say. Something small. Stupid. Hahahahaha. He's such a boy. In the three weeks since she saw him last she's become more man than he is.

I was thinking, she says, maybe I'll come up there and visit you.

That shuts him up. You could, he says, finally. If you really want but you'll hate it.

You can suck my fucking cock, she says, and hangs up as hard as she possibly can.

A pale thin girl with mad pierced lips glances at the violence and nods in maybe solidarity. Alma tries nodding back but her face starts to leak instead. A quake rattles through her chest. Not sounding very manly now. How do you keep your shoulders up and arms out and jaw square when you sob, how do you do that? Mr. Montes puts his hand on her arm and pulls an Xacto knife out of his pocket. He steps past her and slashes the phone cord and tosses the yellow receiver to the ground.

Ya, he says. He kicks it over the curb and puts the knife back in his pocket. *Ya está.*

She stares at him as he kicks the air and she kisses him on the head. Thank you. And then something about the way he nods makes her do what she thought she wouldn't do. Has been trying not to do for days. She moves around to the other phone. Montes wags his finger saying no no no don't do it.

It's okay, she tells him. This is different.

It rings a couple times and then it sort of hiccups and starts to ring again in a different tone. She's not sure she likes the sound of that but then he picks up right away.

Truitt Price.

Daddy.

He barely hesitates. His voice is soft and cool. Hey baby. Where are you, hon. She almost chokes. The quicksilver tyrant, this daddy of hers who you can't trust but who can handle anything. He can handle this.

I'm safe, Daddy.

Well that's something. I'm glad for that. I hoped hard as I could.

The urge to say she's sorry is so strong she has to hold the phone out away from her, but Montes looks like he might slash it and she pulls it back.

You know where I am, huh?

Wish I didn't. You coming home soon?

I don't know, Daddy.

Sounds like it's a party.

No. There's music.

You and your concerts. I hear there's good ones in America too.

Just music outside.

Anything decent?

It's like a punk rock flea market, you'd hate it.

I hate it cause they get you and I don't.

She holds her face with her free hand. She's never had to fight a word so hard. Tell Mama I'm okay.

I will. Now Allie, listen to me. She can't help it, that voice of his freezes her in place no matter how much she should hang up. All these Goths and punks around her, they'd hang up so why can't she? I was wrong about the whole going abroad thing, the voice is saying, and I'm sorry for that. The truth is, Allie? I didn't think you were ready but man I was sure wrong. Now I'm not thrilled about how I how I had to learn that, I won't say I haven't had sixteen heart attacks a day, but did I learn? My god what I did learn. About you. About us. Bottom line, the only thing I care is that you're safe, and that you're happy, and I know you can be both or at least close. Has he even taken a breath yet? If he would just take a breath and she could hear it maybe she'd pull free. So here's the compromise, he says. We'll set you up down there, okay? get you a place, a program if you want it or I don't know, whatever you want to do, but somewhere we know you are, and you stop looking for your grandpa because he's either dead or dangerous, your mama won't say which, and I can shove my heart back in my chest, and you can do your thing, and your mama won't string herself up to a shower rod. Can we please do that?

She hears the hiss of the serpent, the liar's air pulled up slowly through the nose. He would drag her like a dog. He would lock her up. That's all I wanted to say, she says. I'll call you in week, Daddy. Montes is holding out the knife and she takes it from him.

Allie, let's do this then let's—

She slashes the cord in two.

The telephone is not worth, says Montes, taking the receiver from her and dropping it with the other one, shaking his head sadly.

Yes. Maybe Nathan's right, she thinks. You are who you are no matter how you try. Do you want to go home? she asks the old man.

No, it's okay, look, enjoy, the music, the youth, no hurry, whenever you want.

She tries. Browses. At least she's in good company. Everyone here has something fucked up with their father, for sure.

You know those guys? A kid with bad skin's talking to her, pointing at the CD in her hands. *Los Rateros.* She smiles.

No. Good?

He shrugs. You like *Las* something something? She shrugs right back. He half pinches the state fair prize pimple on his cheek. Montes leans over the CD cases, checking out the merch.

I don't know the things from Mexico. I like Fungicide, Screaming Panda, I like—

Ehscreaming Pahn da is my favorite, he says, and bam, she's got a friend. He jabs his finger at some old used T shirts of bands she likes lying on the side. Mexican bands are shit.

All?

My brother sells it. Here's his group. Her new friend hands her a case with an eagle standing on a rock holding an electric guitar over its head. *Banderas Rotas.* Pure shit, he says. The only reason we sell anything is I bring the good stuff.

Can I hear this?

He kills the stereo and swaps the disks. Shit might be a little strong but she can see his point. If it was her brother's she'd probably hate it too. Needs more noise, she says, you know?

Where are you from.

Texas. Everyone's in a band where I live too.

They're made of shit, aren't they.

Yes. Not much of my type music.

That's how it is. This city, all this music but pure shit.

Stay. She can stay here. With the kids who see shit everywhere. Her hotel's not far. Send the old man home alone.

Who's this.

The big brother boss man has returned, or arrived, or something, shoving his dermatologically challenged brother aside. He's eating a little brown banana and it looks hilarious. His hair's a choppy sea of Saudi crude. His skin is alright.

I was asking about your band.

What about it.

When are you playing.

We play all the time.

Where.

All over.

They have a show next week, little brother says. With the Ultrasonics. He jags his lewdest eyebrows and cups both hands over imaginary tits.

Meow, says Alma. She no longer blushes anymore.

That's right, her new friend says. His big brother smacks him hard on the head, that dull sound of some fool deep in a forest chopping wood. He slips a paper flyer from beneath the table and hands it to her. Whoever the Ultrasonics are, they get the biggest lettering. The Broken Flags are tiny. Leave the ancient at home, big brother says.

Of course. She shrugs at her buddy who is still squinting theatrically in response to the attack. Buys a T shirt and a disc. Maybe I see you there, she says.

The rocker doesn't respond. Maybe I'll see you in hell, the little brother says, raising his rock fist high.

She grins and turns around to leave and tell old Montes he's on his own when a familiar guy brushes past her through the crowd.

A familiar looking guy.

A familiar looking guy.

What the fuck?

The hair is gone and the shoulders—she recalls these massive equine knots swelling from a black and purple wifebeater—have melted into something strictly functional. Time has been at his face with a putty knife. The thin lips that used to make him look cruel now have a slight feebleness about them. Her eyes peel back the layers of the years like that in half a second flat.

Brack Aster?

He turns to her, not surprised exactly and only slightly curious. But slightly. He looks her up and down, trying to decide how far he wants to let this go.

You're Brack Aster, she says. You're the reason I had any friends.

He almost smiles. Never heard that one before.

No, really. You. She was going to say *changed my life* but you can't actually say that, can you, not to Brack Aster, lead singer of Gored By Bill, you can't say *three years ago your screams for blood were the soundtrack of my life*, you can't. Thanks, she says, instead, thank you so so much, and that's where she wants to stop because that would be cool, just thank the guy, be that one fan that doesn't want anything else from him, but it doesn't turn out that way, wow, she's saying but that's too girly isn't it, dude, dude, I can't believe it, what are you doing here. She does her best to fight her body's squirmy adulation.

The brothers at their table are watching carefully. Their English may be null but they know something's happening.

Just checking out the scene. We're at the Hard Rock tonight.

Oh man. Oh man, I didn't know. That's so cool. It's all she can do to keep her voice from slipping up eight registers or so. It's all she can do to not blurt had no idea you were still alive.

All right now.

No wait, will you, will you sign something for me. She looks around her desperately, praying for something Gored By Bill close by, but nothing. They've got your shirts here, she says, I saw them, I just saw them, I swear, I got two at home, she lies.

Hey, all right, listen, gotta jet.

Okay, wait, how about this. She pulls the *Banderas Rotas* T shirt from her bag. MexiThrash, she says, these guys the best. A little crowd is gathering. The rocker brother stares at her holding his band's shirt in his hands. She spreads it out on the merch table there beside them.

Yeah? These guys? Brack produces a pen from somewhere—not just any pen, a fucking big black Marks A Lot, *güey*—and signs the shirt so fast she barely sees it happen. She stares at the signature: Brack Aster, absolutely legible. And that's not all, somehow he's also dashed the international sign for Gored By Bill: the modified anarchy rune where the A punctures the circle like a missile. Fuck yeah. Fuck yeah. The older brother is watching with amazement and that's when she sees her lost Fungicide shirt, folded sloppily on the little brother's corner of the table. The same color, the same size, the same age, the same little black marker dot on the bottom hem. That's her shirt! That's her fucking shirt! Globalization and Beelzebub have somehow brought it here! Brack isn't going anywhere just yet—a seriously cool looking Indian in an Earth Needs Slaves shirt has come up alongside, slapping his brown paw into the rocker's meaty hand—and what she does is grab her fateful, rightful shirt and hand it over to Brack.

Please. She's not even pleading. Just low and steady, one man to another.

One side of his mouth goes up and the lips are cruel again, cruel for old times sake, and Brack looks like he did on that first album cover, all those years ago, sans hair, sans shoulders, sans everything except the living scream just beneath the skin.

You like these guys? he says.

Yeah.

He nods and scribbles quickly across the fabric. There you go. And there goes Brack, striding off with a trail of recognizants behind him.

Both brothers are staring at her, and a lot of other people too. Brack Aster. Gored By Bill. She holds it up high for all to admire the shirt that would not die: pale blue fabric worn toward white like a sun bleached sky, the red circled mushroom cloud with a line drawn through it, and FUNGICIDE in black lettering up top. Below that Brack has written:

SUCKS MY ASS

And then his signature—Brack Aster—and the rune of Gored By Bill.

Who? says someone.

But for the older brother with the head of crude there's no who about it, which she realizes too late, as he reaches out and yanks the shirt from her hands.

Not for sale, he says.

She makes a swipe at it but he holds it out of reach. Their arms collide and you can feel the difference.

He, she says, he signed for me. I'm going to pay, but the shirt is not yours.

Not for sale, gringo.

You want this one? She holds up the *Banderas Rotas* shirt and he yanks that from her too.

That's not for sale either, the big brother says.

What would daddy do? The snake. Big ol' Truitt Price from Beaumont T X. Option one is out so what's she supposed to say? That one's yours, she tries for starts. But let's pretend the other is for sale, she says, yes? For a moment. Maybe in two weeks, two hours, maybe now. The Spanish is coming like she's drunk. And we pretend you are talking to the correct person, a person understand the value of the shirt you have in hand. She keeps her eyes on his and puts a hand inside her pants, all gangster like but also zipping open the money belt beneath. Well I could go and buy another shirt, she says, I could follow him and ask another signature, and that shirt in dollars is the same. She shakes her head slowly, shakes it like her daddy does when he's about to get his way. But not to me, she almost whispers, and sure enough the guy leans in. Because for me, one more whisper and then her volume's up again, for me what happened here is a special moment in my life. A decent audience is watching now but Alma doesn't care. She's got the roll of twenties in her hand but she might as well be holding Mother Teresa's beating heart the way everyone is staring—the thief, his friends, Mr. Montes at her shoulder, the strangers stopped in their tracks as they pass by. Because you're right, she says. We're not talking about money. We're not talking about buying and selling. Our world is not this. *Our* world. She waves her hand in a grand circle that encompasses much more than the whole ecosystem of cool around them. No, her daddy says in Alma's fake boy voice, this is respect. This is heart, this is deep, this is. She smacks the money fist into her hand. Now, I've got respect. I've got so much respect for you and your table, and I've got respect for that man who appeared like a beautiful devil in this city so big in the world. When he looked at me, do you know what I saw? Like he recognized me. He recognized himself in me. That's why he did the shirt. He. Recognized. Himself. In me. In all of us. And that's why he's here.

The little brother's mouth is hanging open. The big brother doesn't say a thing. The urge to look away is strong but instead she gazes steady through his stony face to that two bedroom apartment he shares with little and mom and three sisters, plus the oldest girl's two kids, and all he wants is out, all he wants is stick his finger in the socket and feel the infinite and rumble of a D chord ripping through the crowd in front of him, which is the only time he's himself, and for that he needs freedom, he needs a new guitar, a new amp, he needs to get his useless family off his back. She's understanding all that as she pulls the roll of twenties apart, one, two, three, crumpling them slightly in her other hand and holding them out to him. Here, she thinks. Take it. Choose freedom. Give me my shirt.

He looks at the money and he looks at the shirt and he looks at her. Fuck your mother, he explains, you little faggot.

The crowd cheers. Sixty eight eyes.

Fuck *your* mother! she explains, and then again in English, no fuck your fucking mother you fucking piece of fuck. Give me shirt, she yells, Spanish again, her voice harder than she's heard it in her life, take the money and give me shirt, rat, or run home and tell your peasants you're a rat and robbed a baby and left a hundred dollars on the street! Go tell your peasants that!

He's yelling at her and she's yelling at him and she knows what happens next but she keeps yelling just in case. Brack might consider coming back, mosh this jerk into submission. Things look grim. She moves her arms and legs in the most violent ways imaginable. The big brother just laughs. He dances there around her, laughing with his fist cocked. He is wearing a simple silver ring with three ridges in the middle of his hand, and now the ring zooms toward her stopping just short of the bone beneath her eye as a long gray wolf springs from the crowd and knocks back her assailant, batting him onto the table which shakes off CD cases like a wet cat. The big brother screams but when anyone else leans in like they might do something the wolf whirls around so quick and ready you know he would suck their blood and bite their eyes out too.

Mr. Montes tugs on her sleeve.

Let's go, daughter.

The crowd is thinking the same thing, half scattering and half leaning in to see what happens next.

The wolf is tall, and his gray suit coat hangs off him like there's nothing there. He is a morose looking fellow and he's still got the big brother pinned against the table as he turns to look at her.

My shirt, she mumbles. But she's backing away. Because the wolf has picked up the brother and tossed him like a horseshoe into the crowd. The shirt is there behind him but the way he's looking at her! What kind of giant looks at her like that! With recognition!

She grabs Montes and they run.

When she was little she used to nightmare about a chase through some strange empty hospital, running and running and running through white florescent halls, with two sets of footsteps there behind her. It's been ten years since that dream but that's where she is now. They always caught her and the wolf will catch her too, except something's happening back there to the eight foot Mexican calling out her name—Alma Price! Alma Price!—and having a little trouble moving through the crowd, and it reminds her of this time on Guadalupe with cops chasing this kid with weed and then—

Police! she yells ¡policía! ¡policía!

The crowd freaks out. The sea that parts in front of her closes there behind. Black Chuck Taylors and combat boots crisscross the ground like horror vines. The wolf is so close now but stumbling. He falls. He falls desperately and hard down to the pavement. Somehow he reaches one long arm out and grabs her.

She screams. When the wolf lets go she sees Montes throw aside his Xacto knife as her Mexico City map goes flying and she takes off faster than she's ever taken off in her life.

Down they plunge, into the metro, deep into the ground. The escalator lolls out like a dragon's tongue but they make it to the platform where she moves through the comforting crowd. It's a dead end until the train comes but the train is coming soon.

> on a dark desert highway.
> cool wind in my hair
> warm smell of colitas
> rising up through the air

No one seems to notice the subway DJ's choice. She moves toward the end of the platform where she can peer into the dark for signs. A teenage girl there starts singing along with the chorus in crazy accent-ed English.

welcome to the hotel california

The girl knows more than the chorus. The girl knows all the words.

It would be nice to sit here and imagine the whole platform burst-ing into song and dancing like some twisted musical called *Ah Mexico!* except when she looks back the wolf's head is poking up above the crowd in the middle of the platform, periscoping around. She squats down quick and low, inching back toward the wall, pressing her head against the greasy tile.

please bring me my wine…he said

we haven't had that spirit here since 1969

Alma listens for a train but a train won't come. The wolf man is coming. She can't see it but she's sure.

My daughter.

Montes squats beside her. She grabs his hand.

Come, my daughter, come, don't be afraid. He tugs her toward the edge of the platform. Together they hop down onto the tracks.

The goop there is incredible except along the third rail shining like a bulging vein, down in the canyon which seems deeper, wider, bigger now that she's in it. They are on the tracks. The wolf man surely sees them now, who doesn't see them, a cry goes up behind, rippling through the place, echoing off the deep drilled tunnel walls. Surely the wolf man's running now even as Montes pulls her into the darkness, down the tracks.

they stab it with their steely knives

but they just can't kill the beast

She's sure she's never heard those words before.

The rumble is coming, coming from deep inside the earth ahead of them. A hot wind blows. Beams of light reach out around the gentle curve like long arms in white protective gloves, feeling their way through night. Behind them is behind them. The old man's head is on fire in the white light as he parts the wall nearby. He pushes the door open. A thin chute stretches there before them, down and down and out of sight. Montes steps through until only his hand remains. She takes it. In the bright flash of Linea Siete braking toward the platform, in the howl of the crowd and the electric guitars whining overhead, in that moment before the metal snout bursts screaming into the station, old man and child vanish.

Twelve

From the rooftop Hermelinda could see the park, immense and green. It did not take much to get a view in this city. They were afraid of earthquakes, afraid of heights. Here and there—around Reforma, out toward Santa Fe—a tower or two stood up straight and tall, but for the most part, the rule was three and four stories. There were eight floors here at Bitu and it felt like she was on top of the world.

The rooftop bar was clean and white and rich and perfect. An enormous uplit marble fireplace sat surrounded by couches draped in soft white terry. A few other Americans were staying at the hotel, and Europeans, but mostly it was Mexicans, pale and knowing, visiting from their kingdoms out there in the republic. The truth was they were all the same, wherever they were from. If a person ended up here— gringo, euro, *chilango, provinciano*—there could be little doubt about who they were.

She sat at one of the modernist tables that fringed the edges, out near the clear glass wall that shielded wind but still made anyone think they could step right off the edge, if that was what they wanted to do. Why would anyone want to do that? This attractive, healthy, wealthy woman, traveling alone, who went for long runs through the park each morning, long chauffered trips through the city by day, returning in the evening to her glass of chilled rosé, lounging on the couches like a bathed newborn wrapped in towels, why step off the edge? But every night since she'd checked in alone a week ago, after a few drinks, she was glad the glass was there.

Can I offer you something more?

She shook her head at the young waiter. Do you have the time?

Quarter after seven.

Thank you.

It's still early. The music. He nodded to the soft sounds in the air around them and sure enough, there was the familiar voice she had requested the other night.

Qué labios te cierran los ojos
Los ojos que a besos cerré

Thank you, she said again. Just until the kids get here. Then you can put on the *pon-che pon-che* again.

My boss is a big fan too.

Either old or a romantic fool.

The same, no? He gestured to the empty seat. Someone is joining you tonight? She looked at him sharply and his long black lashes dipped servitude again. It's just that there's a lot of Friday traffic. It could be that they're delayed.

Yes. Could be. You better find me a mojito, then. Not too sweet.

With pleasure. And the phone?

Not tonight.

She would not call him. She would enjoy her drink and her *boleros* and take one night vacation from his lack of news, not that he lacked things to say, if she let him, the catalogue of streets and new ideas and strategies, or the embassy folks and DEA agents he networked with at his hotel so of course they were going to help. But she did not let him. Ever since they had lost her daughter at the El Chopo, she did not like to hear Truitt's voice. She did not even like to hear English, and stared down anyone who tried. She would tolerate it in her husband, she decided, only on the phone, only until they found Alma, and after that she was not sure what she would tolerate anymore.

Aunque sigas viviendo

Ya olvidé tus ofensas

She knew she hated this music but she wanted someone to sing and that was the problem with Mexico.

The bar was filling up, a little bit, but at this time of night it was mostly hotel guests, and then later, much much later, the local young heirs and heiresses of the Mexican valley would pour out of the elevator and drive the foreigners and old folks to their rooms. She did not know if the boy would come—she thought he would, she was not sure—but whether he did or not she would not stay late tonight. She always left before the party started, down to her room to watch the *telenovela* about girl's soccer or the Mexican *Family Feud. 100 Mexicanos Dicen.* A hundred Mexicans say a top five cause for traffic jams is *manifestaciones*—protests, or more like demonstrations—she would have never gotten that. She could not stop watching the show. She wondered what a hundred Mexicans would say about her. *If you left Mexico and never looked back, what would happen?* BUZZ! These people had no idea. Tonight she did not care, she was going out, one way or another, boy or no boy, to see what she could find.

Your mojito.

The mint swept over her, washing her in a scent as white as everything else up here. The mint was Mexican but this was not a Mexican cocktail.

Tell me something, she said.

Yes of course.

Do people still mix tequila with Squirt?

He smiled. Everyone. All the time. And sometimes vodka with Squirt, even *whisky* with Squirt. He barely twitched his pretty nose like he might like to wink at her.

And you?

No, he said. Not me. He smiled again but not with any suggestion and when she did not say more he retreated imperceptibly with expert waiter form, and she watched him until he finally turned around and she could admire his ass shimmy across the floor. That first night she thought he reminded her of the boy there in *Catorce*—something about his lips—but she knew that the reminder did not come from him.

Sometimes we call them *frescas*. Do you have any interest in trying one?

Her neighbor—white pants, white shirt, beautiful gray sweater draped around his neck—seemed like he had stepped off the set of something with the word Miami. His accent was not Mexico City, slightly northern, she thought, although not too strong. His skin was shocking, smooth and dark and shiny with health. His true age was somewhere between thirty-two and fifty-five, she could not accurately tell. He was on the Indian side of the color chart with the jet black straight hair to match but his nose and cheekbones were all wrong and his gel was not too stiff, and his cologne was more citrus than the usual leatherwood floating in formaldehyde. He was smoking a cigarette but not as if he smoked them all the time. The smile he flashed her now made her think his whole skeleton had been removed and bleached. Something with Squirt? he said, to remember Mexico by?

My father used to drink that. It was the last thing she planned to say but she said it anyway. Glasses, ice, a bottle of Hornitos, and a bottle of Squirt. Listening to this music right here. She touched the rim of her drink like it might ring along.

While they played dominoes on Saturday.

Dominoes, no. He did not play games.

An intellectual, then.

He thought so.

I'm Claudio. Villafuerte.

Hermelinda.

Hermelinda, nothing more?

Hermelinda Linda.

Of course, the beauty from Bondojito. I thought you retired.

Witches don't retire.

What do they do?

They leave Mexico.

For?

The other side.

Even the witches. How intelligent they are. He shifted closer to her somehow without moving, a perfumed wave of tangerine and cayenne. I'm from Sinaloa, myself. I spend a lot of time in New York and Miami. I'm not a *narco*.

Me neither.

I'm meeting a friend.

Me too.

Not my favorite place, he said, but the waiters are cute.

Yes. Very cute. She could feel herself relax. A rich gay not-a-*narco* from Sinaloa. Her luck was starting to change. Shall we have a tequila with Squirt, then? The fact is I never tried it.

Don't, he said. It's disgusting. Our fathers were idiots.

Pues, salud, she said, and they clinked glasses.

He was telling her all the things she should do and see and hear during her stay—the new things, a lot was trendy and overrated but there were many new good things, he said—and the people she would get along with super well and he would introduce her to them if she liked, and his favorite places to eat in Soho and South Beach—did she know them?—plus a resort down in Huatulco worth the trip, and some punning jokes—Bin Laden loves us and Monica Lewinsky sees frogs and Barbie needs a maid—and she leaned back into the stream of easy words she had not heard for so long in any language. For six days there had been only the voices of her driver and the guard and waiters and sometimes strangers answering her questions—*no, señora, lo siento, señora*—as they inched through traffic to the national library and the university and the used-book stores on Donceles. Truitt and his army were scouring the Zapatas but that was like finding José Garcia. That was not thinking straight. If Alma went to El Chopo how could they think she was still looking for Hermelinda's father?

No. Hermelinda knew. It had nothing to do with her father. At the beginning, perhaps. It was like shopping for a car or a house or something that the buyer thought would tell them who they were. Hermelinda could have told her that what she was looking for was not Mexico but a place like Harvard or Oxford or the Sorbonne if it came to that, somewhere that judged her for her mind and mind alone. Not Texas. Not Mexico! Mexico cared about all the things that did not matter, except for family, which did, and Mexico cared obsessively about it, but what good was family in a place that just destroyed it? Alma did not know these things. She had come here instead of Harvard, and what that meant to Hermelinda, in these days driving the city she was born to, was that the life of the mind was more about folly and imagination than knowledge or reason or anything else. Alma could come here and look around and believe she had found the worldly incarnation of imagination without bounds. If Hermelinda had never lived here, maybe she might believe it too.

They had lived first in the Roma and then Doctores, on the street where for the past three days now Hermelinda had sat watching in the car for an hour or so, late afternoon, not so much for Alma, she did not think she would come, but just to think and watch and remember. Their Roma place on Zacatecas was no more—she barely remembered it—turned into a parking lot by the quake of '85 or so the driver said. But the Doctores place was there. A sickly colored three-story apartment building that no one entered or left. The neighborhood was worse than she remembered, or the same, perhaps, the same piece of rotten meat that had simply rotted for another thirty years. She did not have to leave the car to know the skim of stagnant water that still lingered in the yellow tile of the ground floor hallway, tracking the tenants' filth everywhere, even after her mother poured and mopped soapy water down the three flights of concrete stairs and skimmed it to the side. The humiliation of watching her mother clean that filthy building. *Portera.* It was almost worth losing a father to never have to watch that again.

Alma used to say she was a Russian princess, back when the girl was five years old. *My real parents will come and find me. I have a palace. I have a crown.* She could have her Russian palace but Alma had no right to Doctores and no right to Hermelinda's father. But Mexico? All of it? Maybe some of Mexico. Not here, though, please not the Mexico of Doctores where most cars did not seem to dare slow down. She could see her daughter walking—still terrible to think of but possible at least—through other parts of town, past the table-tarps around the library, where the booksellers spread out or hung their paperbacks like brightly colored fruit, she could see Alma in the library, with its ancient façade and glass-steel interior beneath the floating ceiling, and most of all she could see Alma on dirty Donceles where the line of used-book stores stretched for blocks, browsing the stacks, maybe even getting up the nerve to talk with someone, she could see Alma in all those places but no one there had seen her.

They think I could have showed her this, Hermelinda thought, and saved us all the trouble, but maybe not. How proud she must be to have found it on her own.

I can tell by the way you move, Claudio was explaining, I'm a type of physical therapist.

What other secrets does my body tell you?

No secrets. You don't only run, though, maybe bike or swim too? Your pelvis tilts a lot but I'm surprised your body is in more or less good balance.

For my age.

Your age. He swatted the words away like gnats. Do you work with someone?

I used to.

They taught you well. If you want to keep running, though? I would work with someone. He patted his hands on his hips and drew two little square around his core. With more awareness you could continue a long time.

I'm not sure I want to be any more aware of my body than I already am. He did not laugh. She tried grinning to get that cheerful voice of commercials on the radio. Can't you tell this is the body of someone in serious trouble?

Claudio did not look away and did not smile. He nodded softly. Yes. Yes. I was afraid to ask you why you are here.

I'll tell you if you want. It's a problem with my daughter.

He shook his head. Mothers and daughters. What a mess. *Desmadre.* She could not remember hearing the word before but there was no doubt what it meant. My sisters and my mother, Claudio was saying, from the time they turned thirteen? My mother is very beautiful and she only wanted sons. Look what she gets. Three girls and this.

He did not want to talk about her problems anyway. Yes, well thank you for asking. Everything will be fine.

Please, said Claudio, if I can help in any way. He placed a business card on the edge of her table and his eyes skipped past her. My friend is here. Won't you join us?

No. Thank you.

Call me for anything at all. We'll lunch together.

Yes.

Promise me you'll work with someone. He tossed the words over his shoulder as he glided across the cool white marble floors.

She did not promise. The way you move, she thought, I can tell you are a real live *maricón*, is that what you're talking about? Even the homosexuals pitied her. Even homosexuals looked at her and knew she was a bad mother.

> *Everytime I think of you*
> *I feel shot right through*
> *With a bolt of blue*

Ancient drum machines were tsking overhead. She still recognized that one but her father's music was long gone.

The rooftop had filled with clinking glasses and the roaring murmur of the rich, but still no Rogelio, if that was really his name. Look at this place. There was no way he would come. She tried to decide if she should have another drink or sign her check and go down to her room to get dressed or maybe cry. Call Truitt. Let him know he could still have her if he wanted.

Tequila and Squirt, please.

Really?

Why not.

Of course.

Why don't you just join me, she murmured as he left.

Young princes were arriving, spilling away from the bar and out toward the pool, where she had never seen anyone swim, although its view was the most majestic and the water must be perfect like everything else here. Beautiful filters somewhere. She took her new drink over and kicked her shoes off and dangled her feet inside. She could see someone on a balcony across the street, sitting alone outside without a cigarette or cocktail or anything, just watching the city. She tasted her disgusting drink of gasoline and grapefruit and watched it with him. In the months before she left Doctores with her mother and brothers, there was a teenage boy who used to practice his trumpet on the roof across the street, she could barely hear him over the traffic. She used to think about him her first year in Nuevo and wonder if he still played and whether her father could still hear him. For one year she believed her father was still coming and after that she did not think about the boy with the trumpet anymore. She never thought she would see this city again, but the city she saw from here had nothing to do with what she remembered and what she knew. She would never have seen this if she had stayed.

I better not, she told the waiter.

Something to eat? The ceviche is very good.

I'm sure it is. Bring me another tequila first.

The house invites you to eat whatever you'd like.

I'd like nothing.

Are you well, Señora?

No. The truth is no. Get me my drink.

He bowed his head and backed away. I don't want to be her mother anymore, Hermelinda thought.

The rich Mexican children were everywhere now, cutting her space away on all sides. Raised by maids and servants. If their mothers had really loved them they would know the rich bitch by the pool should be left alone. Alma would know. Truitt had offered a reward, how intelligent was that, to put a price on her daughter's head in this desperate city? He was ten steps behind Alma. Hermelinda was one. She had left El Chopo an hour before Alma called—one hour, one—after walking that strange strip most of the afternoon. She had walked that strip and realized the city in her chest was frozen in a jar. She had been to London and to New York, she had seen the punks down in the Village and in Trafalgar Square. But Mexico? It had staggered her. And that was why she left, finally, staggering from El Chopo because if she did not know Mexico or Alma then how would she find either of them. That was why she let the boy—Rogelio, it was Rogelio—talk to her and lead her away. He was not going to come, not here, the rich princes would have him killed, these drunken fools would throw him off the roof.

One of the drunken fools was staggering toward her now, smiling as if the two of them had already agreed to something lewd, flipping his short blond hair, the whitest Mexican in the world, his hair and cigarettes imported, his future too, she would have been lucky to clean his genitals and toilet if she had stayed and now he was here smiling at her on the most hip roof of Mexico City, she was one of them, except he was not smiling at her at all, just stumbling in a dazed grin past the old bag to his friends smoking on the other side of the pool. It was late. It was too late for her to stay and too late for her to leave, suddenly too late for her to do anything at all.

Hey *güey* where did all these ugly bitches come from? the whitest Mexican in the world shouted.

From your mother *güey*, his friend shouted back.

Claudio was nowhere to be seen, Claudio and his sweater and his knowledge of her body. The waiter had disappeared too. Her daughter, her husband, her father, her mother, her brothers, her teacher, everyone was gone. She used to think her life would begin again when Alma finally left home.

Give me a cigarette.

The whitest Mexican in the world finally handed her a cigarette and she waited there until he lit it. She could smell his gasoline and grapefruit from here. His friends were giggling. If there was an ounce of muscle on his body he had not used it for a long time. She stood there next to him, tilting pelvis and all, her back arched, one leg forward, her fine calves showing, her breasts expensively suspended, shoulders back.

Tell me something, she said finally.

Me?

Who is your father? Have I heard of him?

He did not like the question. My father's not worth cock, the white Mexican said.

She smiled. Mine neither.

Now he laughed outrageously. Wanna drink? he said.

Would you like to go somewhere with me? She sucked half the cigarette away at once.

Where. He grinned.

You want to go to bed with me?

Here?

Sure. Are you a good fuck?

Listen, old lady, I'm the boss of all bosses.

I bet one of your friends is better.

No, no, these pretty ones all have tiny little pricks, he said. I've got a great big sweet potato here.

Yes?

I swear to you.

Don't swear. How big can it be when you let your friend insult your mother?

Yeah, he's a fucking asshole. He shoved his friend with savagery.

Don't talk about my mother, *güey*, apologize, and when the friend shoved him back Hermelinda stuck out her foot and the whitest Mexican in the world went flying sidways toward the pool, smacking his head on the tile rim, spinning into the water, and sinking like an iron plumb.

Later, downstairs in her room, Hermelinda would wonder who would have saved him if she had turned slowly on her heel and strolled back to the bar for another drink. Maybe no one. Maybe the young rich chattering beautiful crowd at Bitu would have let him die. Maybe she would have too, but as his body hit the water and he sank, she heard a sound there like the familiar hollow pop of a starting gun. It could have been his skull against ceramic, or fireworks in Polanco, or a car back-firing on Reforma, or someone getting shot in the woods of Chapultepec, or maybe the sound was neurons popping in her head. Wherever it was, it was the sound that released her from herself. It was the sound she heard when she was no longer Hermelinda Montes Figueroa or Westlake's lovely Lindy Price, not rich or poor or young or old or even male or female. Oblivion. She leapt. Her body entered the water with the tiniest splash as the gasps and shrieks of the crowd muffled overhead. She was flying through the liquid in a gentle corkscrew and slipped behind the body and wrapped her arm around him, pushing off for the surface, rolling onto her back. His head was leaking gently on her shoulder and her chest. She swam the length of the pool in three big strokes, her strong legs muscling them through the water. She held this stupid child in her strong arms and rolled him up to bleed on the white tiles.

Don't do that to mothers, she whispered to him, pressing her lips to his ear, you hear me? Don't do that to me. She lifted her wet body out of the pool and stepped over his coughing body, making her way to the elevator, dripping, silent, and alone. In twenty minutes she would be showered, lipsticked, tucked tight into a black leather skirt and long red turtleneck, a scrap of paper in her hand, room phone tucked under her chin, the ring tone ringing, her car already summoned, but right now, as she walked across the rooftop amidst the stares and whispers, she was the strongest person in the world, a Mexican, an American, an orphaned college graduate, a beautiful woman, a mother unlike any other, a friend to her daughter and enemy to her enemies, a devil, a life-giver, a cunt, a mind, a saint, a soul that lied and wept and sang. There was nothing she could not would not do. Ready, she whispered to herself, as the elevator closed its doors behind her, ready or not, Rogelio, here I come.

Thirteen

He used to think you brought a gun along not just for protection but because you could always kill yourself if things went all too wrong. He used to think all-natural toothpaste on an electric brush tasted like young pussy. He used to think to have her followed, to see if she was cheating, because he was why not her? He used to think shame was how his whole sciatic nerve lit up every time he took a shit, or the hard-ons that sometimes visited when he held a baby in his arms, or the time he called Jim Petrus stupid nigger or drunk hit-and-ran the lime-green Chevette with Louisiana plates, the night he turned twenty-one. He used to think he could not say out loud how much he loved these two, because his wife would never believe him, and his daughter, if she really knew, it would blow her head right off. He used to think he could not live without them but now he wasn't sure. He could. But it was going to be a much smaller, faster, angrier kind of life.

"There's the car," said Charlie. Truitt didn't see it yet but the kid should know, he'd been staked out over here ever since Eguren had tracked the wife down and Truitt sicced Charlie on her. What Truitt saw was Lindy, tarted up and stepping through the quartz crystal of her tony hotel doors. The big black car slid in and swallowed her up. Truitt reached down for the ignition.

"Alright then," he said, grimly. "Giddyup."

Fourteen

Dean is still sleeping when she wakes, asleep or dead, it's hard to tell. He's lying face down on the floor as if he fell from a great height, blotto to the noise she makes in the kitchen and the bathroom, where she showers, makes some coffee, dumps out the mashed and nasty butts, pours off bottles and slots rinsed empties back in crates. She wouldn't mind a vomit but it all came out last night. She doesn't miss old Montes, or his rathole, or that whole part of town, she doesn't miss the poor, she doesn't miss the stench, she doesn't miss that Mexico but it might be nice to have a day without too much to drink.

Through big French door windows, the sun lights up the clean pine floors, recently redone, here in Big Red's deco wonderland off pretty Parque México, on the edge of cute *Condesa,* the prettiest spot in the prettiest place in the prettiest part of town. The Beats would loathe it if they were still alive today, except for all the girls, and poets, and drugs and late night talk and beer and tequila without cease. She would hate it too, except she's weak and happy. For now she's sitting around all night gabbing about Article 27 and the history of clowns and Balzac and Argentine shaped mouths. Writers. Artists. Mexicans. It's been only three days so far since she came back from Montes. Three days of this. They treat her great, better than she deserves, this child, this gringo, this sketchy friend of an acquaintance, with her lies and her deceptions and specks of throw up on her pants.

Where'd you go last night?

Alive, unwell, in tightie whities only, Big Red busts into the room with his hangover buzzing over him like a mushroom cloud. That coke was terrible, he says. He runs a hand through his head. Where's D.

Right here. The hairball stirs.

We're meeting Goofy at the House of Gold in an hour.

The House of Gold?

Neighborhood place. Old school *botanas.* You'll like it. You too. He nods at Alma.

I was going to visit this. She can't think of something they'd think worth visiting.

Disappear tomorrow. His bareness blinds her as he passes. Goofy invited you.

Sure, she says. The word *invited* almost knocks her down.

The bathroom door is open and she hears Big Red in the shower, making those owl sounds that means his head must hurt real bad. Dean pries himself off the floor.

Did you see a young lady around here?

Did you misplace one?

I guess. Ah well. He smoothes back his blond shag and zips closed his duffle bag. My flight's at midnight. You staying?

I guess.

Big Red don't care. You're like his little mascot. You guys and your books and history and shit. Awful cute together. You and your whole lit crowd. He shakes his stupid head. Or maybe you miss Grandpa.

I miss beer, says Big Red from the doorway, dripping, naked, and hirsute. She has not seen a whole lot of men naked and this is not the way she hoped to start. I miss *lomo* and Isolda Dosamantes. Let's move it people, now.

The Friday streets of the Condesa are warm when they emerge. 4:00 PM is the new noon. Big Red leads them out of candyland, winding through treeline curlicues until they hit an enormous ten lane street that turns everything poor and filthy. People gather around sausage carts of death, eyeing the severed devil's thumbs that float in muddy moats of grease. The poor don't care. Fat and smelly, they wrap coli and trichinosis in tortillas and cram them in their maws. The secret to her health is that she simply does not eat.

Transvestite bar, says Big Red, pointing at a red door like a tour guide. See what you might miss, he tells Dean, we could end up there tonight.

Hate to miss out but Al loves all that shit. Don't you Al.

D says you're a fag.

In his wildest dreams. No I'm just a loser, see, it's different.

Dean shakes his head but Big Red laughs. That's why you're the great white hope, he says. Kid's gonna write the real thing while all the rest of us chase pussy. Dean shrugs and shakes his head. She's glad he's leaving soon.

There have been times these last few days—but this not one of them—when Alma has believed she could come clean with Big Red and his friends. Except when she sees them talk to women she sees she must be high. They do not like girls, not really, and not girls like her for sure. They would never forgive her. Or maybe? She can't decide. For now she's being cautious, although she's tired of hiding tampons and compulsively taking out the trash, tired of heavy clothing, tired of swearing, tired of what talk turns to late night when it's just gringo boys around. She's tired of not talking to anyone about anything, about her mother, her beautiful, strange mother who must hold all this inside her, all this country, all this city, all this impossibility.

Will you take me one day?

Maybe. Except for me there's nothing there.

Nothing why?

It's no place to live. No place for you and me.

That was your Mexico. But I got mine now don't I?

The House of Gold has frosted glass and Old West saloon doors to Hickock through up front. Everyone's there. Not just Big Red's crew from the night before and the night before—Goofy, Hugo, Luis Miguel,

Elena, Sara, Isolda Dosamantes—but the whole *colonia* seems. Tables packed. Domino men in their paunchy sixties slap down double six gunshots. Men throw their cheap suit coats on vinyl seatbacks as if they just quit their jobs. Everyone drinking, smoking, eating, shouting. The only women in the place are at Goofy's table, except for a few old matrons in the corner.

¡Rojo!

¡Niños héroes, que han llegado los gringos!

Bienvenidos, queridos traidores.

El dólar es fuerte, caballeros.

Rising from Christ's last supper spot in the center of the table, Goofy unfurls his long limbs and stands and leans across to manhug Big Red. He is dark and unattractive, with a thick black beard and eyes like red hot meteorites struck down ten million years ago. His mouth is big, his lips are full, his ears not unlike Spock's. She has met him once before. He's wearing a red kung fu shirt with a phoenix on it and olive green fatigues. His name is Spengler Castro but everyone calls him Goofy.

I didn't know you had a son, Rojo.

I was young, she was fertile.

You should have aborted, Spengler Castro says, eyeing Alma with a smile. He taps the girl next to him on the shoulder, a midget with enormous glasses whom Alma has never seen. Go away, he tells the midget. You come sit next to me. We can be ugly together. Everyone's looking at her now like they haven't seen her three days running. If he shows interest in this gringo they may have to reconsider. Sit down, sit, says Goofy, gesturing with vigor to the vacancy beside him. His hands are huge and make his Spanish easy to understand. He gestures her forcibly into the chair and puts one of those big mitts around her, on her shoulder, man to man.

All good?

Yes.

What do they call you?

Al.

Al. Qaida. Of course. The table laughs. You're the one America fears most. You like Bukowski?

Burroughs better.

He shot his wife here.

I know.

I wish someone would shoot mine. Will you do that for me Al Qaida?

Okay, she says.

I like him, says Spengler Castro. We'll raise him as our own, like wolves. It's too late for that one, he says, pointing at Big Red.

Very late, says Big Red, settling down at the other end.

The Beats, says Spengler Castro. Is that what the kids read there?

Kids don't read, she says. Kids don't read at all.

Kids like you.

I don't know them.

I don't believe you. You want people who really know how *not* to read, come to Mexico. Books are sacred in this country. No one touches them. I've seen your Amazon.com. Of course it's all shit but there must be a new Burroughs or Bukowski somewhere?

No one, she says softly.

It will have to be you then, he says, pushing the tequila toward her.

This is it. This is what she wants. Not Nathan and the end of history, not a bunch of prep school kids in Cambridge bored by their success, running in the morning, geeking out at night, the sterile halls of knowledge wrapped in wealth and ivy, getting fucked up stupid from time to time to try to keep it real. This. This table of real writers with nothing but their words, no shame, no Oprah, nothing cute, nothing left to lose. This is where it happens. This is why her grandfather stayed. This is what her father can't imagine and her mom will never understand. This is why Alma's Mexican. This is why she's different, and always has been. This is where great minds meet the profane. This is a drink worth drinking. This is what she's looking for. Her grandfather's right here. He's in the bathroom, at the next table, on the other side of Goofy.

She belongs. With them. With Goofy. Something terrible's bound to happen.

You could start with *Las Muertas,* he is saying, or *Lodo,* or *Bartleby y Compañía.* He's writing on a napkin, titles, authors. She has never heard of any of them.

No? says Goofy smiling. You're young.

Yes. But.

I understand, he says, putting a big hand on her shoulder. Don't you worry about all the books. Go to the horse races. Borrow my bicycle. Find a girl. We'll all be dead soon.

I'll start tomorrow.

Start tonight. Go home. Don't waste your time with us. He leans over to whisper in her ear. She expects a stench but the tequila conquers all. This isn't where it happens.

No?

No. And watch out for your friend. He's a fake. We only keep him for his credit card.

They talk about an architect named Barragan who knew overhead lights made women look bad, and Brett Easton Ellis, and why Mexico will never win the World Cup or anything for that matter, and Goofy speaks slowly, making sure she follows, taking care of her, generous, good natured, enunciated. She wants him all to herself but so does everyone else, and the new guy who takes his chair needs to explain that September 11th was the day they killed Allende and this is why the CIA destroyed the towers. The poet from Kosovo says no, your country saved my country, the rest of the world would have let us die! The USA is terrible. The USA is great. Dean's hitting on Isolda, Big Red is drunk, Luis Miguel argues the upside of *sacrificio humano.* Three mariachis sing a song the entire neighborhood knows. She doesn't understand but Goofy says it doesn't matter.

You have time, he says, and doesn't seem to notice when she shakes her head with violence. I'm Mexican, she mumbles, I need to know, but no one hears.

It's pitch black when they stagger to the curb. Cabs. A big Friday night stretches ahead of them, a bar a party a band. The streets are time lapse photos of blaring neon lights. The bar's in a huge Soviet concrete building somewhere off Insurgentes, and Big Red grabs her arm as she says goodbye to Dean and everyone heads inside.

I have to talk to you.

Okay. The taxi with Dean speeds off to the airport. She wishes Big Red went with him.

Be careful of Goofy.

Why.

Because he's dangerous.

I thought you liked him.

What did he say about me?

Nothing.

You should just go home.

Home home?

You remind me of myself, he says. And look at me.

You? She wonders what drug he's on. You're the king. You gave me Mexico.

You should give it back.

Be psyched to be like you, she tries.

Not what you think.

Next to the bar is a little semi vacant lot, a building that crumpled in the quake and the world left it alone. They look like squirrels at first, the two shapes she sees darting to and fro. Rats.

They're almost cute, says Big Red, aren't they.

Like puppies. She tries not to freak.

The little one's about to get raped. He laughs. That's Mexico for you.

Okay.

He laughs again, and whacks Alma on the back exaggerated football style, sending her staggering two steps forward. The rats leap in unison like Sea World dolphins and disappear. We're free down here, says Big Red. You're like my little brother.

I never had a brother.

I can tell. You're hungry.

For? She tries not to back away from him.

I'm just saying I can only protect you so much.

Been protected enough, she says.

You're the real thing, aren't you. That what Goofy sees in you?

No way. She turns for the door so he won't see her blush.

Yeah, he says, you're right, let's go and get fucked up.

Inside the girls are waiting but the men have disappeared. The bar is hectic. Steel ice buckets of *Coronas* and drunks beyond belief.

They went for coke, says Elena.

Why do they call him Goofy?

He has a big tongue. She winks at Alma.

Dance with me, Al Qaida. Isolda Dosamantes grabs her by the ass.

They dance. The place is tiny but a live band crams into the corner with a drum, a keyboard, and a trombone, playing salsa music and The Doors with a chanteuse singing on the side. She's got a move or two from Nuevo Laredo and Isolda is impressed. The woman's hands feel like a skeleton's.

HELLO I LOVE YOU WON'T YOU TELL ME YOUR NAME!

The whole place is yelling. She jumps and whirls in this great long paragraph the Beats would have written if they tried.

YELLO!

What if she stopped looking? Brought him to life herself?

YELLO!

What if she lived here? An old guy across the room catches her eyes and flashes her the thumbs up sign.

YELLO!

She does not even realize her eyes are closed until someone touches her on the shoulder.

Gringo. The bartender stands before her, looking grim. Gringo, you'd better come outside.

I want you! sings the chanteuse, *I need you!*

Yello! screams the crowd.

Gringo, please, quickly.

This is the end, thinks Alma as she follows.

Outside, traffic storms by on the insanely busy street. She expects to see Big Red dead or something but there's no one in sight. She expects to see everyone she's met since Austin out there waiting for her, like the cast of *The Wizard of Oz*: the boy in Laredo, the ass from Arkansas, Dallas, Lee, The Witches, the wolf, the goddamn bastards, Montes, Dean, Brack Aster and Spengler Castro, arm in arm, semi circled around her parents, clapping politely, with a little old man between them, bravo Alma, that's it, finished, over, time to call it quits. But there's only her and the barman and some drunk staggering their way.

There he is! *Gringo*! The bartender steps forward and grabs the drunk.

Him?

Yes, *gringo*, he stole your girlfriend's camera!

What camera, says the drunk, limp in the barman's grip.

What girlfriend, says Alma.

From his girlfriend's bag, *cabrón*!

The thin man shrugs and tries to turn away but barman flippers him in place, bending the guy's arm back like they do on *Cops*.

Okay, the drunk says improbably. It's over there.

Alma looks. Sure enough, sitting beneath the scraggly bush is a little cheap camera. She steps past the barman and the drunk and picks it up, half expecting it to detonate in her hands. She puts it into her pocket and turns around and there they are.

From Catorce, from Laredo, from the East Side of Austin they have come. Men. They crowd the whole world like electrons. Most of them are angry. It occurs to her—too late—that this is the only thing you need to be a man. This real and actionable anger. There are maybe nine there, pretty much surrounding the drunk, the bartender, the boy girl trying to figure out where to put her hands. And you were there, she thinks. And you and you and you.

The bartender releases the drunk man and pushes him down on the ground. As he goes down one of the scarecrows smiles and nods at Alma and points at the man down.

Kill him, the guy says.

She must look confused.

Kill him, another man says calmly, and everybody nods.

The thin man lies on the ground.

I have the camera, she says. He. He is not worth. He is a shit. He doesn't matter. Let him go.

You do not live here, a scarecrow explains. You do not know the consequences of letting him go.

Yes, *gringo*.

You must, the bartender echoes patiently. You must complete your honor.

Honor. What honor is there in him?

They shake their heads in shame. Kill him.

Kill him.

Why? She yells again in English. Why? Why is that the only thing you know! What's wrong with you! All of you!

The nine start to bob like gentle pistons. The traffic barks on all sides.

Don't be a faggot.

Don't suck the tit.

Kill him.

What's wrong with you.

Goddamn *gringo*.

Come on!

No one comes out of the crowd to save her now. The drunk looks up at her with years of tears behind his eyes. She takes a step back.

Now!

Yes!

Kill him.

Kill him!

She can do this. She must do something. But before she does a long arm reaches out in front of her, and at the end of the arm is a huge gunmetal knife, not much smaller than a machete, with a black wood grip that's pressed into her hand.

Do it, *gringo*.

Kill him.

She holds the knife. Someone shoves her from behind. The drunk begins to scream. The knife is heavy in her hands. Her arms are rubber hose from chem class. Her father must have wanted a son, she thinks, and maybe her mother too. A son would be at Harvard. A son would kill someone. The drunk staggers to his feet but they throw him against the wall, which rises up above him, story after story, concrete without windows, a blind monolithic tombstone with deep alarming cracks. She thinks of all the scumbags in the world but still she cannot move. No one has ever loved me, she tells herself, and she closes her eyes and slams the knife up to the hilt and lets it go.

The light turns red at the big intersection and the traffic stops. The men are quiet. The handle of the knife vibrates like a tuning fork, the blade buried in the wall. The drunk falls down on his knees crying with relief. The building seems to groan. Alma feels hot mercury of belief firing through her veins, stepping slowly backward as a scarecrow steps forward and tugs the knife with all his might. It does not budge from its new home in the wall's deep crack. Another one kicks the drunk but his heart doesn't seem in it, and she leaves them without resistance, pulling and kicking in vain.

What was that?

Big Red stands there watching, has seen the whole thing perhaps.

Alma shakes her head.

No really what the fuck was that?

A miracle, she says. There's Isolda now, and Elena, and Alma hands the camera over.

How did you do that? says Big Red. How could you let him go?

Well let's get out of here, says Elena, and find our fucking coke, and Alma hurries out of Big Red's glare to follow. What happens next? she thinks. What happens next is that I find what I've been looking for. Here. Tonight. She feels sure of it even though she doesn't know yet how.

But when they find Elena's fucking coke, she understands how it will happen.

Apartment. Modern. Glass. Steel. Concrete floors. The colors are hues of pink and gold she's never seen before. The great room has windows fifteen feet tall with red theater curtains drawn. There is no furniture, just dozens of pillows that have been pushed off to the side. People are busy here. Taped onto the floors is a laminated satellite map of Mexico City, blown up large enough to see every street, every building, even cars. The photograph fills the whole room, which is the size of a small barn. The party is on all fours, crawling around the city to find their grandma's house and first place they fucked and childhood schools and homes and other landmarks of their lives, and when they do, they snort coke off them.

Come try Victor Hugo Street!

Or Vesuvius!

Who wants Shakespeare!

Who can handle Reforma!

They shout and snort and Alma closes her eyes.

Now you Al Qaida.

Goofy and Isolda stand in front of her, nostrils pulsing, as the animals graze around them, pawing the coke like cats.

Choose, says Goofy.

Give me Zapata.

Zapata, says Isolda.

Zapata, says Goofy.

They look around them. They start walking in opposite directions but Goofy pulls Isolda with him.

No, says Alma, not that one. I know that one already.

Goofy laughs. Isolda frowns. There's another over here, she says.

No.

Goofy looks annoyed this time and shakes a coke smudged finger at her. Which one do you want?

The one you'd live on. If you were old and done and dead.

He puts his head down and Isolda tugs on his sleeve. Come on, she says, don't suck the tit.

No no. He waves her off. I know.

They start walking. North. Toward the mountains. They pass parks and churches, railroad stations, industrial mess, huge elevated highways scarring the city below. Goofy's starting to look around, look around. Isolda's eye is twitching, she keeps pushing her deranged sexy librarian glasses up her nose. When she blinks the corner of her mouth jumps with electric current.

Ah, Goofy says, here we are.

Alma looks down. There's not much there except huge highway tubes leaking out of the city, there at the mountain's edge where the houses dwindle up the slopes. But Goofy is down. He's pointing to a constellation of streets. There are no names here but the pattern looks familiar. She remembers this quadrant of the map. There is one up here. Goofy knows.

This is it. He taps one long finger and traces a street about four blocks long. Emiliano Zapata. Should be a little village or a suburb but it's the most typical middle class neighborhood in the world. A few old artists from around here moved there about twenty years ago. A good cantina. A café. That's the one. You should move up there and write your book, Al Qaida. There is Mexico right there.

I'd rather light myself on fire, says Isolda, squatting to dollop the coke, not even bothering with a credit card, just pinching the white crumble together with her fingers in a caterpillar line. There's your

Zapata Street, she says.

Alma gets down on her hands and knees. He didn't end up in the projects. He didn't end up with the strawberries. He's up here with the middle, waiting for her. Waiting.

Come on, Isolda says, hurry up. Goofy has already retreated, and Alma waits for Isolda to leave too.

Come on, Isolda says again. What are you waiting for?

Alma barks, twice, like a large dog, and Isolda twitches again, her mouth jerking to one side. Then Alma drops her shoulder in a deep press and snorts the line as best she can with a new blue twenty peso note. Her face is inches from his house now. A reddish roof sitting amidst the concrete. Leaning slightly to one side, or is that the shadow distortion of the satellite whirring by? That building. That's the one.

Big Red hauls her to her feet. My god, these fucking overhead lights but do we think these girls look good?

Fucking gringos, Isolda says. You must be nobody back at home, but you come here and think you're someone.

I don't, Alma says, but Isolda isn't listening.

Who knows why Goofy let's you hang out with us, the coke crazed harpy says as she retreats. The United States is a fucking shark!

Somehow the whole room hears her and now is when the musical number begins. Coked up. Drunk. Angry. Happy. Free. They all take up the chant, another song she's never heard.

> *It's the shark that comes a hunting*
> *It's the shark that never sleeps*
> *It's the shark that waits in ambush*
> *It's the shark of bad luck*

I was somebody back home, says Big Red. Why do you think I'm here?

> *Shark! What do you seek in the bay?*
> *Shark! What do you seek in the sand?*

Fucking Mexicans, says Big Red. How can you not love Mexicans?

I'm part Mexican, she says.

Bullshit, says Big Red.

No. Really. I am.

Hey everybody, Big Red says, Al Qaida says he's Mexican, he's one of you you fucking fucks.

The sharks are Mexican!

I don't believe it.

Not me. Al Qaida.

She can't see Goofy in the crowd that's turned its face to her. He would know she's telling the truth.

What do you mean, Mexican?

I don't believe it.

Let me see his cock.

What's cock got to do with it.

I know a Mexican cock.

She does, she does, she's not lying.

Long live the Mexican cock!

Cock cock cock cock!

And they've got her now, they actually have her by the arms, pulling her around the room and then away from the table with its cool track lighting that keeps the cocaine trainyard spectacularly lit, pulling her into the shadows, Big Red on one arm and someone on the other.

Cock cock cock cock!

Come on Al Qaida, show us!

Stop, she says, in English now, English all she has. I can't.

He's shy!

He's Mexican!

He's just a kid!

Grab his pants Elena!

Elena reaches for her but Alma jerks herself away and then strong arms drag her off again and the music muffles behind.

The room they're in is a bedroom with a black stained dresser, and for a moment she thinks there's not one face she recognizes except there is Big Red behind them. They're all laughing and chanting cock

cock cock until one guy she doesn't recognize has unzipped his fly and reaches in and flops his penis on the dresser top, where it sprawls out on the surface there, limp and brown and pink.

Ay you fucking pervert!

Ass faggot!

Put that shit away!

They all recoil. The guy is laughing outrageously as everyone scatters now except the pervert and Big Red.

Let's see, says the pervert, and Alma starts to cry. Not with noise though. Just all her tears of Mexico bubbling out like dew.

Listen, Big Red says. Enough.

You then gringo.

Get out, says Big Red although he's staring right at Alma. When they're alone he reaches out to touch her tears as if to see they're real.

I'm sorry, she says.

He nods, and then reaches down with both hands and hauls down her pants.

My god.

She looks down. She thought she was out of miracles but she can't believe what she sees.

Magic, she says. Miracle, she says. She bends to pull her pants up but before she can Big Red says you little fuck and throws her against the wall.

You make a noise, he says. Don't you fucking look at me. You shut up.

She bends her head like prayer. Five fingers on her throat are steel and stone. Remember this, she whispers to herself, as he reaches out to close the door.

PART FOUR

Fifteen

There used to be more rock clubs in Mexico. Everyone remembers one that is no more, that rumbled a neighborhood for an era before the yellow *clausurado* sash fell across its door. The Insurgentes Metro had a great one, a punk rock club right there in that crater, where the music ricocheted at night like Christians' screams. The golden age of rock is done. DJ Tal and DJ Cual are in charge of parties now. The megashows still blow through town, but for everything else there's the Hard Rock and the Palacio.

The Palacio sits on the hinge of Roma and Doctores, just north of Álvaro Obregón. This is a neighborhood in doubt. There are worse parts of town than Doctores—far worse—but that does not mean it isn't dangerous. Obregón is a famous avenue for catching crooked taxis. Grab a *libre* headed east and somewhere near Drs. Vertiz and Erazo the taxi stops, door opens, and armed men hop inside. Then it's off to the ATM machines and maybe overnight to get a fresh day's maximum. The kidnappers can be cruel for cruelty's sake. They don't kill often but they like to mess folks up.

A shopping mall sits north of the Palacio and another one sits south, near the sprawl of General Hospital, where during the day an abundance of cripples limp and roll the streets. Good cantinas—the kind with free five-course meal *botanas, pierna, lomo, camarón*—like the *Auténtica* are nearby. The Hidalgo market of Doctores is cheap and comprehensive. Some of the better *fichera* joints—the cleaner ones, not too sleazy, although men do pay the almost whores for dance and con-versation—are still open. And then there's the Palacio.

On the first floor is the bar, not expansive, but with enough space for drinkers and for transit. It's dark and black inside, and darker upstairs, which opens up to square around a stage in the front. Maybe a hundred people pack in there on an extraordinary night. The ceilings are low, the walls are hung with thick fake-velvet curtains, the air is scarce and split with smoke. A washed-up American band is playing, no one's ever heard of them and no one ever will, but no one came to see them anyway. Half the people don't know why they're here. The other half has come to see the *Ultrasónicas*, who are milling about in the crowd, sneering at the gringo band and drinking with their friends.

Outside, on the curb, a young man with black spiked hair leans his cigarette toward the wall. He does not live close by. His home is with his family in Santa María La Rivera, a middle-class neighborhood to the north. His father teaches secondary and his mom stamps papers for the State. Rogelio works mornings in their neighbors' corner store, where he no longer lets his friends steal stuff, and in the afternoon hangs out with the parking guys down the block. On the weekend he rocks. He rocks at the Chopo and he rocks at the Palacio, where he knows the door guy and doesn't have to pay.

What's interesting about tonight is not the Ultrasonics—he's seen them plenty of times—but the big sedan that's pulling to the curb with the woman there inside. The door opens and the *señora* swings her legs out, straightens her leather skirt, and stands, finding him immediately in his spot against the wall. He doesn't know how old she is—older than his girlfriends, younger than his mom. She wants something from him and he can't wait to find out what.

Hola, Rogelio. She has a vaguely northern accent. She has money. He's thinking Monterrey. He's thinking somewhere with preservatives to make her look like that. Her legs seem excellent. Her tits are good, even in this red turtleneck. He's not sure he's ever seen anyone wear a turtleneck in the Palacio before.

Cómo andas, guapa.

Con mucha sed, mi amor. Her eyes scan his face, moving from eye to eye to mouth to cheek and finally to his hair. She smiles. *¿Aquí estamos?*

Estamos aquí. He reaches out and takes her hand. *Qué fría está tu mano.*

Soy vampiresa, she replies, *¿no te dije? Tengo 620 años. ¿Y tú?*

22.

Perfecto. Seguro que tu sangre está sabrosa.

Son of a whore mother, thinks Rogelio, as he pulls the *señora* inside.

A few doors up the street, parked in front of a booming taco town with green plastic sidewalk tables and young kids mauling *al pastors*, the two Texans watch her enter the Palacio. The young one glances back and forth between the window and the computer on his lap. He's a soft-skinned boy, with straight brown hair that flops over his ears and eyes and flat features that make him look even younger than he is. He hasn't shaved for a few days, but no one would know. The older one, the father, is hunched up tight, craning his head against the glass, trying to see what's what. He taps his big class ring against the glass.

"This a club, is that it?" Truitt says. "Looks like a club to me." He hands the kid a black sweatshirt and a silver walkie-talkie. "Put this on. Why don't you go in and check it out."

Charlie stares at the sweatshirt.

"Go on now," says Truitt. "Buy yourself a drink. Check out the scene, relax. Chat up some señoritas as long they ain't my wife."

Charlie pulls on the hoodie and zips and steps out of the car. Good kid. Truitt watches him square his slim shoulders, put his head down, and push into the club. When the door winks open Truitt gets a brief glimpse of a crowded bar, dark and smoky, packed in tight, with no one coming out.

He waits.

Upstairs at the Palacio, the gringo band is finishing. Limp applause sweeps them from the stage. They brush by the lukewarm audience, heading for the bar to claim free drinks. On the stairs, a small collision—the young buck leading a lady won't give way. It should be a scuffle, but the *señora* holds his arms back as the gringos mumble asshole and disappear where they belong. The señora is pretty strong. When she releases him she smiles.

I need you here with me, she says.

Rogelio nods in compromise. If they're still here when he goes downstairs to piss he can try to kill them then.

Downstairs, the Americans grouse up to the bar, all rocked out and unhappy with their ignominious lot. They never made it as a band but rock still keeps them young, or youngish, despite the wiry white chesthairs that squirt atop the black metal beaters, puffing up like ancient lion's mane. The drinks are on the house at least. Charlie is surprised to hear English, and sidesteps toward the sound, sliding down the bar.

"Was better in Gwadela Hara."

"Better in my basement."

"This is Mexico fucking City?"

They clink bottles loudly and suck them down. Charlie cradles his Corona in both hands, rolling it back and forth, mustering the courage for whatever's next. He reaches for his wallet but bumps his walkietalkie instead, activating it by mistake.

Outside in the car, Truitt's unit squawks to life, the unmistakable sound of a dive in full swing. Truitt turns the volume down until it's a low, comforting static hum. The SUV is quiet. It's the only one on the street. Some Mexicans have money but not in this part of town. Whatever Alma came here looking for, it wasn't a better way of life. The walkie yelps. Something's going down in there? Something loud. On the curb outside, a crush of new blood is arriving, a happy gang. Enough, Truitt thinks, reaching for the door.

Hooting. Shouting. The chanteuse snaps her gum and slaps feedback from her guitar. *¡Somos Las Ultrasónicas!* she whines, and the big bad chords begin. Her hair is long and wild and hangs down to the frets. They're loud, they're really loud, power trio all the way. The drummer girl is portly, maybe even fat, although she looks just right pounding on the battered kit in front of her. Her crush on the guitarist is undisguised and unrequited, and she ignores the crowd to watch the girl with lust. Long live the girl band, Rogelio thinks, long live the girl band that rocks. He stands with the *señora* at the back, his arm around her waist. She's a bit still, holding her drink with two hands like a chalice. The music is too loud to think but she does not need to think. She needs to watch the crowd. She slides along the wall, brushing against the curtain hanging there. She imagines wringing it out and the liquid smoke and sweat and alcohol that would run in toxic rivulets through her hands. She is too close to the speaker now, her ears are being damaged, but at least the faces of the crowd can be seen. The young. She might have been that girl with long black hair standing near the front in the black and white panda shirt, ears pierced up and down, tattoos on her neck. Her parents might have lived and stayed together and sent her to a *prepa* down in Mixcoac, and then on to a third-rate *secundaria* where some fourth-rate teacher would try to molest her, but she grows up smart and quick and escapes unscathed by men and education. If she was lucky she would be a secretary but until then, why not not rock 'n' roll? And Alma? There would be no Alma. That's why Mexico was impossible, why did her girl not see that?

The boy is shouting in her ear but she cannot hear him until he pulls her in close and drags her toward the back again.

Do you like it?

Are there other shows tonight?

Here?

Other places.

The Hard Rock. But it's expensive.

I've got money. Let's go.

Okay, the boy says.

Every show in town, I want to see them all.

A couple more songs we'll go.

Now, she says, but he does not seem to hear her.

No one can hear anyone. Charlie can't. The boss's wife moves her mouth but he can't read her lips She might be saying terrible things. She moves nervously as if she knows she's being watched. He's got his hood pulled down as far as it will go. She makes him nervous. Charlie has never been proficient at meeting people's eyes, but usually folks give him a break. Not Mrs. Price. He's naked when she looks at him, naked with his hands tied up in knotted bras behind his back. She wants to play with him. She wants to play with everyone. The boss's wife. As long as she doesn't do anything he has to lie about. He can't lie worth beans. The guy she's with does touch her every now and then, not too serious, but contact, definitely, and she doesn't seem to mind.

I should just tell her, Charlie thinks. I should just go over there and tell her what's going on.

The Palacio is dancing now, dancing from the head up at least. The crowd is dialed in. Rock me *Ultrasónicas*, rock rock rock. Charlie tries to make his move but a new crowd of people is pouring in, a tight posse of revelers who dance for real as they crest the stairs and pogo their way in front. They own the joint. They totally disrupt the crowd. Charlie's not the only one brushed back, and a rumble and grumble bubble in their wake. Charlie waits for them to pass, but someone, one of them, a short young woman with big breasts and insane nerd glasses reaches up and cuffs him on the head. She doesn't mean to, not exactly, what she means to do is yank back his hood which is also what she does. She yanks back his hood and grins at him and yells something he didn't learn in Spanish II. Then she's gone, headed for the front row, and right behind her there goes Alma.

Charlie starts to shake. He's reaching for his walkie but he's shaking so bad he can't work hand in his pocket. The posse still streams by, pushing Alma with them, and then they're past him, leaving an open space there in the center of the crowd. But he's got it now. He's got it and he's yelling. She's here she's here she's here.

Through the briefly open space, just before it winks and disappears, Hermelinda sees him in a clear red rock 'n' roll light. Charlie is supposed to be somewhere but not twenty feet away jabbering on his phone. This is not right. Messages are firing down her spine. She lets her drink go and it falls with a mighty splash and smash, the shards ricocheting off her boots across the greasy floor. Alright Charlie boy, let's talk, she thinks, as she fights her way his way.

The lead singer of the Ultrasonics is elated. The bass player is elated too. Their favorite person's here tonight, their favorite man around town. Spengler Castro! Rogelio's never heard of him. Is he in a band? The Ultrasonics do not say. What they say is he's their favorite, and they've written a song about him, which now they're going to play. It's called Spengler Castro Doesn't Care! One-two-three-four!

Fuck Spengler Castro, Rogelio thinks. Song sucks. Lead singer's dirty dancing on the guy like a bitch in heat. Now's the time to leave. But when he turns to tell her the *señora* throws her drink at him and starts plowing through the crowd. It stuns him for a second but then he grabs her as she goes.

He doesn't care he's Spengler Castro
He doesn't care he's Spengler Castro
He doesn't care he's Spengler Castro
He doesn't care so why do you!

The din in there is absolute. The only reason Truitt knows his walkie-talkie's squawking is he can feel it vibrate pleasantly against his hip, where it rests in a high-tech holster he bought from a catalogue. The stairs disappear beneath his feet two at a time. He pops up into the big room just as the music stops, or doesn't stop exactly. Something's happened to the drums. It's packed in there, but he's a head taller than most. What he sees explains things—a big girl with drummer's sticks has abandoned her post and is beating on some guy in front while the audience cheers her on. But that's not what concerns him. What concerns him is the piece of shit laying hands on his wife.

No one sees Truitt coming, not Rogelio who feels something crack in his face as he heads for the floor, and not Hermelinda either, who is watching Charlie try to fight his way into the mob. But she sees Charlie cannot get very far. She watches him, a body moshing in the pit, pushed around, with everyone singing now, chanting the words to this simple song and flailing out at one another. They dance and fight, every one of them. Everyone except the figure standing stock-still at the center of the storm, who does not move until someone clips her and she spins toward Hermelinda like an old revolving door. She has seen that expression on Alma's face before, when she was a little girl who sleep-walked into their room at night and stared right through her. And here she is.

The hand on Hermelinda's arm evaporates as Rogelio leaves his feet and Truitt follows him to the ground and Hermelinda sleepwalks toward her only daughter staring through her from the fray.

Up front, by the stage, the drummer beats on Spengler Castro, Isolda beats the drummer, the gringo band thrashes happily, bloodying lips and ears and other parts. Truitt smacks Rogelio side to side. Hermelinda takes an elbow to the gut but keeps on going. The baggy jeans, the big sweatshirt, the baseball cap, Alma has even got her hand shoved down the front of her pants. Her little gangster. A short girl with big breasts and glasses is in her way and growls at her and Hermelinda grabs her by the bra and tosses her aside. Almost there. A shoulder hits her in the head but she reaches down and squeezes two big testes as hard as she can and the obstacle moves aside. Alma bounces back and forth like a lottery ball in the little chamber of bodies until Hermelinda reaches her and wraps her in her arms. She is smaller than her daughter but she expands now to cover her like a magic cloak.

I got you, love, I got you.

From his knees, Truitt tries to give the kid another bash, but his victim squirms out of his grasp and leaps away. Before Truitt can stand, a flying munchkin lands on top of him, drops to a sitting place and slips into his lap. It's a little girl, or a woman actually, with intelligent fury sparkling in her hard-to-focus eyes. She blinks at him, reaching out one hand to feel his face.

You okay? he says.

She chirps back something Spanish. A pair of thick glasses lie on the floor beside him, and he hands them to her. She crams them on her face and looks at him and winces.

Yeah, he says, now get up off me girl. He heaves her off him just in time because here comes the kid he's been beating on, back for more, and more is what he's going to get except the girl with glasses has grabbed a broken bottle off the floor. For me? he thinks. But it's not for him. Girl with broken bottle is charging through a break in the crowd, heading for his wife.

Hermelinda does not see her coming. Everything she sees and feels is that her Alma is elsewhere. The girl's flesh is there beneath her mother's hands—her baby skin, her baby breath—but she does not make a sound. Her daughter starts to rock back and forth like she still hears music, like somewhere plays a song and she rocks slowly to the beat. There is something wrong with her.

Are you hurt, the mother says. She puts an arm around her and takes her hand and somehow holds on despite the blood she finds there.

The first shot is loud enough and the second one louder. It's a good loud gun, no doubt about that, with no translation necessary. The room drops to the floor and heads for the exits. It doesn't take long. It happens fast. And when it's over, the only bodies left behind are the nuclear family standing together in the middle, the father with his automatic aloft, ready to put another shot into the ceiling, if that's what Mexico wants, the mother still wrapped around the daughter, holding her back, as the daughter blinks hard in the harsh red rock 'n' roll light, searching for the bullet holes and reaching for her daddy's gun, staring at the ceiling, staring and staring and staring.

PART **FIVE**

Sixteen

For twenty days, since she moved Alma from the hospital, they have barely left the hotel suite. When Hermelinda goes to bed at night, Alma is still writing, and when she wakes up in the early morning, there is Alma writing again—or maybe still—at the desk, or on the floor, or curled up on the window ledge, staring at the city. The hotel windows do not open. Day by day, the color of the air outside may shift but Mexico looks the same. The desk and the valets downstairs know not to let her daughter leave, although Alma does not seem interested in leaving, as she fills the small black notebooks and piles them on the nightstand, one on top of the other, in a stack of charred and crooked vertebrae. The stack contains her Alma but Hermelinda has not touched it. She does not read one word her daughter writes. She has not asked permission and it has not been offered.

Alma.

Sí.

Will you eat something?

Chilaquiles, Alma says without looking up, still scribbling away.

Again?

Alma does not answer. Instead she stretches and leans her wide forehead against the glass and lets the vibrations of the city seep into her skull. Closes her eyes. In the darkness there, where she's been living, the shapes and shadows soar. Not the past. The future. Mechanized drones with jet propulsion buzzing through the megasphere. The future will need these smogbots to cut holes in the sky. The future will need cellophane, Mexican kids wrapped up in the stuff for fashion's sake. Alma can't wait to get to the future. She's making the future come to her. She can't wait to look back at her teenage years from a formidable distance. She can't wait to tell the next generation how cool girls used to pierce their tongues and blog and sodomize. What else can she imagine? Cellophaned kids with devil's horns and jaw spurs and maybe even tails. Skintint. Digigraphs. Nokia noserings corner the non implant cell phone market and there's designer Kevlar everything. No one uses verbs anymore. The army has been privatized, homemade viruses from Albequerque escape into the wild, monsters roam the deserts near the border. Bergman the Poisoner kills off half of Fresno, Iran is part of France. Her mother's turning sixty and having half her cells replaced. Alma an old lady, living in a refurbished art deco apartment, with a maid named Juana stewing tomatillos—she can smell the seedy acrid tang—in the ample tiled kitchen, in Mexico City, in Santa María La Rivera, Alma's neighborhood. What will she remember about running away to Mexico?

That was the year Maria Felix died, and the line wrapped around Bellas Artes to see Mexico's biggest movie star lie in state. It was the year the civil rights lawyer Digna Ochoa y Placido was murdered in her office, the killer never to be found. Scandals for the first lady and PRD potentate Rosario Robles. A lousy year for women. Endemic groping plagued even the female only subway car; murder rape continued in the *maquiladores* of Juarez; schoolchildren were ruined on the streets and in big screen hits like *Perfume y Violetas* and *De La Calle.* It was the year Alma dressed in drag and learned about the Donkey Punch and Dirty Sanchez and the hearts and hands of men.

She will remember how she used to think the world was all fucked up, but the older, wiser Alma will see things a little differently. There are no miracles without pain, she'll say. No truth without lies. Everything will make more sense, one day, even if people still believe in virgins, in Mary appearing to Juan Diego ten years after the Conquista to burn her image onto his back. Science will never disprove miracles and it might even prove them. Maybe not immaculate conception but there are many cases of fairly spontaneous sex change in the natural kingdom, including echinoderms, crustaceans, mollusks, and polchaete worms. The clown fish will switch from male to female in order to take over as queen. Gobies do it when one sex is not available. Reed frogs and grouper. Oysters. These things happen all the time and Alma thinks that in the future maybe people will understand that.

The food's here.

Okay.

Do you want to eat at the window? Or at the table?

Wherever.

The future may be more open minded but in her bestselling memoir Alma will not discuss the miracle or her explanations. No one's ready for that. What sells is not the miracles. People want to hear about the hospital, about the Demerol, about the blood and semen samples, the nurse combing her for evidence. They want to hear about the importance of holding back your pee. They want to hear about the trial, even if there wasn't one, and how she did up there on the stand. They want to hear the defense grill her on the *coca* floating through her system, about her deceptions, her poor parents, her wildness and lies. They want to hear about what happens in her chest when she's alone in a small space with a stranger—an elevator, say—or when sudden footsteps startle her, or better yet, when she's at a party and sees a group split off and close the door. They won't give a shit about gobies. She'll give them what they want. She'll lie and stretch and fabricate and watch the hardcover sell like hotcakes. She'll give them their memoir but the much anticipated novel will be the book that tells the truth.

The novel will outline how a plain girl from Austin, Texas can also be the love child of Sor Juana and Emiliano Zapata. Juana, the courtly virgin, floats giddy in verse through the vicereine court, with its intrigues and its intellectual spark. Peasant warrior Zapata loves the field, the dirt, the man behind the plow. He believes in land. He believes in crop. She lies in her convent cot while he slumbers under cypress when suddenly a great crack of lightning pollinates them across the centuries. In their own times, soon, both will give their lives for others, Sor Juana committing suicide by tending the sick, Zapata walking into the ambush with Guajardo. But this night, through an accident of time, they fall into each other's arms. Just that: their arms. He presses his weary head into her beautiful body, closing his burning eyes, while she whispers sweet 1660 verse in his good ear. From this union, Alma is born, to soar as they soared, and suffer as they suffered.

Dear reader! she will write. This is the story of a runaway who dashed headlong through the present as long as it would last. You will see strange brothels in the north, and men dancing round and round with panties on their heads. You will see witches and ghosts. You will see Sor Juana slinking around in disguise and William Burroughs kill his wife. You will see Zapata cry for justice as he falls, and tables piled high with coke, and singing, and dancing, and men itching for a fight. You will see a girl who changed into a boy when she absolutely had to, because we come from the sea, where these things happen all the time.

She writes until her brain bleeds. The sweat pools beneath her breasts, where beautiful curves are waiting to arrive along with hips and calves and tapered thighs. Her true body will emerge from its disguise. The strange suede sack and little hooded thumb disappearing. And then the little growth spurt. Two inches in a couple months. The ugly duckling—her mother will be right. A gentle neck. The magic of the body. Her hair will grow again and its color will turn redder, the texture thinning and straightening a bit. Her skin settles into something a little more beige, a little less pink. The fat in her face and ankles melts away. Only the nose will remain, and it won't look too bad, big, for sure, ugly, but the rest of her will be actually pretty nice. Her mother will be right: Alma is extraordinary, an almost beautiful woman, a big success, a thinker, a voice, a happy lover, a well off expat living on royalties beneath the Tropic of Cancer.

The notebook fills up. She pushes the untouched plate of green *chi-*

laquiles to one side.

You have to eat something.

I will.

Promise?

Yes. But you have to leave me alone.

Hermelinda backs away from her daughter. Alma does not touch her food and does not look up and Hermelinda wonders if it is wrong for a girl to eat nothing but *chilaquiles* eight days in a row. She wonders what room service must think. Room 316, the crazies, toast and *chilaquiles* again.

Hermelinda did not think that this was what shock looked like. Sometimes she wonders if it would be better in the hospital, where at least the walls and curtains told them something was still wrong. The hospital was private and the treatment was superb. They said Alma would be alright. The attack was not trivial, they did not say that, but physically she would be fine. Of course that was good news. Without that there was nothing. But once Hermelinda stopped worrying about the body, the worrying got worse. Skin heals. Swelling shrinks. The attack. She could not say the other word.

The first week she flew down a therapist but the therapist got nowhere. Alma would not talk to her at first. And when she did it was to discuss books, literature, getting her notes into some structure. The therapist spent hours with her, at the hospital and the hotel, down in the restaurant or in the rooftop garden, scribbling diagrams on butcher paper. She's coping, the therapist said. She's doing her best. She's making things make sense. After ten days Hermelinda sent the therapist back to Austin but they talk every other day. I think she's doing well, the therapist opines.

She's in another world, says Hermelinda.

She's where she needs to be.

She won't come home with me.

She's strong, the therapist says. She's more than strong, she is absolutely incredible. She knows what she's doing. Trust her.

I can't.

I know.

She won't talk to me. She won't let me in.

She will.

Okay. I can wait.

Good. And Truitt?

You can update.

Don't you think you need to talk to him yourself?

No. I don't.

He's still there, you know.

I know.

Truitt is indeed still there in Mexico City, although not in their hotel, not in sight. He keeps his distance, but Truitt is still here. Where else would he be? Every day he chats up the concierge at their hotel, the guy's got a cousin in Dallas or something, is hell bent to get his butt up to the States. You help me out I don't forget a favor, Truitt says.

Your wife and daughter do not go to anywhere, the concierge says.

You call me when they do.

Yes.

Twenty four seven. That means anytime. You call me. You'll like Dallas, Truitt says, good looking women in Dallas. You like blondies, doncha?

Yes, sir.

Who doesn't. Don't forget to call.

Eguren's fired. Truitt's got a new guy. All business. Connections up the zinga. Rafa something or other. Suits made out of glowing flower pistils. Eguren's fees now look like chump change. Maybe if he'd had Rafa on the case to start with. It's an unthinkable thought. He doesn't think it.

He meets Rafa in some hip neighborhood full of kids, not too far from the hotel. His new PI regards the folks around them with plain lust and disdain.

Children of the rich, he explains.

Gotcha. They're sitting outside on the sidewalk on a sunny afternoon. What do you know?

You see that cantina?

Yeah.

There's a group that hangs out there. Journalists and writers.

Course there is.

She was spending time with them.

I'm not surprised. Got a contact?

I know the names. Some of them I know. They are degenerate, but. Not.

Not what.

Not what you are looking for, I think.

People can surprise you. People do the damndest things.

That is true.

When they get together?

Every night.

Time?

Five, six. Seven, eight.

I'll meet you at five.

It's not possible for me tonight.

Well you know where I'll be.

Yes, Mr. Price.

He's got a few hours to kill. He could call Austin. He needs to. The biz don't run itself. And what would he say? He's better off not calling. The parts of life he's been neglecting are the only ones that haven't fallen apart. He calls the concierge again.

You like the Cowboys?

¿Señor?

The Dallas Cowboys, how do you feel about them?

I don't know.

Well make sure you keep that to yourself.

He chats up the concierge, who isn't listening much, who's busy after all, greeting people, making guests feel welcome.

I should be working, the concierge says finally.

Of course you should. You're a good man. You take care of my kid. And your wife.

But Hermelinda does not need taking care of at the moment. She is feeling better than she has for a long time. She has left the room. She is in the pool. She has been eyeing it for weeks, but has not dared to leave her daughter behind. She leaves her now. Alma was still in the window, like a cat, curled up with her knees against her chest, writing and then staring and then writing again.

I'm going for a swim, Hermelinda said.

She expected silence but instead her daughter lifted up her head and looked her straight for the first time in Mexico.

It'll be good for you, Alma said.

I know.

You go swim.

I will.

I'm getting to a tricky part, her daughter said. Be good to be alone.

Okay.

It took some nerve but Hermelinda grabbed a towel and her blue two piece and walked right out the door. A tricky part. If I can do this, Hermelinda thought, if *we* can do this, what else can we do. Now she is swimming laps, lots of them, the chlorine shrinking her skin, swimming and swimming and not thinking about a thing.

The tricky part is what happens underground with Mendes, walking through the city's sewers, the enormous tubes of profound drainage. A great tunnel, fifteen feet in diameter, with a string of lights at three o'clock curving out of sight, built in 1900 to carry sewage and floodwater thirty six miles into the rivers flowing eastward to the Gulf of Mexico. But there was an older sewer there. A secret door into catacombs from four hundred years ago. Sixty thousand Indians built it in ten months. Who knows how many lost their lives. Who knows how many stayed. They were still there. Small people, with big hands and beautiful oval eyes wide open in the dark. She could hear the voices swishing softly behind them, the chuh chuh chuh and shuh shuh shuh. She could see the runes cut in the sewer sides, their grafitti, literature, who could tell? A secret city that will not be discovered until a Mexico City sewage diver is sucked into the ancient system and rescued by these lost tribes seventeen years later.

She throws the notebook across the room. Fuck this. Tell the truth. The truth! The truth is what I say it is, she thinks. In the street below, she can see real people walking down the clean Polanco streets. A rich and purposeful part of town, but there is a beggar down there too, the ubiquitous Indian mother and child. Was there a single moment when that woman became the woman she is now, one fucked ghost in thick wool color on the curb of a luxury hotel? Filthy Indian. Raped. Notebooks can't really rescue her from that. Words. Dulcet, keening, the shit and melody of blood, kites that tear and flutter in her throat, the syllables of skin, of hatred like a razor top that spins and cuts all things to strips. Fear and shame are just words to smear like acid on the gums, acrid, pulicous, a needle fucking flesh, his penis floating in a jar at the Grizzly Death Museum. Teeth, fulvous. Mariachis and cocaine. The words are here and I will find them. I will. Mine. Ours. She reaches out with two hands and pushes back from the window. Swooned. Slowly. The truth may be it's all her fault, but she knows what she must do.

Across the city, at the Lobo, the long table of familiars grows. Now fifteen of them, now twenty. It's six thirty, and the place is pretty packed, except for the four top near the door where Truitt sits alone, sipping a *Bohemia* and watching suspects carefully. Which one? From face to face he gazes, not caring who knows. He's ruled out some. There's daddy intuition, and the only other thing to go on is a single word his girl said in the car. Someone walks in front of him, blocking his unrelenting view, and as the someone passes Truitt hears a phrase he recognizes, something in English, an American, talking to himself. With interest he sees the guy sit at the table under question. Truitt can barely hear his cell phone ring for the blood all through his head.

Yeah?

She is going, Mr. Price.

Who is.

Your wife.

And my daughter?

No.

Call my wife a car. Get in bed with the driver.

Mr. Price?

Pay off someone to tell you where she goes. What she does.

I'll try, sir, but she is out the door.

Well hurry then. Don't let my daughter leave. He terminates the call and gets up for the bathroom. Let me see your face, good ol' son of a whore.

The concierge calls her a car and confers briefly with the driver, opening the door, taking her hand to help her in. Her hair is still wet. There's no time. It's an unmarked car, a big black sedan with no sign of taxi anywhere.

What did you tell him? Hermelinda asks.

That he must treat you like the Queen of England.

Why do you need to tell him that?

This service is the best in Mexico. Please, don't worry. He nods with easy servitude. Meanwhile, I will look out for your daughter, he says quietly.

It is important that she does not leave.

I understand. She will not leave.

They pull away and out into the viscous evening traffic. She tells the driver the address. He purses his lips unhappily but says nothing, flipping his phone between thick fingers.

They slice east across the massive city. On the highway, off the highway. Down the thick *calzadas*. Up the *eje* five. She stares out of the window but does not see what she sees. The sky is darkening slowly. The air is unusually clear. To the east an enormous plain slopes up gently in the distance, slopes and slopes and slopes until the city finally peters out. The lights are coming on. A vast parking lot of trucks, hundreds upon hundreds, encircles a makeshift city to the right, with buildings made of wooden crates piled thirty high. Spotlights shine.

What is that, she asks.

Abastos. Everything the city eats passes through here.

Really.

Almost.

My father had a market. Here in Mexico. When I was a little girl. He bought his produce right there.

Maybe. He did not think he was a grocer. A very bad businessman.

The driver considers this. Well, that's the best place, he says.

Hermelinda does not answer. If they had stayed she might have gone there with him. They would sell fruit like only a father and daughter could. She would have reached out her arms and kept the family together. There were moments when that was possible and moments when it was not. The moment of impossibility had come for her father. She does not know if she will know the moment when it comes.

The city is getting strange outside. Big strange parks and a fenced compound for the national telephone company. And then the communist buildings, stacks and stacks of them.

Prison? she says.

Habitation Units of the State.

The black car climbs a sudden hill, winding around through streets named first for battles and then Aztec kings. Then the road ends suddenly at the base of a blasted cliff, and she is staring at Habitation Units again.

Here?

The driver shrugs.

She takes a deep breath through her nose and catches her own scent, chlorine and sweat and the rose perfume from Creed. She opens her mouth and blows the air out. With one breath she managed to cross the Rio Grande for her first day of American school. With one breath she managed to watch her mother buried. With one breath she could

229

sit at her damaged daughter's side and smile and hold her hand and rub her arm and not say anything at all. With one breath she can do this. She opens the door.

The door of the Lobo is swinging back and forth, back and forth in front of Truitt as the drinkers come and go. He keeps his eye on the prize. This guy used to be an athlete, Truitt can tell, he's got one of those bodies that's not used to being small. A body that does not move around a whole lot anymore. Not fat but soft. Truitt's soft a little bit but this guy's too young for that. Dude speaks Spanish like a motherfucker. If his wife were here she could tell him something about the guy, his accent, grammar, what he's saying.

It's silent in the long dim hall where Hermelinda walks with Eguren's final field notes in her hand. 108. 107. 106. Here it is.

She knocks.

¿Sí?

She breathes in through her nose and opens her mouth and pushes everything out.

¿Sí?

She knocks again and the door swings open into the dark and dingy room.

You are Mr. Montes, she says.

Come in, my daughter, come in, sit down, sit down.

Truitt's not sure he can just sit here any longer, but turns out he doesn't have to. There's a crew leaving, a pod of folks that splits off from the table and scampers out the door. Truitt drops a couple red ones on the table and goes after them. The four guys stand on the sidewalk, doing their Spanish, trying to decide what's next, and then they split in twos and head in opposite directions, with Truitt following the American and his buddy close and obviously behind. They don't seem to mind. He follows them through the park where they again swap wisdom and subdivide and Truitt's mark slips into a corner store. Truitt waits outside. He hits the speed dial.

I need to talk to my daughter.

Yes, Mr. Price.

Right now. Run the phone up there and hand it to her. Break the goddamn door if you have to.

Yes, Mr. Price.

He can hear the concierge running, moving fast. Good man. The American's chatting with the storekeep, buying liquor. From the phone he can hear knocking, talking, shouting.

Daddy?

Allie cat.

She can't remember the last time he called her that. The phone is tucked tightly under her chin as she pulls all the big bills she can find out of her mother's leather bag. She shoves them in the back pocket of her jeans.

What's wrong, Daddy?

Need your input on something.

She feels suspicion cinch behind her eyes. Where are you? He doesn't answer and she sits down on the bed. This new silence feels so rare between them. She wants to tell him it's not his fault but instead she says, You ever think about where we'll be in thirty years?

Try not to. She can hear him thinking of something funnier to say. Here's the thing, he says instead. I know you wouldn't tell the cops but that's different from telling me.

I don't want to talk about it.

Just a name.

No.

In thirty years I'll be a sad old man.

You're already an old man.

He doesn't laugh. Alma. I need you. To open. Your fucking. Mouth. And tell me right now. Or I swear I'll never speak to you again. And all the hatred he deserves will boil you and me. Say it. Alma Katherine Price. Say it.

Red, she whispers, and then her heart goes back to beating again.

Okay. Okay. She can almost hear the veins thumping in his throat.

I'm so sorry, baby.

You shouldn't have done that, Daddy. She can barely hear herself.

I know. I know. I'm sorry. There so many things I shouldn't do and that's definitely one of them.

And what's the worst? What's the worst thing you shouldn't have done?

He doesn't hesitate long enough. I don't know. Lots of competition, baby. She's not going to let him off but he's too quick for her again. I know the best thing, though, he says. Best thing I ever did was you.

You're so full of it.

I may well be but it's the truth.

Right. So tell me this. Don't just say something, think about it. Do you think, Daddy, do you think our best thing's always related to our worst thing?

You're on to something there. He's concentrating now. Okay. You're right. The worst thing I ever did and do was not to trust you. The people I love.

You just make that up?

He almost laughs. I probably heard it somewhere. A car honks past him, wherever he is. Some ol' country song. Sounds about right, though, doesn't it?

Let me think.

Thank you, Allie.

Why should anyone trust anyone?

No idea. But I trust you now. Not too late, is it?

I don't know. Daddy. But whatever you're doing, stop. Stop and let me handle it.

I love you, her daddy says. He hangs up.

She gives the concierge his phone back, and when he turns and pads back down the hall she sneaks out there behind him. Quiet. Quiet to the stairwell as he hits the elevator. Plunging to the lobby door. Mexico's lights are there to blind her, close her eyes. She sees spots and somewhere in the spots are Spengler Castro and her future maid Juana and her father and her mother, who should be upstairs swimming but is sitting there with Montes and a painting in her lap.

Which year is this from? Hermelinda asks.

What? The old man is deaf and upstairs elephants are dancing. He leans in to look at the painting. Year? He shakes his head.

There must be something earlier. Earliest you ever did.

Yes, I have those too, he says. He pulls a stack of canvases from behind the refrigerator. Yes, I have old paintings, old old old.

These paintings too are of the house, the recurring house and street again and again and again. You had a visitor, Hermelinda says, pretending to examine the canvases in front of her. A young visitor. A month ago.

Yes?

She was looking for her grandfather. She was looking for Zapata Street. Do you remember?

He points at the painting in front of her. That's the house, he says, the house I grew up in. All changed. Everything has changed.

Maybe so. You've been painting your whole life.

Yes.

There must be more.

I sold many.

There must be more. From earlier.

You can help me. Under the bed.

Under the bed lie canvases thick with dust. With her bare hand she swipes and gray webs up between her fingers. She is peering through wiper crescents in a storm. But that's not the house this time.

Who is this.

He doesn't say anything.

Do you remember this painting? Do you remember painting this, old man?

I know who you are, he says.

I know who you are, she says.

Do I know you? Truitt says. I think we might be acquainted.

He has followed the American along the edge of the park and to the front door of a pretty building, one of those Paris buildings that don't belong down here. The American stops fumbling with his keys for a nano to glance back Truitt's way.

No, the American says.

Red?

The guy stares at him and Truitt sees the current jump the gap. The American's eyes jump up and down, taking in this middle aged man so out of place with his jacket and his boots.

Is that you, Red? My god goodness gracious. What you doing down here? Truitt's voice sounds just the same to him but his mouth tastes like rotting meat.

The guy says something quick to him in Spanish and Truitt shakes his head.

Excuse me?

People like me don't know people like you, the guy says.

Is that true? My daughter introduced us, Truitt says, sliding the gun from the small of his back, beneath his jacket, where it's been gouging him uncomfortably. He flicks the safety off with his thumb like he's done it a thousand times. You remember my little girl, don't you. The gun bobs gently in his hand, and his lower back feels marvelous, expanding to fill the space the steel's been hogging up all day.

I don't forgive you, Hermelinda tells the old man. I don't forgive anyone.

You're not an artist.

You're not either.

That's what your mother used to say.

She's dead. We all died up there.

He leans over the small canvass and uses his filthy sleeve to wipe it clean, gently and methodically scraping the dust from left to right. The painted Mexican girl stares back. Her cheeks are sucked in slightly and her lips freeze there half-puckered as if she's trying not to smile.

Beautiful, no? I wrote to her.

The girl is beautiful, Hermelinda thinks. The girl doesn't know what's coming. No one does.

We died here too, the old man continues.

That's what you wanted.

No one wants that.

You could have told her. You could have told my daughter and sent her home.

How sad she would have been. Look how sad you are.

I'm sad I ever saw you again. You could have told her. But you didn't. Not her. Not me.

You can tell her. She and I have something in common.

You both hate me? You both hurt me?

Ask her.

To her, you're just a little old man. To me too.

Then why did you come.

To see where I would be. She glances at the ceiling. The dancing up there has stopped. The music too. In hell, she says.

The American bangs his fists against the door and yells out something Spanish. Truitt didn't realize how quiet it is, how quiet the biggest city in the world can be, until this man shouts out for help. But this is not a man. This is a vicious animal that must be put down. He's beating on the door right now and he's going to turn and attack. But when Red turns around he just looks at him. Forehead wrinkled up with cosmic worry. This is a man. This is what a man does.

Red opens his mouth again and Truitt puts a bullet in it.

Hell is everywhere, the old man says.

Hermelinda stands. I came back to life, she says. Old man.

Truitt runs, is running in his boots like they used to tear down Grooms Street late at night, when he was just a kid, and Lindy was the sleeping beauty on the couch outside, the future just a glimmer in their bright unencumbered eyes. He runs three blocks like that until he's winded and his lungs are full of shit. Then he walks to the big avenue waiting there and flags a cab and gone.

The black car is waiting for her as Hermelinda steps out of the Habitation Units into the night outside. The lights of the city are galactic. Out there, among the twenty million, every kind of thing is happening tonight. She calls the hotel as the driver takes them back the way they came, through the kings and battles and the biggest market in the world.

Your husband just called, the concierge tells her. He's leaving. He's going home.

Good.

He says he trusts in you.

And Alma?

In the room.

I'll be there soon. Her daughter's pages, scrawled onion skin plucked from the old man's hovel, crinkle in her hands.

Alma is not in the room. She is in Mexico, walking down the street. There's no cellophane or smogbots here, not yet, there is just the reek of soap and gasoline that reminds her of mistakes. Will it always be like that? The guilt is deafening. Her eyes are down, down on the pavement, down on her own shoes that she has never seen before. The shoes are black and big and beautiful. Her mother must have bought them for her, even though her mother's never bought her shoes like these before. And the dark new jeans with gentle flares that make her legs look long. Her body curving there beneath the T shirt. This is not who she really is, this is what her mother sees, this is just a lie until she glances at her image in the shiny hotel window. The girl there looks like Alma. Looks like someone she could talk to. Looks like someone who should stay. Not in this rich neighborhood, which lacks the yelling gas man, the loud water guy, the tinging triangle of the knife sharpener, the night steam whistle of the *camote* carts. Not in his neighborhood either. But somewhere in this city is a place where she could live and write and stay.

The Indian woman is in front of her, begging on the curb, legs bent back beneath her like a tiny little kid. Her hand's extended but barely, at a weak and sloping angle, as if she expects nothing or someone broke her wrist. The beggar's child who was there before is nowhere to be seen. Alma stops in front of her but the woman doesn't look up. Up close, the shawl looks fake, factory made from Wal Mart. This might not even be an Indian. The fact she's begging here might be her own fault.

Alma squats down and the beggar looks at her. The face is wide and flat and dark as an unfamiliar moon but tells nothing. Alma plucks the wad of bills from her left back pocket and hands them to the woman. Must be a couple thousand dollars there.

I'm not trying to save you, Alma says. The truth is I don't care who you are. I probably will one day, but right now, I'm just doing this for myself.

The woman's eyes hum with static.

Leave this city. Leave it. I'm going to stay, and I don't want to ever see you again. If I see you again you have to give the money back. You must leave. You sold your place, you understand? I paid for it. It's mine. Go. Leave. Get out of here. If you don't go right now then neither of us have a chance.

The woman doesn't move until Alma reaches out to take the money back.

The city! The woman shuffles to her feet and buries the bills under her clothing, mumbling words that Alma does not understand. Shuh shuh shuh. Maybe that means oh my daughter may the gods exalt and bless you in whatever language she's speaking. Maybe that means fuck you. Maybe in this old language of this ancient valley exist three syllables that mean exalt and bless and fuck you all wrapped up into one. The woman retreats only a few paces and lingers, held by magnets to this spot.

It's mine now. Go! What are you waiting for?

From around the corner, the little boy comes running, who knows where he's been but he comes running now, vaulting past the gringa and into the arms of his mother or sister or aunt, waiting for him there, who calls out one last time for Alma—shuh shuh shuh!—before tapping her forehead twice, and turns and disappears.

Alma sucks the yellow air down deep until it hits the bottom of her lungs, until every inch of her is filled with the world around her. Remember this. This is the place to start. She brings her left hand up and leans forward until her fingers touch her brow and taps there, gently, once and then again, and her fingers are soft, her skin is soft, the skin feels younger than she remembers, the skin belongs to her. Remember. Learn. She will go and find her mother but not now. Muscles in Alma's face tug wild at her eyes and lips. She lets them. And sits down in her place there on the curb.